GEDDIN THE HOLE!

A NOVEL BY
FRAZER GRUNDY

Geddin the Hole!
by Frazer Grundy

Published by Frazer Grundy
www.geddinthehole.com

Copyright © Frazer Grundy 2011
Print book ISBN: 978-0-620-51065-3
Ebook ISBN: 978-0-620-51118-6

Front cover illustration by Warwick Goldswain
www.krop.com/warwickgoldswain

Edited by Natasha Curry
natashacurry@telkomsa.net
Set in Museo and Adobe Garamond Pro
Designed and produced by Mousehand

www.mousehand.co.za

All rights reserved. No part of this publication may be reproduced, stored in a retrieval system, or transmitted in any form or by any means without the prior permission of the copyright holders.

A percentage of the proceeds from this book will be donated to the
Gary Player Foundation.
To find out more, or to make a donation, please visit www.garyplayer.com

For Michelle, Scott and Ben,
without whom this book would not have been possible

Gary Player

FOREWORD

Golf can be a serious game and golf books can be serious reading; and that's ok. But every once in a while it is nice to sit down with a novel about the sport I so love and just enjoy the read. I am happy to say that Frazer Grundy's new book allows you to do just that.

Geddin the Hole! is a tale of four average club golfers. They are not professional golfers, just regular club players – probably guys just like you. But in their own way, they end up experiencing many of the challenges that professionals like me face – dealing with pressure and figuring out how to use it to your advantage, what the difference is in playing to win and playing not to lose, and most importantly learning how to step onto the tee box on the 18th hole knowing that par wins the tournament, and making it. For me, there was nothing like competing, especially during the majors. For these four guys their goal is much simpler – revenge against a dastardly character who has deceived them. But despite the obvious differences in our backgrounds, there is something which I do have in common with them – a burning desire to succeed.

The story of the Ferkaryer Four unfolds into a caper of note; at times making me laugh and then turning and almost bringing tears to my eyes. It is an enjoyable read that really captures the highs and lows of golf, business and life. I hope you enjoy it as much as I did.

Gary Player

GARY PLAYER

---

c/o Black Knight International (Pty) Ltd
PO Box 785629, Sandton, 2146, South Africa
Telephone (011) 883 3333   Facsimile (011) 883 7250
www.garyplayer.com

Golf is the greatest of games. You are not playing a human adversary; you are playing a game.

Or so I thought...

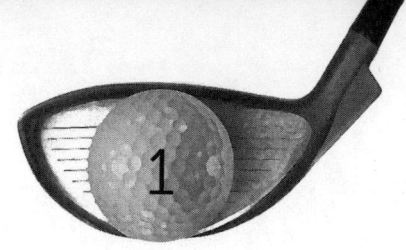

1

We'd lost. I still couldn't believe it. Talk about snatching defeat from the jaws of victory. The match was there for the taking and then Lofty had ...

I couldn't bear to think about it, but it came back and nagged away at me as I sped into my driveway. I slammed hard on the brakes and the car skidded to a halt, gravel spitting out from underneath the tyres.

It's a stupid word, isn't it: 'sped'? One of those words that sounds more and more stupid, the more you say it. Sped, sped, sped, sped. Well, stupid or not, I did it. I sped right into my bloody driveway. I hardly ever do that. I hardly ever 'speed' anywhere actually. That's why they call me Speedy: a kind of ironic nickname. If you extend that logic, then today they should be calling me 'Happy'.

To say that I was annoyed was like saying that Tiger Woods had a bit of an eye for the ladies. In golfing parlance you might say that I was teed off. On a 'teed off' scale of one to ten, I was about a forty-five.

I sat there for a moment and sighed. I hated coming home in a bad mood. It wasn't fair to Shelley and the kids, was it? But I knew that I wouldn't be able to hide it from them, no matter how long I waited in my car. Sitting there was futile; I had to go inside.

I climbed out of the car and slammed the door – a touch harder than was really necessary – before trudging up the driveway towards the house. The sweet aroma of the jasmine plants that flanked the path didn't have its usual calming effect on me this time. It would have taken something way stronger than that to lighten my mood. Probably something illegal.

As I opened the heavy wood-panelled door I was greeted enthusiastically by our beefy little Staffordshire bull terrier.

Buster didn't understand 'teed off' and was as happy as ever to see me. Normally I'd humour him, but I didn't feel like it. Not today. Shelley was in the kitchen, merrily concocting something or other for dinner.

"Hi, darling! How did it go?" she asked with cautious optimism.

"Don't ask," I replied solemnly, still trying to fight Buster off.

"Oh dear. I'm guessing you didn't win."

It seemed that she was slightly more perceptive than Buster.

"That's what I like about you – you're just so insightful. How did you learn to read me so well?" In truth, she did read me well. Like one of those Mills and Boon novels where you just *know* what's going to happen next.

"I guess it's just ESP. We're soul-mates, remember?" She could see – although to be fair, anyone could have – that I was seriously unhappy and that she would have to be subtle if she wanted to coax me out of it. Either that or take me straight to the bedroom and give me a good seeing to. That might work. I'd probably have settled for it, but the kids were running around the house so it looked like we were going to have to stick with plan A for now.

"Was it really that bad?"

"Worse! It wasn't just that we lost, it's *how* we lost. Unbelievable." I gazed through the window and shook my head.

"You want to talk about it?"

"You sure you want to hear about it?"

"I do have a plan B," she said, motioning towards the bedroom. She *was* perceptive, wasn't she? "But I'm not sure it's viable right now. Why don't you give me the whole nine yards?"

"I thought it wasn't viable?" I quipped. Not unusually, I was hoping that a cheap gag might provide some sort of tonic for my bad mood.

"Okay, if you want the full post-mortem, here goes," I sighed and proceeded to tell her the whole sorry story.

Geddin the Hole!

As Lofty and I walked to the seventeenth tee, I had an extra spring in my step.

"Let's bring it home, partner," I said eagerly. I'd just made a long putt on the sixteenth to win our third consecutive hole and square up the match. With only two holes to play, I felt that we had the momentum.

"Yeah, okay," replied Lofty in a detached kind of way.

I glanced across at him and wondered whether his nerves were getting the better of him. However, this was not the time for a pep talk. I had to concentrate on my tee shot.

I checked the height of my ball against my driver ...
I walked behind my ball and took two practice swings ...
I picked a spot and lined it up ...
I addressed the ball ...
I waggled the club twice ...
I stood there for a few seconds as if frozen ...
Then I finally pulled the trigger and smacked the ball ...
Crack!

A good drive, straight down the proverbial middle. I followed the ball's flight with relief as it sailed along the fairway, but my reverie was rudely interrupted by the voice I loathed most in the world.

"Good grief! Now that you've won a couple of holes, you're taking even longer than your usual five minutes!"

"I'd probably say the same thing if I was staring defeat in the face, Mr Bingley," I replied, gritting my teeth.

Derek Bingley just smirked in a patronising kind of way. He's such a smart ass, I thought. It would be so nice to whup him at last. I'd been waiting for this for years.

The Directors' Cup was an annual golf event hosted by African Tobacco, the company where Lofty worked. Most of the company's *directors played golf and the idea was that ten of them would take on ten 'staff' – otherwise known as 'plebs' – in a Ryder Cup-style match. This year there weren't enough golfing plebs to make up a team, so a couple of ex-employees were invited to make up the numbers.*

That's where I came in.

Our opponents that day were Derek Bingley and Paul Hammond, Directors of Marketing and Corporate Affairs respectively. They always played together – and boasted a personal unbeaten record. Moreover, in the ten years since the competition's inception, the plebs had never won the trophy. I was well aware of those particular statistics and was determined to change them in the next hour or so.

Hammond was a fairly affable character, if a little timid. He spoke with a mild stammer which gave him a slightly nervous demeanour, but most people quite liked him. Bingley, on the other hand, was a bombastic asshole. Nobody liked him. After what he did to me, I hated him.

Today I was determined to exact revenge.

I'd worked at African Tobacco a few years previously, but had left the company rather ignominiously. More of that later. Suffice to say that after I left, I didn't stay in touch with many people – Lofty was one of the few. In some ways I had no choice; he's my brother-in-law after all. But, despite that complication, we'd become very close friends. He helped me a lot when I first came to South Africa, not only in business but as a mate too. As a result I would do almost anything for him, which was just as well really because our relationship was about to be severely tested.

At this stage in the competition, the director and staff teams were tied at two matches each. Ours was the last match and the stakes were clear: if Lofty and I won, not only would we inflict the first ever defeat on the Bingley-Hammond partnership, but the plebs would also win the coveted Directors' Cup for the first time. And of course, I'd have my revenge on Bingley. To achieve this, I needed Lofty's help. He wasn't a great golfer – a twenty-three handicap in fact – but he could putt pretty well, and I'd placed all my hopes on him being good enough.

○

Lofty looked nervous as he teed up his ball.

"Don't worry, I'm sure you know exactly what you need to do for the next two holes," chirped Bingley sarcastically.

What a tosser, I thought for the umpteenth time. When it's his shot, there has to be total silence. When it's our shot, he can chirp all he likes. Arrogant prick. He won't be so bloody clever when he's explaining to his colleagues how he lost the trophy.

Lofty managed a weak smile. Then he carved his tee shot into the rough.

"Looks like the pressure might be taking its toll," smirked Bingley as he teed up his ball.

"Pressure is my middle name," I shot back, unable to resist the bait.

"Ah, yes, but you don't work for us anymore do you? Your partner here has his career to worry about."

I couldn't believe Bingley's arrogance. He hadn't changed. I just hoped that this flagrant act of gamesmanship wouldn't continue to affect Lofty. He looked ill.

"It's okay, Lofty. I've got it covered," I told him before Bingley could rub further salt into the wound.

Bingley and Hammond both got their drives away okay, before Lofty and I headed for the rough to find his ball. It actually wasn't lying too badly.

"Don't let that supercilious prick get under your skin," I said. "We've got them by the balls."

"Easy for you to say. You don't still work for African Tobacco. Bingley doesn't control your career."

"Lofty," I said as reassuringly as I could manage, "this is a golf match for heaven's sake. Let's win it. Tomorrow it will be business as usual *at the office. And in a couple of years Bingley will be retired and you can have his job."*

"Yeah, okay," replied Lofty, but he didn't look convinced. *He played an ugly but effective shot which trundled safely onto the green. Not close, but safe. He still looked ill though.*

The rest of us found the green. Crucially though, Hammond and Bingley were both a long way from the hole, whilst I'd hit a decent shot and left myself about fifteen feet for birdie.

In the ensuing putting contest, Lofty left his putt about four feet short, whilst Hammond ran his six feet past. He then tried to hole out for par, but after taking an age to line it up, he missed again and made bogey. Advantage us.

"Hammond, you're bloody useless. You could have screwed that up in half the time," Bingley said, *without a trace of humour. He was even obnoxious towards his fellow directors.*

His admonishment of Hammond turned out to be rather premature though, as he also raced his putt past and left himself a slippery – and imminently miss-able – downhiller for par. The initiative had shifted further in our favour.

I had a quick look at my putt, but then decided to get Lofty to hole out. If he made his putt, then I could have a real go at my birdie and it wouldn't matter if I three-putted. A real advantage.

"Try and get me the par, Lofty," I said.

Palpably fighting his nerves or his demons or both, Lofty somehow holed the putt, then strode over to pick his ball out of the hole. He'd made his par and given me a free look at birdie.

I could barely believe what happened next.

Lofty pocketed his ball, then picked up Bingley's marker and handed it to him.

"You don't have to putt that one. I'm sure you would have holed it," *he mumbled unconvincingly.*

I was speechless. A downhill three-footer? I'd seen professionals miss those putts hundreds of times. I couldn't believe he'd conceded it.

I wanted to say something, but chances are it would have been along the lines of "What the hell are you doing, you asshole???" so I stopped myself.

Bingley glanced over at Hammond and gave him a smarmy but relieved look. This just incensed me even more. Rattled, I just couldn't get comfortable over my putt and made a bad stroke. The ball didn't even reach the hole, let alone go in.

"Hole halved in four!" declared Bingley, in possibly the most pompous voice he could have mustered. "Still all square."

As Lofty and I walked together to the next hole, I could no longer contain myself. "What the hell were you thinking, giving him that putt?"

"I didn't think it was in the spirit of things to make him putt it. I'm sure he wouldn't have missed it."

"Well I would have loved to give him the opportunity to try. That could have been one up to us!" I shook my head and tried to forget about it as we walked onto the eighteenth tee box. No-one spoke a word as we prepared to tee off.

I went first and unleashed all of my pent up anger on the ball. Fortunately, I caught it flush and it sailed down the middle of the fairway. Lofty remained totally out of sorts – I couldn't work out if he was even trying or not – but he composed himself well enough to find the fairway. He was followed there by the directors, although I was pleased to see that Bingley's ball seemed to take a bad kick right.

Lofty was first with his approach. He hit a pretty decent shot, about thirty feet from the hole. He seemed to have gotten his act together just in time.

To my delight, Bingley had found a shocking lie in some thick grass about a yard off the fairway. A bad break, but it couldn't have happened to a nicer guy. He had plenty of experience – he had been playing golf for many years – but he didn't have the skill to handle this shot. He smothered it, and we watched it trundle right across the fairway and into the little stream that guarded the green. I allowed *myself a discreet fist pump.*

Hammond was next and the pressure seemed to be getting to him too. He seemed to take ages to choose his club and even longer to play his shot. When he did so, it was a rare bad one, chunked along the ground and also into the stream. I opted against a fist pump this time. Instead, I concentrated on sizing up my shot. A hundred and thirty-five yards into a slight breeze. A simple nine-iron. If I could hit it close, we'd almost definitely won.

I pulled my club from the bag and went through my usual routine.

Two practice swings …

Pick a spot and line it up …

Address the ball …

Waggle the club twice …

Stand frozen for a few seconds …

Then pull the trigger …

As soon as I hit it, I knew it was perfect.

"Be right," I murmured and then, as the ball lasered towards the flag, I said it again, louder and more confidently: "Be right!"

The ball landed like a bag of sugar, less than two feet from the pin.

I didn't say anything. I didn't do anything. I just stood there and felt my heart pound. We'd done it. We'd done it!

"Fine shot," Hammond offered graciously. Bingley just bowed his head and set off towards the green. I'd shut the wanker up at last.

As expected, neither Bingley nor Hammond could produce a miracle. Bingley took a penalty drop behind the stream, but then found the greenside bunker. From there he couldn't get it close and two-putted for a triple bogey. He was red-faced as he retrieved his ball. Hammond also took a drop, then hit a reasonable chip but left himself twenty-five feet and was unable to convert it. He eventually cleaned up for double bogey.

I was a bit surprised that they hadn't conceded my putt, especially after Lofty's over-generous concession on the previous hole. Quid pro quo and all that. I could even have three-putted and we'd still have won. I was tempted to walk up and tap it in just to get it over with, but Lofty had an outside chance of birdie so I thought it better to let him finish them off. Allow him to redeem himself and have the glory.

Boy was I wrong. What happened next would live long in my memory.

Having marked his ball, Lofty now walked over and prepared to putt. He replaced his ball, picked up his marker, and crouched down to look at the line of the putt.

Then it happened. The scene seemed to unfold in slow motion, like a horrible nightmare. Much as I wanted to intervene, there was nothing I could do. With the precision of a watchmaker, Lofty gently placed his thumb and finger on the ball and rotated it, ever so slightly. You've probably seen the pros do it, to align the writing on the ball with the hole. That would have been all well and good except for one small detail: he'd already removed his ball-marker.

Moving the ball under these circumstances is not allowed. I froze. I knew what the penalty was: loss of hole. Unfortunately, I wasn't the only rules expert.

"Hold on there!" Bingley called out. "I'm afraid that's not permitted under the rules. You can't move the ball like that! I'm afraid that's our hole – and the match!" he proclaimed.

Bingley had a sign above his desk at work that said, 'I may not always be right, but I'm never wrong'. On this occasion, it was true.

I felt sick. I could barely bring myself to shake hands. Lofty looked extremely sheepish. We all knew that he'd done it deliberately.

"Bad luck, old chap," said Bingley, grinning from ear to ear like a Cheshire cat.

"Well played," offered Hammond, looking embarrassed. He knew it was a hollow victory.

○

"… and for the rest of the evening," I fumed to Shelley, "Bingley was *so* full of himself, going on about how they had toyed with us. Then we had to sit through his speech. I hated it."

"That sounds just hideous. What came over Lofty?"

"I talked to him about it afterwards. He just bottled it. He admitted that he'd done it on purpose. He said he was terrified that it would be a career-limiting move to beat his boss."

"Oh dear. It's so sad. But that job means so much to him, I suppose I can understand it in a way."

"Well, I bloody can't! What about me? That was my chance of revenge that he took away! And just you watch: it won't make a blind bit of difference to his career."

I couldn't have been more wrong.

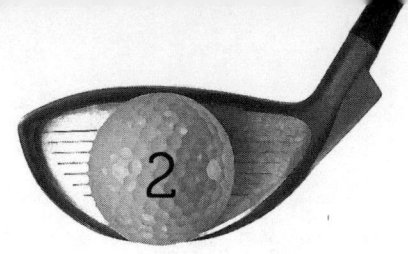

2

Speedy isn't my real name, but you'd probably guessed that. I was christened David Holmes and only acquired my nickname when I took up golf. Although I became interested in the game at a young age, I only started playing fairly late – in my early twenties, just before finishing university. Not unusually, I took up the sport because some of my mates had started playing. It seemed like a good way of spending my time during the long vacations. Being brought up in the North of England though, the weather was often too miserable for golf. Nonetheless, we played whenever we got the chance.

All of my buddies knew me as a very fastidious character, so the way that I approached the game was no surprise to any of them.

Carefully.

Meticulously.

Painstakingly.

Bloody slowly.

I saw it differently. I reasoned that if I was going to play, I was going to do it properly. I made sure I had the correct grip, that I was aligned properly, that my stance was right. But I did take my time doing it. *Boy*, did I take my time! I made Bernhard Langer look like Usain Bolt. People called me 'anal'; I preferred to think of myself as 'thorough'. It only took me one round of golf to earn my rather creative pseudonym. Soon enough I got hooked on the game and set myself a goal of getting to single figures. My 'thorough' approach paid off: within a few years, I'd made it to a nine handicap.

I had a few golfing heroes, but my idol was Gary Player. When I first became interested in golf during the late 1970s, he was already in his forties, but he was still winning tournaments. As a golfer he was great in many ways, but the thing I really liked about him was his attire. In those halcyon days of Rupert Bear-style checked trousers and badly clashing shades, he nearly always wore black. Not only was it pretty cool, it was also practical, especially for me because I'm colour-blind. Whenever I risked wearing a multi-coloured outfit, disastrous results ensued. So, as soon as I took up golf I emulated Player's all-black garb.

During my formative golfing years, I graduated from university with a lower second class honours degree – I liked to call it a drinking man's degree – and secured myself a job in a small management consultancy near London. I enjoyed the work, which basically consisted of analysing and solving business problems for corporate clients. I did well at the firm, and after five years I had become an associate director. About the same time, I met Shelley.

I was working on a project at a large IT services company, when one day this new contractor started in my area. She arrived in the office in a flurry, rather like the Tasmanian Devil on steroids. Except she was better looking and had bigger tits. Anyway, it was a long time since there had been so much energy in the place. It was as if someone had told her that the building was on fire and she had come to put it out.

But she didn't put out *my* fire. Far from it. We started dating and quite quickly it got serious. Her initial contract at the company was only for six months, after which she had intended to leave and return to her native Cape Town. However, at the end of the six months she agreed to extend the contract and, later, would admit that the main reason was so that she could carry on seeing me. Clearly she was insane too.

At this point, however, she ran into a problem. Her contract wasn't the only thing that had been valid for just six months: the lease on her flat also expired. Fortunately, I had a spare room in the house I was renting. Problem solved: she moved in with me. Not that the spare room got much use.

Within another year we were married. One year later we had our first baby, Danny, and eighteen months later along came our second baby boy Jamie. Crash, bang, wallop. My life was suddenly very different. Not that I minded – we were all very happy. I even managed a bit of golf, although with parenthood and the dubious English weather, it was a little too infrequent for my liking.

Then, rather suddenly, things changed again. One day I got called into the Managing Director's office out of the blue and was told the news: the firm had been bought out, swallowed up by a much larger consulting practice. This presented me with a choice: stay on and take a role as Divisional Director in the new parent company or take the money and run.

I chose the money. What's more, I did run – to Cape Town. Shelley and I had been talking about the possibility of moving there for a while. Up to then it had just been talk, but when this retrenchment offer came around it seemed like a sign. It just felt right.

I didn't have any work when I landed in South Africa. The only business contact I had was Shelley's brother, Lofty, who worked at the African Tobacco Company. Through him I got a foot in the door. They interviewed me, liked me and I agreed to join.

My job at African Tobacco was in the Internal Consulting department, which was known within the company as 'IC'. My role was to work with the other 'real' business areas such as Production, Logistics, Finance and Marketing to make them run more efficiently. My first project was working with the Marketing team – Lofty's department. Or to be more precise, Derek Bingley's department. Remember him?

I enjoyed the work, as much as one *can* enjoy work, that is, but I was keen to rise up through the ranks. Problem was, it was pretty difficult to do that at African Tobacco, especially in IC. Dead men's shoes and all that. So after I'd been consulting to

Marketing for a couple of years and couldn't see where my next move was coming from, I hatched a brilliant plan. Well, *almost* brilliant as it turned out.

I arranged a covert meeting with my boss and the Managing Director, and cunningly engineered a sideways move to Marketing, where there were much better long-term prospects. I set it all up beautifully and put the final piece of the jigsaw in place just before I went on a two-week holiday. There was, however, one problem: Bingley hadn't been consulted. I returned from holiday to discover that the pieces of my jigsaw were scattered all over the floor.

I was shocked to learn that my plan had been modified somewhat. Instead of my dream move to Marketing – the department of deep shagpile carpets, designer suits, bouffant hairstyles, fancy cars and inflated salaries – I would be moving to a 'special project' in Production – better known for its noisy machinery, all-night shift work, crew cut hairstyles, room temperature IQs and industrial language, not to mention the ubiquitous odour of tobacco leaf. I'd be based in the factory.

No prizes for guessing who'd arranged this for me.

I knew almost nothing about production, and before I had even worked out what the hell I was supposed to be doing, the six-month project had reached its end. Hardly anything had been achieved and my new assignment had run its course. With my old position filled, I was out of a job and there was only one real option left: all roads led to redundancy. I left under a cloud and, whilst I subsequently found gainful employment with Rivlin & Lloyd Consultancy, I still couldn't forgive Bingley for what he'd done. I hated him with a passion.

Ironically, and rather unfortunately for me, African Tobacco was one of my new firm's clients and as part of my new job I had to put in the occasional appearance there. I tried my best to keep this to a minimum: once a month, twice at the most. It was quite nice to go and visit Lofty, but I couldn't bear to even breathe the same air as Bingley.

The Director's Cup was going to be my chance for payback. Maybe it wouldn't wipe out the debt entirely, but it would be a sizeable down-payment nonetheless. I'd been determined to beat Bingley. I was one short putt away from doing just that, but then, as you will recall, along came Lofty.

○

Alan 'Lofty' Jacobs had never been very good at anything, or at least that's what he'd been programmed to believe. He was actually fairly good at a lot of things, but for some reason his parents had compared him – unfavourably – to their other two kids. He never quite measured up, literally or figuratively.

He was short for one thing. That didn't help. He was quite bright, but not quite as bright as Shelley. He was quite good at sport, but not quite as good as his older brother, Nick.

Unfortunately his 'I'm no good' mindset had followed him into adulthood. His grades might just have been good enough to have gotten him into university, but instead he went to the local technical college and did a marketing diploma. He figured that he would have more 'discretionary' time that way. I forgot to mention that he was a bit of a lazy bastard too. But whilst he was studying, he was forced to get a part-time job as a waiter in a local restaurant to help pay the bills. That's where he met Abigail.

Like Lofty, Abigail worked at the restaurant part-time to support her studies. Unlike Lofty, she was a top law student at the University of Cape Town and, again unlike Lofty, she worked incredibly hard. It took a few weeks, but Lofty eventually plucked up the courage to ask her on a date, and no-one was more surprised than he was when she agreed. For reasons known only to herself, by the time their graduation came around they were engaged.

It was during this time that she gave him his nickname. He was certainly not the world's tallest fellow, but in comparison to her he was, well, short. At nearly six foot tall she towered above him so, rather creatively, she named him 'Lofty'. It stuck.

Abigail graduated *cum laude* – which I think is Latin for 'top marks' – and slotted straight into a job at a big law firm. The closest Lofty ever got to *cum laude* was a rather embarrassing incident at the seedy Green Point gymnasium when he tried to bench press too much and got trapped under a barbell, in the process arousing a great deal of unwelcome attention from some of the more liberally minded clientele. But let's not go there.

Despite an obvious lack of commitment, he scraped through too and did well to get a pretty decent job as a marketing analyst with African Tobacco. Soon afterwards, he and Abigail were married. Lofty had to stand on a box for the photos.

The other area in which Lofty's nickname didn't quite fit was his ambitions. Whilst Abigail went from strength to strength, eventually setting up her own legal practice, Lofty was happy to plod away slowly, which he continued to do for the next few years. He climbed the career ladder in a pretty traditional fashion and ended up being one of several Marketing 'second in commands'. He did okay without ever setting the world on fire.

His boss – Derek Bingley, in case you'd forgotten – was in his late fifties and everyone knew he would be retiring in a few years' time. He'd been there since he was about sixteen and there would be no point in him staying any longer. His retirement often seemed a long way off, but all the potential successors – Lofty among them – had to get their ducks in a row to make sure they were best placed to step into his shoes. This basically meant lots of brown-nosing, which to some extent explained Lofty's actions on the golf course that day.

That didn't necessarily mean that I could forgive him any time soon.

When I woke up the next day, I was still battling with this whole forgiveness concept. I always play 'Kahula Slack Key Guitar' as my wake-up music, ever since we bought it on honeymoon in Hawaii. It is soft and gentle, and usually has a calming effect on me first thing in the morning. But not that day.

I'd had some weird dreams the previous night. Most of them involved Bingley meeting an untimely end. In one version, he got sacked from his job and then committed suicide. Shotgun in the mouth. In another version, I kidnapped him, hung him from a rope by the feet in my garage and beat him senseless with a nine-iron. It might have been a pitching wedge, actually. I couldn't say for sure, but I'm sure you get the gist. And in yet another version, I tied him to a chair, covered him in petrol and cut off his ear whilst listening to an old Stealer's Wheel song on the radio.

Nothing too unusual really.

As I gradually reached consciousness that morning, I was still having visions. In the latest instalment – there were even more episodes than in the Rocky series by this stage – Bingley was driving his Jaguar XJ over the edge of a cliff. I'd fiddled with his brakes I think. And if I'm not mistaken, my mother-in-law was in the passenger seat. I managed a quick wave goodbye as they disappeared from sight. I was actually a bit disappointed to wake up.

My first clear thought was that I wanted to get even. With Bingley, not the mother-in-law. Mind you … Nah, on second thoughts, that will have to be another story.

Remember what Bill Shankly said about football? 'Some people say it's a matter of life and death, but it's more important than that.' That's how I felt about that particular golf match. There was so much more to it than just being a game; the whole thing just didn't seem fair.

Bingley was a scheming bully who had ridden his luck for his entire career, sitting in his ivory tower wondering who he was going to pick on next. He didn't seem to work very hard or very long, yet he had risen up the ranks and stayed there. He had developed this reputation of being bombproof. No-one really knew how he'd done it. Yet done it he had, and what's more he had shafted me in the process.

My theory was that Bingley did all the boring stuff that the Managing Director hated. This seemed to be the thing that protected him, rather like an 'immunity idol' in one of those dumb reality shows. But not only had Bingley acquired this immunity, he'd used it over the years to mess up the careers of numerous people. I just happened to be the latest. No-one had ever successfully taken him on. A few had tried, but Bingley always seemed to have the last laugh.

It was outrageously unfair.

Winning the Directors' Cup, taking it from Bingley in front of everyone, would have been perfect. It could have been my moment: The underdog rises up and overturns the odds at last.

And it so nearly happened. If I'd just putted out …

But Lofty had committed the greatest act of appeasement since the days of Neville Chamberlain. Peace in our time, my arse. He lost his bottle, lost us the match and denied me the chance of retribution that I longed for. It hurt like a kick in the bollocks. And if you happen to be one of the fifty-something per cent of the population that don't actually have bollocks, just trust me: it hurts.

I had a big stretch and remembered how I'd felt when I went to bed. I thought about it quickly to see if the feeling of vengefulness had passed.

It hadn't. I was still mighty peeved.

I opened my eyes and looked at the ceiling, sat up, scratched my nuts and inhaled deeply.

Aaaah, the unmistakable smell of freshly ground coffee: Shelley was already up.

Then the sound of a cereal bowl smashing on the floor: so were the kids.

I settled into my familiar morning routine. I've never been a morning person. My philosophy is always to stay in bed as long as humanly possible, then get up at the last minute, rush like hell and get ready in the shortest feasible time. As a result, I have invented a few creative techniques to make this routine as efficient as possible.

For instance, whilst most people first go to the loo and then brush their teeth, I do both together. I even manage to gargle with some mouthwash. It's the only time I ever multi-task, really. I reckon it saves me a couple of precious minutes every day.

So on this day I dragged myself out of bed, executed my well-practised routine, then dried the end of my old man with a carefully folded square of toilet paper. I always did this to avoid getting a 'wet penny' – that horrid little blob you get on your undercrackers when you haven't quite gotten rid of the last drop. For some reason I seem to be more susceptible to it these days. Maybe my prostate is giving up. Anyway, I flushed the toilet, spat in the sink, rinsed my toothbrush and then gargled noisily one final time.

"I still don't bloody believe it," I told the bathroom mirror as I spat out the minty-fresh mouthwash. "If I had just putted out, it would have been over. But how could I expect Lofty to do *that*?"

I stopped talking abruptly as Shelley entered the bedroom. I felt a bit stupid, not for the first time in my life.

"You're not at it again are you?" she asked, accustomed to my habit of talking to myself.

"I was, but then I heard you coming so I stopped and got out of bed," I said with a smirk. You can't beat a good knob-joke first thing in the morning.

Shelley just cast her eyes heavenwards.

"You know what I mean. What were you yakking on about this time?"

"I'll give you three guesses. The clue is that it involves your brother and me trying to get a little white ball into a hole."

"Oh, *that*."

"Yes, *that*. I still can't believe he did it."

"No, neither can I, but there's nothing much you can do about it now. Look, it's Friday. Just try and forget about it for today. Keep your head down and by Monday it probably won't seem like such a big deal."

I doubted that very much, but I didn't have time for a long and probably futile debate. It was time to get going. I finished getting ready, said goodbye to Shelley and the kids, then climbed into my silver 2005 Honda Jazz and zipped out of the drive. I glanced at the clock: 06:22. I should just beat the rush hour.

I always set the clock seven minutes fast – a technique I learnt on a time management course. Of course, my brain should surely have known – sub-consciously if nothing else – that it was actually 06:15. But for some reason this little trick seemed to successfully deceive me on a daily basis.

Twenty-three minutes later I arrived at the office and parked the car right at the front door. While getting up early for golf is tolerable, doing it for work is a real challenge for me. Despite my aversion to it, however, I do derive more than a little satisfaction from achieving a stress-free journey, as well as the bonus of being able to park more or less wherever I want.

Today there was another downside on top of the usual early morning blues: it was my monthly visit to African Tobacco. What timing! There were only about six other cars there when I arrived, but my mood dropped down a notch when I noticed that one of them was a champagne-coloured Jaguar.

Derek Bingley's car.

"You've got to block it out of your mind," I told myself. "Shelley's right, by Monday you'll have forgotten about it."

I walked through the grand reception area and up the stairs – I never take the lift – then through the double doors to the Marketing Department and into the open-plan office. It was still pretty deserted, but as I walked in I could hear someone talking over in the far corner by the coffee machine. As I got closer, the words became clearer.

"… in truth, we should have had it wrapped up by the fifteenth, but Hammond couldn't putt to save his life!"

Bingley.

I gritted my teeth.

As I walked to my desk, Bingley and three of his sycophantic hangers-on came into view. I didn't look up, but it didn't matter. Bingley had seen me.

"Ah, Mr Holmes, what an unexpected pleasure. I was half expecting you to call in sick today!"

Several rather direct responses went through my head, but I resisted. "Good to see you in such high spirits," I replied instead.

"High spirits? You can say that again! I was just telling the boys here that we're going to enter the *Golfing Journal* Subscribers' Challenge next month after our inspiring win yesterday. Maybe we should team up with you and Jacobs? Mind you, on second thoughts I'm not sure that you'll be able to handle the pressure!"

He turned round and sniggered in the direction of his colleagues.

"Mmmm, maybe we should do that," I said with no conviction whatsoever, willing myself to behave professionally.

"Yes, I think we'll be hot favourites for the Subscribers' Challenge," Bingley went on to his audience. "If only Hammond could learn to drive, chip, putt and hit his irons properly, he'd be a half-decent player!" he guffawed.

"Anyway, you lazy good-for-nothings had better get back to work. Our brands aren't going to market themselves you know! What are you all waiting for? Let's go to it!"

I wanted to go over and punch him in the face, but I realised that probably wouldn't be the best idea. Instead, I sat down, switched on my laptop and immersed myself in my work, determined to avoid Bingley for the rest of the day. By the time Lofty came in to work at 08:30, I had so far been successful.

Being a fairly senior manager, Lofty was entitled to his own personal office and didn't have to sit in the open-plan area with the clerical staff and the consultants. He looked rather dishevelled as he unlocked his door.

"Morning, Lofty, how's it going?" I called, genuinely concerned as to his state of mind. I was still in a pretty foul mood, but after Shelley's pep-talk I'd decided that I didn't want to take it all out on Lofty. I was sure he felt lousy about the whole episode. I got up and walked over.

"Aw, okay I guess. I feel a bit bad for your sake. I know you wanted to whup his ass really badly."

"You got that right," I said as I followed him inside his office. I was unable to deny it.

"But it *is* only a game after all," Lofty went on, unaware that this would push my buttons. "I've got to make sure I'm in the frame when Bingley hangs up his boots. I just *know* he would have shafted me if we'd beaten him."

"Yeah, well, just as long as you're ready to put up with his gloating for the rest of the day. He's started already."

Suddenly Bingley's triumphant face appeared around Lofty's door. "Aaaah, Mr Jacobs! What an unexpected pleasure. I was half expecting you to call in sick today..."

Good grief, he was going to start all over again. What an asshole! That was the cue for me to leave Lofty's office and return to my desk. I wasn't going to stick around to hear it all a second time.

Otherwise I think I might have strangled him.

"Throwing the game isn't going to help you, Lofty, just mark my words," I murmured to myself as I slid out of the door, before switching my attention back to my work.

I pretty much kept myself to myself for the rest of the day. Trying to ignore Bingley certainly improved my focus even though I couldn't help hearing him blab on every five minutes about how he was going to win the Subscribers' Challenge. Every time it happened I went to get a cup of coffee so that I wouldn't have to listen.

I drank a lot of coffee that day.

A last-minute problem with one of my reports meant I was still at my desk at six o'clock. Way too late after such an early start and I was famished too. Time to head home. As I was starting to pack away, Lofty rushed up to my desk with a huge grin on his face.

"Bingley's just asked me to go into his office. He says that he 'wants a word'. It could be good news – a pay rise or even a promotion!" he enthused. He was like a child on Christmas morning.

"Go get 'im, Tiger!" I said, trying not to sound too cynical. I was still angry about the golf match and I was also now a bit annoyed that Lofty's plan seemed to have worked; it looked like he might get promoted after all. I didn't like being proved wrong. I'd probably have to eat humble pie in about ten minutes' time.

I suddenly lost my appetite.

I decided to wait for Lofty to come out. I didn't think he'd be in there long, whatever it was about. What's more, if it was a promotion then he would probably want to go for a quiet beer. And several loud ones.

I called Shelley to let her know I might be late. "Hi love. It's me."

"Hello *me*," she said, as usual.

"I was just about to set off home, but now Lofty's been called into Bingley's office. He reckons his ship might have come in."

"Wow, that's great! So it paid off after all?"

"So it would seem," I admitted begrudgingly. "The bad news is that he's probably going to want to go and get plastered with me tonight."

"Maybe you'll stop being such a misery as a result," she teased. "Lofty deserves a break and it'll be nice to share the celebrations with him. Go and enjoy it."

"I'll try and make sure we just have a quick beer to be honest. I won't be late."

"Just try not to break anything on your way through the front door, whatever time that may be."

I put the phone down and waited, utilising the dead time to delete old emails and then throw scrunched up bits of paper into various nearby rubbish bins. I was just starting to get good at it when sure enough, about ten minutes later, Lofty emerged.

But the look on his face was not one of joy. He looked like he had seen his own ghost.

"Lofty? What happened?" I asked with real concern.

He looked back at me blankly.

"I've just been fired."

3

As we sat at the bar, Lofty continued to shake his head in wonderment.

"I still can't believe it," he said for the umpteenth time that evening. "They just can't *do* that to me."

I could empathise, of course, but I knew that they could do it, and that they had. However, I thought it best not to say so. Technically, Lofty had been made redundant. They had decided to 're-organise Marketing Intelligence' to make it more 'nimble'. The number of management positions had been reduced, and Lofty wasn't one of the chosen few. What's more, they had decided that – 'in everyone's interests' – he should leave with immediate effect. He would get paid for the coming month and would receive a further three months' wages as a lump sum payout, but that didn't seem like much compensation, considering he'd given them fifteen-odd years of his life. I knew that Bingley was behind it all. Again.

I knew how Lofty felt, but I really was lost for words. I wanted to give him the 'told you so' speech, but I resisted the urge. I figured that I'd have to do a lot of 'resisting the urge' that night. I knew that Lofty must now feel extra bad about throwing the golf match. Not only did he fail to get promoted as he'd hoped, he actually got canned instead. It was quite funny really, in a sick sort of way.

"Maybe you should see what Abigail says," I eventually said. "She might be able to find some sort of legal loophole for you." I didn't necessarily believe it; I just wanted to keep the conversation going.

"Nice try. She's good, but she's not that good. They'd never have done this without covering all their bases first."

Lofty was right and we both knew it. So we just went over

and over it, time after time. The only real progress we made was towards a state of drunkenness.

After talking and drinking for hours, it suddenly dawned on me that we'd planned to play golf the next morning. We had a tee time booked at 7:15.

"Crikey!" I exclaimed. "We're supposed to be teeing off at sparrow's fart tomorrow! Don't you think we'd better cancel?"

"No, man, don't be soft!" Lofty replied, borrowing one of my Yorkshire expressions. "I'm not letting this stop me from having a totally miserable time on the golf course."

With that, we paid the bill and staggered out of the bar.

It must have been after midnight by the time I arrived home. As I drove into the garage, I remembered that I hadn't phoned Shelley to warn her that I was going to be quite this late. I tiptoed into the house, hoping that she'd gone to sleep. No such luck – when I staggered into the lounge, she was sitting there watching TV.

"A quick celebratory beer was it?" she said, clearly unimpressed.

"Hmmm, yeah, well, it washn't quite ssho sshimple," I slurred.

"I can see that!" she replied, suddenly lightening up a touch and trying not to laugh.

"No, you don't underschtand. Lofty'sch been bloody well schacked!"

"*What?*" she said, taken aback. "Sacked? But you said …" I watched denial, acceptance and finally sympathy cross her face.

"Oh no. Poor Lofty. How? Why?"

Shelley and I then spent half an hour or so revisiting the same ground that Lofty and I had been over.

"What makes it worse," I said, at last managing to speak without constant slurring, "is that Bingley keeps blabbing on about how he and Hammond are the best thing since sliced bread and how they're going to beat everyone at the Subscribers' Challenge."

"What's the Subscribers' Challenge?"

"It's this big golf competition run by *Golfing Journal*. Anyone can enter. You pay a few hundred bucks and you can play in the tournament. It's the prize that makes it such a big deal: the winners get to go to the States and play at Augusta National.

"Bingley has obviously decided it's the competition to win this year. I think all the corporate big-wigs will have entered. There'll be a lot of kudos for the winners. Bingley actually asked me if Lofty and I wanted to play with him, although I think he was trying to wind me up a bit more. He'll play with some of the other directors I would think. Besides which, I don't ever want to share the same golf course with him again."

"I've got an idea," mused Shelley. "Why don't you two enter the match and kick his ass?"

"Hah! Nice thought," I said, not taking her seriously.

"But why not?" she insisted. "If it's such a big deal to him, then why not go and beat him? You know, *schadenfreude* and all that."

"Huh? *Schaden*-what?" Was this another Afrikaans word I needed to learn?

"It means 'pleasure derived from the misfortunes of others'. It's German," Shelley explained knowledgeably. She saw the blank look on my face and decided to get back to basics. "In other words, even if you don't care about winning for your own sake, it will still be worth it just to see him lose. Why not give it a go?"

"Well, for a start, there are only two of us. We need four. And what's more, I'd rather break into his office and put a virus on his PC. Get him sacked. That would give me much more *schadenfreude* than beating him at golf. But I have to say that's not what's on my mind right now."

"Really? What is?"

"The fact that I've got to be out of bed *and* sober in about five hours." I swayed down the corridor in the general direction of the bedroom.

Shelley started to follow me, but before she turned off the kitchen light, she put two aspirins and a glass of water out on the counter. With them, she left a note which read 'Enjoy your game – here's your breakfast.'

My alarm went off at 06:15. I got up, whizzed through my 'get ready quick' routine, then gobbled down a bowl of instant oats. All whilst nursing a rather severe headache. Shelley's aspirins were gratefully wolfed down too.

I brushed my teeth a second time in an attempt to get rid of the taste of stale beer, then went to the garage to pack my stuff into the car. Ten minutes later I was pulling into the car park at Westlake, the golf club where Lofty and I were members.

Westlake is a fabulous club. Not only is it always in good condition, but it's a pretty stern test of golf, especially when the wind blows. What's more, it's the most social golf club in Cape Town, which is actually the main reason that Lofty and I had joined.

The notorious Cape Doctor – the furious south-east wind that barrels through Cape Town on most summer days – had not yet got itself up to full tilt. And it was set fair. That was good. What with my hangover and the rather depressing events of the previous day, the least we could hope for was decent weather.

I thought about what Shelley had said the previous night. I was annoyed enough when we lost the Directors' Cup. Now that Lofty had been fired too, well, I was officially livid. The thought of Bingley sitting there in his fancy office, plotting this and then gloating afterwards, made me squirm. It made me want revenge just that little bit more. I wondered whether the Subscribers' Challenge might just provide me with the perfect opportunity after all. But the chances of us getting a team together *and* qualifying *and* winning were, to say the least, extremely remote. I still preferred the idea of a virus. Maybe even a real biological one instead of a computer one.

I wandered down to the pro shop to sign in. The place was quiet – it was still only 06:45. The Professional, Nicolaas, was manning the till.

"Mo-ra," I said, slowly and deliberately. I liked to show willing in my adopted country by speaking to Afrikaners in their own language. The problem was that my vocabulary only extended to a grand total of about ten words. And eight of those were profanities.

"*Gooie môre, Mnr Speedy. Hoe gaan dit met jou?*"

"Beg your pardon? Sorry, I've only learnt how to say good morning. I don't know how to deal with the reply yet!"

"Terribly sorry," he said, effortlessly changing to English. "Is the local dialect a bit too complicated for foreigners such as yourself? Maybe we should just stick to a simple language like yours. You know, fewer long words to mispronounce!" He laughed disdainfully.

Oh? He was going to make fun of the English was he? How dare he! Well, if he wanted to play hard ball, he'd come to the right place. I had an ace up my sleeve.

"How about you try and get your tongue round the name of the place where I was born? Then we'll see who's the language expert here!"

I was born in a place called Penistone. I always derive great amusement from the fact that people pronounce it 'Penis-', instead of the correct way, 'Pennis-'. This would show him.

"I bet it's not quite as obscure as my home town," he retorted.

Okay, he'd taken the bait, had he? Brave man.

I grabbed a pencil, scribbled down 'Penistone' and confidently handed it over to him.

"*Pennis*-tone," he said, knowledgeably. "Just between

Huddersfield and Sheffield, isn't it? My wife has family who live near there."

My day was not going particularly well so far.

Okay, fair do's. Round one to him. I could handle it. But I wasn't going to let him win that easily. Foolishly, I tried to salvage some pride.

"Okay, smarty pants. So what's yours then? It has to be 'Something-berg', hasn't it? Every South African town is 'Something-berg'. What is it – 'Randberg'?" I laughed.

"You're close, but no. It's 'Something-fontein'," he replied.

"Well, excuse me!" I said sarcastically. "Is it 'Randfontein' then? That's it, isn't it?"

He shook his head. "Not quite. It's actually Tweebuffelsmeteenskootmorsdoodgeskietfontein."

There was a brief silence whilst I prepared my next counter-chirp.

It never arrived.

"Okay, right," I said eventually. "What time do we tee off?" Best to quit whilst I was only slightly behind. I don't think he noticed. Much.

"Let's see," said Nicolaas, grinning as he traced the sheet with his pen, mercifully deciding not to rub my nose in it. "Ah yes. 07:17 off the first. Holmes and Jacobs. *Yurra*, are you playing with Lofty Jacobs? I haven't seen him here in weeks!"

At that moment, Lofty stepped into the pro shop. I was impressed to notice he was clean-shaven and wearing his brightest shirt. Maybe he was feeling a bit better this morning.

"Speak of the Devil!" I said. "Here he is – early for once! Come on, let's go and warm up. We're gonna need every spare minute to shake off these cobwebs – I still feel a bit ropey. You're looking great though!"

We signed in and made our way out to the first tee.

"Yeah, well, it's all an act I'm afraid," Lofty confessed as we handed our slips to the starter. "I feel lousy."

"Mentally or physically?"

"Both. Mentally, physically, spiritually, psychologically, metaphysically and actually."

"Otherwise okay though?"

He didn't even manage a smile. I was losing my touch. As we marched off towards the first tee, Lofty continued his rant.

"If you want a technical prognosis, I feel crap. Obviously I have a mild headache – I think it was that thirteenth beer that did it – but that's nothing compared to the rest of it. I feel such a bloody fool. I gave over fifteen years to that bloody firm and look what they do to me. What a bloody idiot!"

Much as I wanted to, I couldn't really argue.

"I'm not gonna say 'I told you so'. But you know what? They must have already made the redundancy decision long ago. It was just bad timing." I knew that Lofty's self-confidence would be even more fragile than usual right now so I didn't want to be too harsh on him.

"Bad timing? You can say that again. If only I'd known about it before the golf. If *only*! I'd give anything to go back and kick Bingley's ass!"

Shelley's idea about the Subscribers' Challenge briefly crossed my mind again, but I pushed it aside.

"I don't suppose you've had a chance to think about what you want to do next?" I asked instead.

"As a matter of fact, I have. Abigail's cousin has got this coffee shop and he's been wanting to sell it. I always kind of liked the idea of running a little restaurant or something. His shop would be perfect. I've thought about it before. Abigail and I even talked about buying it, but we didn't have the cash or the time. Now I've got both," he laughed ironically. "I think I might make him an offer. I need to get busy right away and he'd be happy to hand over immediately."

As we walked the course we talked a lot. Well, to be precise, Lofty talked and I listened. He spoke a bit more about the injustice of being fired, but I sensed that this didn't actually bother him all that much, deep down. It was almost as if it had come as a bit of a blessing in disguise. No need to spend another two years sucking up to Bingley, only to have someone else chosen to replace him instead.

What Lofty talked about more than anything, though, was how he had thrown the Directors' Cup. He was clearly mortified about that, and kept going over it time and time again.

"I just don't know what got into me," he said as he prepared to chip onto the final green. "It was already on my mind, but when Bingley made that comment about my career, I just thought …" He tailed off and shook his head. Then he took one quick practice swing and promptly duffed his chip about six inches forward.

"Bollocks!"

He wiped his club on his golf towel and started his routine again. This time he managed to blade the ball across the other side of the green.

"Shit! I can't even bloody chip!" he complained to himself before carrying on about the Directors' Cup. "I really thought he would shaft me if I beat him, just like he did to you. Even after you told me to forget it, I couldn't concentrate. He messed with my head. If I'd known that I was gonna get canned anyway I'd have beaten the smug git. Taken his unbeaten record away. Won the cup. For your sake! Hell, I'd love to have the chance over again."

"Yeah, me too, but we can't. Hindsight is a wonderful thing, but we – I mean, you– have got to put it behind you. Get stuck into that coffee shop venture and within a couple of months you'll be glad this all happened." I watched as he walked up to his ball and nonchalantly rammed in a thirty foot putt.

"At least you're still the best putter in town," I said, trying to find some kind of silver lining for him. He didn't seem to notice it. With the golf out of the way, we went for a drink in the bar.

"Better make it a quick one," I said, remembering that the Lofties – as we affectionately called them – were coming over for lunch. "Abigail will be at our place soon. Besides which, I think we have enough residual alcohol in our systems, don't you?"

We gulped down a quick beer each, then headed home where a yellow Post-it note on the kitchen table announced, 'Just nipped out to get lunch supplies, won't be long'. Next to it, there was a glossy brochure. I picked it up and read the front page out loud: "The *Golfing Journal* Subscribers' Challenge: 26th March and 2nd April".

Stuck to the front page there was another Post-it note. I grinned as I read it to Lofty: "Kick his ass! Shelley xxx".

O

The Subscribers' Challenge was the brainchild of the editor of *Golfing Journal* magazine and some semi-famous ex-golfer whose name I can't remember. It was a competition for the magazine's subscribers that involved a series of provincial games. Two teams from each of these events would qualify for a national final. The winners of that would go to the States and play Augusta National, home of the US Masters. The Western Cape provincial match was to be held at the nearby Steenberg Golf Course. Conveniently, the national final would be held only forty-five minutes' drive away at Erinvale in the Cape winelands.

By the time Shelley arrived back from the shops, Lofty and I were deep in conversation about whether we could – or even should – get a team together. After my initial indifference, I was finally converted; Shelley's note was the clincher. Lofty on the other hand, needed a little more convincing.

"Yeah," said Lofty, "but unless I'm mistaken, there's only two of us."

I pretended to count on my fingers, "Two down, carry the one, let's see ... wow! You're right. There *are* only two of us!" I gave him a sideways look. "I *know* there are only two of us, you plonker, but we can get two more, can't we? It can't be that hard."

"So you got my note then?" asked Shelley, shepherding the kids towards the playroom. "Are you guys up for it, or what?"

"Yes and no really," I said. "I think it's a great idea, but Mr Optimism here is worried about starting his coffee shop. He also doesn't seem to think we know anyone else who'd want to play for what happens to be the most exciting prize ever offered to amateur golfers in this country." I couldn't help the sarcasm; I had seen the light and I needed Lofty to wake up too.

"Surely there are some guys at the office who would like to put one over on Bingley?" suggested Shelley helpfully. "You could just put a notice up at work entitled 'Search for the Fab Four' or 'Seeking the Awesome Foursome' or something that jumps out like that."

"There are already two of us," said Lofty drolly. "If we asked for four, then we'd have six. That's too many." He still looked dejected.

"Then ask for the Dynamic Duo or bloody Gruesome Twosome for all I care," Shelley retorted, kicking Lofty's chair in frustration. "Just get a bloody team sorted. There's only a month to go."

"Awesome Foursome! I like that. It says in the brochure that you're supposed to have a name for the team," I said, getting more enthusiastic by the second. "Come on, Lofty, why not? Let's ask around at least. What about the other guys from the Directors' Cup? You know some of them pretty well, don't you?"

"Yeah, I guess I do," he said in his usual non-committal fashion.

"Then why don't we make some phone calls? Come on, let's do this! Let's create the Awesome Foursome. We can start by filling in the on-line application form right now."

"No need," said Shelley. "It's already done."

Lofty looked at his sister accusingly, but she just grinned and winked at him. "You never know, it might be quite exciting!"

I had no idea just how much of an understatement that would turn out to be.

4

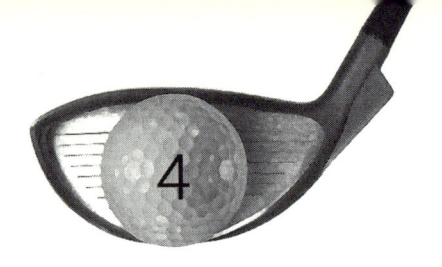

The next few days were frustrating to say the least.

Although the competition itself was a month away, there was a more immediate deadline: we only had ten days in which to submit the names and handicaps of all our four players. If we didn't, our application would become null and void. We needed to get our team together. Quickly.

Lofty was initially reticent in calling his ex-colleagues. Instead he became totally absorbed in his wretched coffee shop plans. By the time he found enough enthusiasm to phone the first candidate, the guy had already signed up to play for another team. What's worse, the next three names on Lofty's list made up the rest of that same team.

Of the remaining two contenders, one guy had just been for eye surgery and the other was booked in for a vasectomy that weekend. I ask you! A bloody vasectomy! If only we were ten years younger, we might have had a different circle of friends. But anyway, that was the sum total of Lofty's efforts.

To make matters worse, I was busy at work and couldn't give the required attention to finding anyone either. It was the end of the month and I had to spend a few days at our head office. One reason for doing so was to catch up on the month-end admin, but the more important reason was to show my face so that they wouldn't forget who I was when the bonuses were handed out.

By the time it got to Friday I had a third objective: it was now only three days until Monday's deadline. I needed to recruit someone – two someones in fact – and fast. I was prepared to pounce on any unsuspecting colleague who might possibly know one end of a nine-iron from the other, but it seemed that no-one did, at least for the first couple of hours that I was there.

Then, just as I was ready to give up, Colin Rivlin appeared at his office door.

Rivlin was the co-founder of Rivlin & Lloyd, the company where I worked, but I didn't know him that well. From what I did know, I didn't like him much. He was originally from Dublin and still had a strong Irish accent. Most Irish people that I had met were good-humoured and easy to get on with. Rivlin wasn't. In fact, he was stiff and usually completely humourless. Worse, on the odd occasion when he *did* decide to crack a joke, he would laugh like a drain. Usually he would be the only one to do so. As a general rule, I tried to avoid him.

The layout of the offices at Rivlin & Lloyd was pretty simple. Rivlin had one office and his partner, Roger Lloyd, had another. Everyone else was either out at client sites or sitting in the communal open-plan office at one of the so-called 'hot desks'. You just came into work as early as possible, grabbed the nearest vacant space and hooked up your laptop. That morning I happened to have found a desk about ten feet from Rivlin's office. I glanced up from my screen as he stepped out of his door.

Scanning the office, he caught my eye.

"Morning, sir," I said, respectfully.

"Morning," he answered disinterestedly, not even maintaining eye contact. He found who he was looking for – one of the other consultants who was sitting just across the office.

"*Phillipé!*" bellowed Rivlin.

The consultant he was glaring at didn't look up.

"*Phillipé!!*" Still nothing. I didn't know the guy very well, but I was starting to get anxious on his behalf all the same. Ignoring the boss is never good for a consultant's career development and I didn't need to witness a second firing in one week.

Rivlin stalked furiously across the room and stopped about three feet away from Phillipé's desk.

"*PHILLIPÉ!*" he roared at the top of his voice. The poor guy nearly jumped out of his skin.

"I need those files in my office – now!" demanded Rivlin before turning and marching back towards his office.

The guy looked around in wonderment, then said to no-one in particular as he followed Rivlin, "But my name is Pierre."

I tried not to laugh. What's his problem? I thought. Phillipé? Pierre? They were both French names, weren't they? Surely that was near enough?

I watched as Rivlin stomped past and something caught my eye: his cufflinks. Silver cufflinks. Silver *golf ball* cufflinks!

I stopped and thought.

Rivlin was a tosser. That much was irrefutable. But if he could play golf then maybe, just maybe, I could overlook that minor detail. I had less than three days. I was desperate. It had to be worth a try.

A few minutes later, a rather dishevelled-looking Pierre came trudging out of the office. He'd obviously just been on the receiving end of Rivlin's infamous hairdryer treatment. Against my better judgement I decided that it was now or never and approached the open door with trepidation.

"Strike whilst the iron's hot, Speedy," I muttered out loud as I approached Rivlin's office.

"Good day, sir," I said as casually as possible. "I wonder if I could have a quick word? I'm sure you're very busy so I can come back later if …"

"Not at all, Donald." At least he'd got the first letter of my name right. "My door is always open. Come on in!"

He was clearly energised after his roasting of Pierre and had morphed into his cringe-worthy 'I'm a people kind of guy' persona. He was even more irritating this way. I was starting to lose my nerve.

"What's on your mind?"

"I just wanted to ask you a quick question. It's not really work related though, so maybe it would be better if –"

"Don't be silly, Hughes!" he interrupted again. "You can ask anything. I'm a great listener. It's one of my strengths, you know. Just ask young Phillipé over there."

"Erm, it's Holmes, sir. David Holmes."

"That's right," said Rivlin, clearly not paying attention. "Of course it is. Yes. Davey Jones. So what's the problem then, Jones?"

I didn't particularly like being called Davey, but Jones? Please! Nonetheless I pressed on.

"I couldn't help noticing your cufflinks —"

"We've all been blessed with two ears and just one mouth, Jones."

"Ah, erm, yes, sir. Anyway, I noticed your cufflinks and it made me think —"

"Listen twice as much as you talk. That's what I'm getting at. Most people just have two modes: 'talking' and 'waiting to talk'. Take a leaf out of my book, Jones. Listen more. You'll be amazed what you learn."

"Yes, sir, you're quite right. I agree. So, I just wanted to find out if you actually play —"

"That's what my wife always says to me. 'Oooh, Colin,' she says, 'you're such a good listener.' She calls me her sounding board, you know."

"I'm sure she does, sir. Which is why I want to just bounce something off you. I'm thinking of entering a competition and —"

"Her soul-mate. She calls me that too. Her confidant. It's quite becoming actually. Rather apt."

"Yes, absolutely. So about this competition —"

This time I was interrupted by Rivlin's cellphone. Without hesitation, he picked it up and peered at the display.

"Just a minute, Davey, that's her right now. *Darling,*" he said, answering the phone, "Jones and I were just talking about you.

No, it's not important, I was just lending Jones an ear. He came in for a chat. Wants to get something off his chest. Make use of the old sounding board, you know." Rivlin winked annoyingly and waved me away. "No, sweetie, it's nothing that can't wait."

Rivlin proceeded to 'listen' to his wife, which ultimately involved him talking non-stop for over five minutes. I eventually decided that it wasn't worth waiting and slowly backed out of the office. Rivlin didn't even notice and I didn't see him again for the whole day.

It was time for plan B. I picked up the phone and dialled Mark Cashen, one of my best friends at the firm. I had always liked his enthusiasm and energy. He always seemed ready to help. He also knew Rivlin pretty well.

"Hey, Mark. Speedy here. How's it going?"

"Hi, what's up?"

"Just something and nothing really. I wanted to ask you something about Rivlin."

"Yes, he is an asshole. I can confirm it," announced Cashen.

"Very funny. I guess you didn't know these phones are bugged, did you? I refuse to comment on that slanderous remark."

"Okay, try me again."

"Rivlin just came out of his office – on some sort of warpath as usual – and I noticed that he was wearing golf ball cufflinks. I just wanted to know if he plays?" To save time I decided to skip a description of Rivlin's subsequent master class in listening skills.

"Ah, so you've got to chapter five of *The Brown-noser's Manual*, have you? 'Play your boss at golf and let him win'?"

"Ha! I could tell you a story about that!" I said, images of Lofty's capitulation flooding into my mind, "but I don't have half a day free. Anyway, it's not that. One of my client's has a golf day coming up and I was just thinking about who I might invite to play," I lied. "I thought about Rivlin, but he doesn't seem like much of a sportsman. I thought I'd check with you before I asked him."

"Well, you were right, he's not a sportsman. He *kind of* plays golf, but apparently he's crap. There was a golf day last year that he played in. From what I heard, he hardly got the ball airborne all day and shot about a hundred and fifty. What's more –"

"Yeah, I know, the back nine was even worse. Very funny." That was one of the oldest jokes in the book.

"So if you want to annoy our clients and lose us lots of business, then choose Rivlin," laughed Cashen. "Otherwise don't bother."

In a way I was pretty relieved. In truth, I didn't really want Rivlin on our team anyway. But on the other hand, there were still only two of us. I was becoming despondent. The Subscribers' Challenge was just over three weeks away. More importantly, the deadline for the submission of the team's names was on Monday at midday.

I had less than seventy-two hours to recruit two more players.

5

Friday night. A party. Just what I didn't feel like.

I looked in the wardrobe for what to wear. As I did so, I let out a huge sigh.

"It's not gonna happen, is it?" I asked myself.

"What's up, love? You don't normally fuss over what to wear. Why don't you just throw on your lime green, striped shirt and your pink cords?" Shelley joked as she came into the bedroom. My colour-blindness was a constant source of amusement to her.

"Very funny. I'm just bummed that I can't seem to find anyone who can play golf, is free on March 26th and isn't a total prick! All I need is two normal blokes like me and we can enter this flippin' competition."

"Normal like *you*?" asked Shelley, in mock disbelief.

"You know what I mean. Is it too much to ask?"

"Look, don't get despondent, Speedy. There's a whole weekend to go. You'll find someone if you just keep at it."

I shrugged. I always admired Shelley's positive outlook and she was usually right too, but this time I wondered if her optimism was slightly misplaced. I didn't feel like looking on the bright side. I felt like I wasn't going to find any more players and that our whole elaborate plan would be over before it had begun. I was like a bear with a sore head. And I felt like staying in and sulking, not going to a bloody party.

I've never been much of a party animal at the best of times. I prefer to hang out with a small group of friends. Big parties aren't my thing, especially when I don't really know anyone. This one was someone's birthday – a mother from our kids' school. Usually I'm happy to make an effort, even if it means putting on an act, but after the week I'd had I just felt like vegging in front of TV. I knew, however, that that wasn't going to happen.

With parenthood came commitments, most of which were quite obvious. But there were some more subtle ones too. Like other kids' parents' birthday parties. Shelley felt that it was the 'done thing' to accept the invite.

To make matters worse, there was a football match on TV: England were playing a crucial Euro Championship qualifier. I wanted to stay at home and watch live coverage of them losing. The highlights of these big match defeats were never as good.

As I was adding my finishing touches – flossing my teeth and extracting any superfluous nose hairs – the phone rang. Shelley answered it in the other room. Moments later she came into the bathroom.

"It was for you," she said, looking very serious. "I said you'd phone back."

"Was it someone about the Subscribers' Challenge?" I said, more in hope than anything else.

"Yes and no really."

For some reason my next thought was that it might be one of my bosses telling me that they'd planned an overseas trip for me and that I would miss the competition. "Not Rivlin? Please?"

"Worse," said Shelley. "It was Derek Bingley."

In all the time that I had known him, Bingley had only phoned me a couple of times and he'd never phoned me after office hours. I couldn't begin to think what he might want, but Shelley was right – it was unlikely to be good news.

"So did he say what he wanted?"

"No. He wouldn't leave a proper message either. He just asked – in an incredibly smarmy and slimy manner – if you would 'kindly call him back as soon as possible,'" she said, imitating Bingley's plummy voice.

I went into the study, took a deep breath and dialled Bingley's number. After about four rings, he answered.

"Bingley!" came his voice, abruptly. He sounded even more self-important over the phone than he did in the flesh. What's more, I hated people who answered the phone with just their surname. My dad used to do it. When Bingley did it, it was even worse. It was so bloody pompous.

"Hello, Derek, it's David Holmes here. You called?" I said, trying to make sure that the call was brief.

"Ah, *Mr Holmes*," said Bingley with a smarm-factor of about two hundred, "How kind of you to phone back."

"Pleasure. What can I do for you?"

I wasn't in the mood for small talk and I didn't mind if Bingley picked up on it.

"Now then, Mr Holmes, don't be a cynic. Who said I wanted anything from you?"

"Call it a hunch. You were saying?"

Bingley's voice finally became more businesslike. Still smarmy, just in a different way. "It's really more a question of what *I* can do for *you*. I've phoned to make you an *offer*."

"Go on." I wasn't buying.

"Well, a rather rare opportunity has presented itself and I wondered if you would be interested."

I said nothing.

"Ahem." Bingley was suddenly not quite as sure of himself. "One of my esteemed colleagues on the Board has sadly had to drop out of next month's Subscribers' Challenge. His wife has been taken ill. Shocking luck, though frankly I don't see why he can't get someone else to take care of her while he's on the course."

Did the man have no shame?

"Anyway, rumour has it that you've not yet been able to cobble together a team. I thought I would give you the opportunity to —"

"Thanks very much, Derek, but we have a team," I lied. "Is that all you wanted?"

"Oh, erm, I see." Bingley hesitated, before regaining his composure quickly. "I would ask you to consider it, Holmes. It's not every day that a chance like this comes along, you know. You do realise that you'd be playing with the *directors*?"

"Like I said, we have a team. Thanks for the offer, but no thanks," I said, without a trace of sincerity in my voice.

"It would be wise to sleep on it at least, don't you think?" he persisted. "Being hasty is never wise. Some might even consider refusal to be a *career-limiting move*." I couldn't believe his arrogance.

"Really? Well, I'm not 'some people' and I take care of my own career, thanks all the same. As for the golf, I've got my own plans like I said. I'll see you next time I'm at the office. Goodbye, Derek."

I had seldom been this mad before. How dare Bingley phone me and pretend that *he* was offering *me* an opportunity? The son of a bitch.

We had to win this bloody thing.

○

The party was being held at a bar just across the road from the beach. It being late summer, the night was fairly balmy. Unusually for Cape Town, there was no wind. I could smell the sea air as we crossed the road, then the aroma of incense instantly filled my nostrils as we walked into Carla's Place. The walls were purple, dark pink and bottle green. The atmosphere was slightly bohemian.

Typically, we were the first to arrive. I still can't get used to how unpunctual Capetonians are. It was five past seven. Technically we were late, but it would be another half-hour before the bulk of the guests arrived. In a way I didn't mind – it gave Shelley and I some time together before we were forced to socialise or, even worse, dance.

We spotted our hosts fairly quickly and walked over to the bar to greet them. I had only met the birthday girl once and couldn't recall her name, although I somehow remembered that her husband was called Roy. Undaunted, I wished her happy birthday anyway. There were no other guests to mingle with so Shelley and I hung around, making small talk.

After a few minutes, in the midst of a scintillating discussion about the merits of the kids' school, Birthday Girl suddenly started waving frantically. "Bernadette and Greg are here!"

I watched, transfixed, as the couple walked over.

I hadn't seen anyone so good looking in a long time. Dark hair and deep brown eyes. Wow. If you liked 'em tall and slim, this was the perfect body. Must have been six feet from head to toe. Maybe more. Wow again. And those legs. Clad in a pair of tight fitting black slacks, they went all the way up to where most people's armpits finish. I could only imagine what they looked like in the flesh. And what a pair of buns! You could have cracked a walnut between them.

His wife wasn't bad either.

She was, in fact, tall, blonde and pretty. But the husband was enviously good-looking, from a purely heterosexual viewpoint, you understand. In addition to all his other attributes, he had a slightly mischievous yet quite handsome face. That's just an objective observation. I didn't *fancy* him or anything! I guessed he was about the same age as me. At least we had something in common.

They came over and said hello to Birthday Girl who did introductions, although I still didn't find out her name. Presently, the guys and girls settled naturally into two subgroups. Maybe it was the fact that he was buying the drinks, but Roy seemed more fun than I remembered him being and I was pleased to note that Greg seemed very down to earth. I was pretty relaxed. Maybe the evening wouldn't be so bad after all.

"So how do you guys know each other?" I asked once we had separated ourselves from the girls.

"Big G and I were at university together," said Roy, nodding at Greg. "We go back a few years."

"Big G? Interesting nickname. Where does that come from?"

"It's from when I was a kid. I was much taller than my classmates when I was young. I never did like the name Greg anyway."

"Okay, 'Big G' it is then. So what do you do for a living, Big G?"

"Erm, well, I'm kind of in property," he replied, rather cagily.

Roy interjected again: "What he means is that he's bloody loaded and doesn't have to work; if he didn't buy and sell houses then he'd just be sitting watching porn on the Internet all day!" Roy guffawed loudly and then added, "Normally, he only watches it for half of the day!"

Big G smiled politely, but didn't really laugh. It looked like he was a bit, well, proper. He reminded me of Peter Perfect from the old Wacky Races cartoon. He certainly didn't join in with Roy's banter, instead looking almost a little embarrassed. He was obviously a bit shy about being a bazillionaire.

When Roy went over to welcome some more guests, I carried on talking to Big G and quickly warmed to him. He seemed to have a fairly good sense of humour and was clearly no dummy when it came to business. We were just starting to talk about the 'who's who' of the Cape Town business world, when his cellphone rang.

"Aw, blast it. I'm very sorry about this. I'm afraid I'd better take it."

I've realised that it's pretty much accepted these days for someone to answer their cellphone whilst in conversation with someone they've just met. I still think it's rather rude, but at least Big G had been polite about it. That seemed to be his style. I smiled and nodded in acknowledgement. Then, equally rudely, I tried to eavesdrop on his conversation.

"No, don't worry, I understand. It can't be helped. We'll do it another time. Okay, cheers, see-ya." He sighed as he put his phone away.

"Good or bad news?" I asked as subtly as I could manage. If he was going to take the call, then I was going to quiz him about it. Screw politeness!

"Oh, it's nothing serious. That was my mate phoning to tell me that he's got 'flu. We were supposed to be playing golf tomorrow."

Golf! My ears pricked up. Suddenly it wasn't just a question of satisfying my curiosity. This had unexpectedly become much more interesting. I'd found a normal person who wasn't a total twat and who played golf! I took a distinct-yet-discreet deep breath.

"Do you play much?" I asked, trying to act nonchalant, but failing miserably. It came out *way* too high-pitched. I cleared my throat rapidly.

"Every other month or so," he answered, apparently not noticing my inadvertent falsetto. "I was up in Johannesburg 'til last year. I haven't got back into it properly. I joined Steenberg but haven't played that much, to be honest."

Steenberg??? The poshest course in town! The venue for the Subscribers' Challenge!

This was too good to be true. I had to try and get him onto the team somehow. Even if Big G was a rubbish player, he HAD to be a better bet than Rivlin.

As you might have realised by now, I'm not the best at thinking on my feet, but despite this I tried to subtly steer the conversation towards the competition. I had to hook him.

"Funny you should mention golf." I said as casually as I could, trying to keep my voice more in the baritone range. "I also got a call from one of my golf partners just this morning. Phoned me to pull out of this competition that we entered. Left me right in the dwang," I lied, hoping that he'd take the bait. He didn't.

"That's a nuisance," said Big G. "I hope he had a better story than my mate. 'Flu indeed! What was his excuse?"

Shit, thought I. Not only had I failed to snare him, he'd gone and put me right on the spot instead. There was no partner and of course no excuse, was there? Now I'd have to elaborate on my little white lie and invent a reason for this fictitious 'partner' pulling out. My mind went blank, and I felt a Pinocchio moment coming on.

I knew that all liars are supposed to end up in Hell, however, at this stage I was prepared to risk it. I tried to think of a plausible explanation.

"Haemorrhoids!" I announced from nowhere.

No sooner was the word out of my mouth than I wished that I could take it back. Haemorrhoids? Was I mad? Of all the possible golfing injuries – twisted ankle, sore elbow, sprained wrist, slipped disc, I had to go out on a limb and plump for good old bum grapes. As if lying wasn't bad enough, I had managed to make a total pillock of myself and create a huge pregnant pause to boot.

Big G looked at me for a few seconds, his eyebrow raised. He wore a bemused expression as he waited for me to carry on. I grinned weakly, lost for words, then decided to buy time by taking a quick sip of my beer.

I sipped and sipped, and carried on sipping whilst I waited for the right words to spring to mind.

They didn't.

About five seconds later, it wasn't just my mind that was empty. My glass was too. Big G looked down at the floor as I stood there with a gormless look on my face, before I eventually broke the silence. Sadly, all I could manage was an extremely loud belch. Damn that gassy lager beer! I knew I should have ordered a glass of wine instead.

Finally I found some words. "So, erm, what's your handicap then?" I said, trying desperately not to look embarrassed. I could feel my whole head glowing bright red.

"I haven't checked lately to be honest, but I think it's probably still two."

A two handicap? My jaw nearly hit the floor. I suddenly forgot about my embarrassment and was dumbstruck once more.

Maybe I did fancy him after all.

6

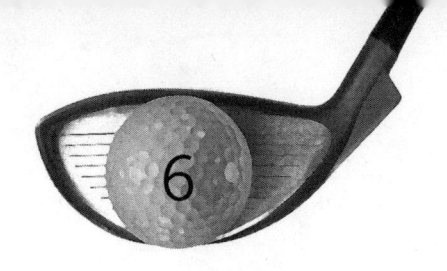

Greg 'Big G' Gardner was born and brought up in Cape Town. His family was, to use a technical term, bloody loaded. He wouldn't have needed to work if he didn't want to, but he was one of those people who is just good at everything. At school he played first team rugby and cricket and was a star athlete. Unsurprisingly he was the school's head boy.

He didn't take up golf until he was about seventeen, but when he did, he was a natural. For his first round, he carded an eighty-eight (by way of comparison, Lofty's best *ever* score is still only eighty-six). Whilst he was getting straight 'A' grades in all his subjects, he was simultaneously getting down to a single figure handicap – a feat which he achieved less than a year after picking up a club for the first time. He has still never shot a round in the nineties.

He sailed through school and decided to study commerce at the University of Johannesburg. Yet again he breezed through and graduated with flying colours. He was basically able to interview several companies and decide which one would have the pleasure of employing him. In the end he chose a large investment bank, also based in Johannesburg. He would have preferred Cape Town, but the business climate wasn't quite as sharp down there. The hours were long and the work was intense, but he relished the challenge. He had no desire to live off his parents' wealth and this seemed to spur him on to work harder, longer and smarter than anyone else. He did well – inevitably – and made a fortune in a few years.

During his time there he met Bernadette. Their first meeting, embarrassingly enough, was in a seedy nightclub. Big G didn't drink very often, so when he did, he got drunk quickly. One of his mates bet that he wouldn't dare chat up the best-looking girl in the place. The rest is history, although Bernadette never found out about the bet.

They dated for a couple of years before getting married and setting up home in Johannesburg's leafy northern suburbs, where they lived for seven years. During this time, Big G made plenty of money and then started dabbling in property. Predictably, he had a talent for it and made yet more money this way. He got to the point where he still made millions without even trying.

Eventually however, Big G pined for something that money couldn't buy: Cape Town. He convinced Bernadette to relocate and she didn't regret it for a minute. In fact she now wonders why it took them so long to do it.

◯

"Wow!" I said, somehow managing to regain the power of speech. "A two handicap! That's pretty impressive for someone who hardly plays!"

I was gushing *way* too much, but couldn't stop myself.

"Yeah, but once I start playing regularly it'll probably go back up quite sharply," said Big G modestly. "How about you?"

"Oh, I'm not quite in your league," I replied. "I'm down to nine, but I think that's as good as I'm gonna get to be honest."

"Well, you're in single figures. That's pretty good!" said Big G kindly. I could see that he was a genuinely nice chap. Not at all egotistical about his own ability, but genuinely appreciative of mine.

"So like I was saying," I continued, remembering the competition and trying to sound nonchalant again, "this bloke has really left me in the lurch. It's only a couple of weeks until the competition and I'm a man down." I could feel my face turning red once more, as images of that fellow with the bad case of piles crept back into my head.

"You're not talking about the Subscribers' Challenge, are you?"

said Big G with a sudden burst of enthusiasm.

"I certainly am!" I said, excitedly. "You're not interested in playing are you?"

"You bet! I've been hassling some of the guys at Steenberg to make up a team, but they've all got some excuse or other. I'd love to play!"

I'd done it! I'd snared him! I'd recruited another team member! One down, one to go! Okay, I'd embarrassed myself a little bit with my ridiculous fable about the guy with the agonizingly sore derriere, but that was all behind me now, so to speak.

Or was it?

"So, who's the rest of your dream team?" Big G asked out of the blue.

Shit. Again. We didn't actually have a dream team, did we? Not a full one anyway. Just me and good old Lofty. I went quiet for a second time. I was either going to have to lie again, or needed to create a diversion, ideally one that wouldn't cause me to burp in Big G's face this time. I'd just about gotten away with my first fairy tale, but I wasn't at all sure that I could get it to work a second time.

In the nick of time, Roy called us all to attention. Time for everyone to gather around and drink a toast to Birthday Girl. Turns out her name was Natasha, although at this moment I didn't particularly care. The only thing that mattered was escaping Big G's probing questions. Shelley raised her eyebrows in surprise as I fairly hurtled across the room to reach her side.

"We're hitting the dance floor as soon as this is over, whether you like it or not," I whispered urgently. Whilst Shelley was still coming to terms with the fact that I had asked her to dance, I took the opportunity to tell her the good news that Big G had agreed to join our team. I even admitted my little white lie about the guy pulling out with piles, at which point she had to quit dancing to avoid peeing her pants with laughter. At least someone thought it was funny.

By the time I had followed her from the dance floor, Big G was safely engaged in conversation with someone else. I congratulated myself on a situation well avoided.

I still needed to firm up our agreement though, so at the end of the evening I located him once more. "So maybe we should have a warm up game at Westlake sometime?" I offered. "It's only three weeks until the competition. Maybe next Saturday?"

"Great idea! But why don't you let me book a game for the four of us at Steenberg? Get some advance knowledge of the course layout. Have you played there?"

A practice match at Steenberg! Wow! Now don't get me wrong, Westlake is a fine course. I love the place to bits. But Steenberg it ain't. If they were cars, Westlake would be a zippy hatchback like a Subaru Impreza, or perhaps a convertible like a Mazda MX-5 or, at a push, a Porsche Boxter Spyder. But Steenberg would be a Rolls Royce.

The evening had gone from bad, to great, to embarrassing and back to great again.

"No, not quite," I replied. "I imagine myself playing there whenever I drive past though! It would be great if you could set up a game for us."

"No problem. Consider it done! I'll book a slot for us. Can't wait to meet the other two guys!"

This last remark bounced around my head like one of Lofty's shots onto the tarmac road outside Westlake. Where I was going to find our final player with less than three days until the deadline?

Little did I know it, but for once in my life the solution would present itself surprisingly quickly.

7

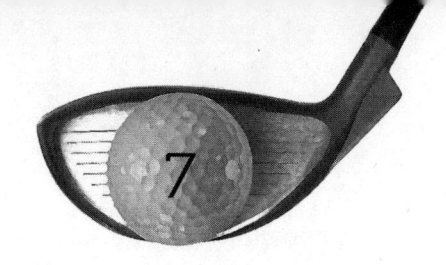

Whilst I'd spent the last week racking my brains over how I was going to get a four-ball together and making a fool of myself by lying to strangers at parties, Lofty had dived headlong into his new venture. Abigail's cousin Alf had been running the coffee shop successfully for many years and it was quite well established, so the risks for Lofty would be minimal. He'd agreed a fair price with Alf and they'd done the deal without much fuss. Alf had also agreed to spend a few weeks showing Lofty the ropes.

Lofty's main objective during this period was to work on business strategy. Blue sky thinking, vision, mission. If that all sounds a bit pink and fluffy, I have to tell you that his efforts resulted in only one tangible achievement: he changed the shop's name. For twelve years it had been known as 'Alf's' and it had become quite a landmark in Cape Town. People would refer to it when giving directions: "Go past Alf's and then turn left." That kind of thing. So rather creatively, and some would say foolishly, Lofty decided to change the name to 'Lofty's'.

Not satisfied with that stroke of genius, he ordered a huge, ostentatious sign to hang up outside. I wondered if he had his priorities right.

But to give him credit, with the 'strategic' side of things taken care of, he then spent every possible moment down at the shop getting to know the customers. In fact, once the signage was done, this became his highest priority. Alf took a back seat whilst Lofty took over all customer-facing aspects of the place; serving the customers and stopping to chat with some of them during the quieter times. This, he figured, would help not only to build a loyal customer base, but would also generate some more 'word of mouth' business.

On Saturday morning, just a week after his unceremonious

departure from African Tobacco, Lofty was at work at six o'clock sharp. He'd always been an early riser, so getting to work at that hour didn't bother him. If nothing else, this whole experience had given him a renewed vigour for life.

Despite having a bit of a sore head – not to mention tired feet – after the party, I decided to surprise him and turn up there nice and early. I was dying to speak to him for two reasons. For one, I wanted to share my good news about recruiting Big G the previous evening. More importantly though, we still needed to work out how we were going to find player number four. Maybe I could tap into Lofty's own very special brand of blue-sky thinking in order to crack this particularly stubborn nut. Hopefully he'd forget about his new business venture for a few minutes and I could get him thinking about our version of the gunpowder plot.

"Hey, guess what? I recruited another player last night. And it gets better! He's a two handicap!" I declared triumphantly as I stirred my coffee, trying my best to arouse his enthusiasm for the Subscribers' Challenge. It worked.

"Jeepers!" replied Lofty with equal fervour. "That's amazing! Who is he?"

"He's kind of a friend of a friend, I guess. I met him at someone-whose-name-I-forgot's birthday party last night. He said he's definitely in. And it gets *even* better – he's a member at Steenberg. He says we can go and play a practice match there as his guests! Awesome, huh?"

"Awesome indeed. This is too good to be true. What's the bad news?"

I should have known that Lofty wouldn't keep his alter-ego, Mr Not-Very-Positive, locked up for too long, and out he'd popped, right on cue. But, to give Lofty credit, maybe he had a point after all – there was the small fact that we still only had three players.

"Interesting you should mention it. What I didn't tell him was that we're still one player short. I suppose you classify that as bad news."

"You're right there. We'd better get on with it. Apart from anything else, this guy will think you're a real idiot if he finds out that it's only me and you, won't he?"

"No shit, Sherlock. Got any bright ideas?"

Lofty didn't get a chance to answer. Our attention was seized by the sound of the door clattering open. A short, stocky man in his late forties barged through it hurriedly. Lofty leapt to his feet. Call me intuitive, but I sensed that our conversation was over. Lofty's bright ideas, if he had any, would have to wait.

"Good morning, sir," said Lofty as he walked over purposefully. "Would you care to look at the menu?"

"No thanks, mate." The man was obviously English, with a strong London accent. What I would have called Cockney. Probably a Millwall fan I guessed. "Just a filter coffee. Bring plenty o' cold milk too. I ain't got time to wait fer it to cool down. I'm already late. Gotta just skull it and get outta here pronto."

Focusing on the challenge of impressing a new customer, Lofty jumped as his coffee machine bleeped loudly.

"I'll be with you just now, sir," he said with a suitably ingratiating smile as the man took a seat.

The expression 'just now' is very popular in South Africa and it's one that I can't get my head around. It doesn't actually mean 'now', which is a term that I can understand. 'Now' simply means 'immediately'. 'Just now', on the other hand, definitely seems to be less than immediate, although I've never really been able to work out exactly *how* immediate it is. The UK equivalent would probably be 'in a moment', but even that would be more precise. From what I can gather, 'just now' seems to mean 'at some indeterminate point in the future' or more likely – 'when I can be arsed'. The Capetonians have another even more esoteric term, 'now-now', but let's not go there.

On this particular occasion, 'just now' seemed to mean 'after I've gone to the counter and switched off that bloody noise'.

Lofty rushed back to the kitchen to get the order as quickly as he could, reappearing with the steaming cup. "Here you go, sir. One filter coffee. My own special blend," he added, rather proudly. "I've just taken over the place so allow me to introduce myself: Alan Jacobs. You can call me Lofty though. Everyone else does."

"I guess that explains the new sign outside," the man grinned, accepting Lofty's handshake. "Simon Rogers. Yer can call me Dodgy. Everyone else does, especially the poor bastards who do business with me!" and, laughing raucously, he lifted his left buttock from the chair and let rip with an ear-splittingly loud fart.

"Keep shoutin', sir, we'll find yer!" he called, cupping his hands around his mouth and chortling loudly to himself.

Lofty obviously didn't know whether to laugh or cry. I knew that he would have found it funny, but he was also desperately trying to establish himself as a serious businessman. What's more, he didn't want to offend the other customers.

Then I saw him relax. This wasn't stuffy corporate life. It was the new Lofty. Man of the people. If people wanted to fart in his shop, he'd fart with them.

"Spoken like a true gentleman!" he said at last. He offered Dodgy a high five and Dodgy responded with gusto.

"Yer only supposed to blow the bloody doors off!!" Dodgy said, sounding remarkably like a young Michael Caine. His laugh now became more of a schoolboy giggle.

Lofty, composing himself and remembering his mission to get to know his customers, moved the conversation along. "Do you work nearby?"

"Not really," said Dodgy, pouring large quantities of milk into his coffee and adding at least four spoons of sugar. "I've just got a business deal goin' on with a big company round the corner at the moment. Should wrap it up in the next week or two. I could tell yer the name of the company, but then I'd have to shoot yer." He aimed his fingers at Lofty before glancing at his watch.

"Oh, I used to be in Marketing at African Tobacco," said Lofty excitedly. "They don't come much bigger than that! I was there fifteen years." He was obviously keen to come across as a real businessman too, not just a coffee shop owner. "What kind of business are you in, Dodgy?"

"Oooh, a bit of this and that. Mainly writin' dodgy software and hackin' into company's systems. A bit like Bill Gates but without the Harvard degree, the billions of dollars or the clean conscience. Anyway, today I'll be doing a different kind of hackin'. Not business, but pleasure. I'm playin' whack-fuck in an hour's time."

Lofty was out of his depth again. He looked totally bemused.

Dodgy simulated a very average golf swing. "Yer hit the ball – whack – then it goes into the bushes and yer shout 'Fuck!' Don't forget though, a bad day on the golf course still beats the crap out of a good day at the office. I play a bit more since I divorced me latest wife. Never get married, I tell anyone who'll listen, just go find a woman that yer don't like and give her half of everythin' you own."

He drained his coffee cup with a noisy slurp, wiping his mouth appreciatively on the back of his hand. Tossing a crumpled bank note on the table, he grabbed his well-used laptop bag from neighbouring chair and got up to leave.

"Right. I'll be back at the same time on Monday morning so get a nice cuppa ready fer me, won't yer? Make it a strong one too – I'm going out on the piss on Sunday night so might need a bit of a kick start in the morning.

"But right now I'm late. I'd better get outta here. Need to get the old joints loose, get practicin'. Remember what Gary Player said?

'The more I practice, the dodgier I get'! I'm desperately tryin' to get onto a team fer this bloody Subscribers' Challenge thingy. That's if any daft buggers will have me!

"But for now, guv'nor, let's just say *ciao, amigo*," he attempted a kind of Spanish-Italian-Cockney accent before looking back and adding, "Or should that be *au revoir?*" as if to emphasise his flair for languages. It didn't work.

At that moment, however, I wasn't concerned with Dodgy's linguistic skills. There was only really one thing on my mind: the Subscribers' Challenge. Here was another golfer! I couldn't believe it! Had our prayers been answered? The final member of our fourball had seemingly just fallen into our laps. We might be teeing it up in the competition after all.

But it was all happening too quickly. Dodgy was half way out of the door already.

"W-w-w-wait," stammered Lofty. He couldn't seem to get the words out. "W-w-what's your handicap?" he managed in desperation.

"A truss, but yer can't see it when I wear these pants!" shouted Dodgy over his shoulder. Then he climbed into an old, beaten up BMW seven series and screeched off into the traffic, blasting his horn and shouting, "Up yours, yer arsehole!" in the general direction of all the other motorists.

Lofty and I looked at each other.

"Are you thinking what I'm thinking?" I whispered.

8

Simon 'Dodgy' Rogers had moved to Cape Town from London about ten years previously. How to describe him? Well, for anyone who has ever seen *Only Fools and Horses*, just think Del-Boy. He was shortish and slightly plump, he wore loud clothing and had an even louder mouth – or 'north and south' as he called it in his rhyming slang. He wasn't much of an academic, but he had an incredible aptitude for computers and had wisely moved into the software industry.

He'd had hundreds of so-called brilliant ideas over the last twenty years or so and had enjoyed varying degrees of success with his different ventures. None of them ever completely failed, but none made that elusive fortune for him either.

A Cockney through-and-through, Dodgy was in his mid-forties, but looked a little older. This was probably explained by the fact that he'd already been divorced three times. When his latest *decree nisi* had become final, he'd decided to get out of England, mainly to escape his growing collection of ex-wives. He'd vowed never to marry again.

His latest scheme was some sort of fancy anti-virus programme that he was writing from within South Africa and planned to sell internationally for a small fortune. Dodgy being Dodgy, however, he wasn't content to limit himself to just this one venture. Once he was settled in Cape Town he dabbled with several other dubious ideas. Some worked, some didn't, but he always sailed very close to the wind.

Lofty and I listened to the cacophony of tyres screeching, horn blowing and profane language as we watched Dodgy pull straight out in front of one of Cape Town's infamous mini-bus taxis. At last, I thought with a smile, I've found someone who drives worse than they do. It had been a brief encounter, but a memorable one. This guy certainly was a character.

Lofty looked at me imploringly. "Should we ask him to play in our team?"

"So great minds do think alike after all! Put it this way, the registration deadline is on Monday, then there are only three weeks before the first round of the competition. If we're going to stand a chance of pulling this thing off then we have to recruit *someone*. And quick."

"Crumbs! Monday? Is that all the time we've got?" lamented Lofty, suddenly realising how urgent it was. "Maybe I should have signed him up then and there? But what if he's no good? What do you think?"

"What I think is that beggars can't be choosers. I'd look pretty stupid if we pulled out now. For one thing, I'd have to admit that there had only been two of us all along. More to the point though, we'd lose our last chance for revenge, wouldn't we? I think we should rope this bloke Dodgy in on Monday. He said that he's coming back, didn't he? You'll have to make it happen. If he's signed up with someone else by then you'll just have to talk him into dropping them and playing with us instead."

"You quite sure?"

"Well we've got two-and-a-bit days before the deadline, and the only other remote possibility is Colin Rivlin. Does that answer your question?"

"Shit! Is it that bad? Say no more – I'm on it!"

○

Lofty opened the shop at 05:45 on Monday morning, making sure he'd be ready when Dodgy arrived. After making another massive effort to get out of bed at this ungodly hour of the morning, I stopped by on my way to work. It was a control thing on my part: I didn't trust Lofty to be decisive enough if things didn't go according to plan.

Lofty got some coffee going and we waited. Ten minutes went by and no-one had arrived. I became slowly engrossed in the newspaper. Some politician or other was under suspicion of corruption – again.

Suddenly there was a screech of tyres as a car skidded to a halt outside. Moments later the door burst open. "Gawd almighty, those bloody taxis. I don't bloody believe 'em!" came a rasping voice.

Dodgy had arrived.

I stayed in the corner, out of the way. Lofty wanted to handle this – for now at least.

"Ah, good morning, Mr Rogers," Lofty said warmly, getting off to a good start, "and how are we today?"

"Lofty, Lofty, please! Call me Dodgy. 'Mr Rogers' makes me feel like a right old wanker. Yer know what I mean – less of the 'old'!" he laughed. "Sorry I'm late anyway. I'm usually very punctual but I had a bit of a cock up with me medication."

"Medication?" repeated Lofty. "That doesn't sound good."

"No it ain't. Last night I got me Viagra and me sleeping pills mixed up, and ended up having forty wanks."

Not for the first time, Lofty didn't know how to react.

"Erm, so what can I *do you fer* today?" His attempt to imitate Dodgy's cockney vernacular sounded rather ridiculous. I hoped that he wasn't going to embarrass himself like I had done with Big G, although it didn't look as though anything could embarrass Dodgy.

"Let's see – a cup of coffee, twenty Rothmans and a blow job," said Dodgy, pausing for effect. "But not necessarily in that order."

"Erm, that's very tempting, but I'm not that sort of gal," replied Lofty as soberly as possible. "One strong coffee coming up," he added, clearly trying to assume control of the conversation.

"Okay, I'll settle fer that then. Bleedin' spoilsport!"

Lofty went into the kitchen to pour the coffee and fetch the cigarettes. "I've only got Rothmans in packs of ten. Is that okay?" he shouted.

"Yeah, mate, that's fine. Just hurry up about it. I'm bloody gaspin'!"

Lofty rushed back with Dodgy's order. "We'd better sit outside though if that's alright with you."

"Yeah, no problem. I need ter wake up a bit. Besides which, I can feel a brutal fart brewin'."

"Let's get outside, quick. I'm going to have to fumigate this flippin' place. I reckon I should give you a permanent table outside."

"Not a bad idea. Yer don't really want the other patrons havin' ter mix with me. It'd be crap fer business. They used me in the Vietnam War when they ran out of napalm, yer know."

Lofty had only just got him to one of the outside tables when Dodgy cracked off the violent trouser-cough that he'd promised. I moved over to a table by the door – close enough to listen, but hopefully far enough away from Dodgy's answer to mustard gas. I buried my face in the paper and tried to remain inconspicuous.

"At least you can enjoy the sunrise from out here," Lofty offered, trying to make up for asking Dodgy to sit outside. "Just look at that! Red sky at night: shepherd's delight –"

"Red sky in the mornin' – shepherd's hut's on fire!" interrupted Dodgy. His customary post-jape laugh petered out, replaced by a rasping smoker's cough. Then he began his sugar-shovelling ritual.

"So how did the game go?" said Lofty, re-opening the topic of golf.

"Bleedin' awful!" said Dodgy, depositing the fourth spoonful of sugar in his coffee. "I couldn't hit a cow's arse with a banjo.

I'd have been better off with a bleedin' hockey stick and a blood orange! Luckily I'm a bloody good cheat – I cleaned up!"

He rubbed his finger and thumb together to signify money, then produced another gravelly laugh-cough.

"Yer've never seen a feller get so many perfect lies in knee-deep rough. I call it the Rogers' Shuffle." He motioned with his foot, as if flicking a golf ball out of long grass. "The Gentleman's Persuader, yer might say."

Lofty seemed a little taken aback, but pressed on nonetheless. "Do you play much?"

"Yeah, now and again. Probably a couple of times a month. I've only got two hobbies: golf and sex. The only two things yer can enjoy without being good at 'em." He paused to chuckle at his own joke again. "Trouble is, I play golf more often than I get me bloody leg over these days."

"So what is your handicap then?" asked Lofty, ignoring Dodgy's banter and doing an admirable job of keeping the conversation going in the right direction. He was better at this than I had given him credit for. "I reckon you're better than you're letting on, aren't you?"

"I suppose I'm alright. Me official handicap is seventeen, but I like ter keep it – how can I put it? – a little on the uppish side, if yer know what I mean," and he winked knowingly over his coffee cup. "I can break eighty on a really good day. It all depends on what the stakes are."

"Well, in that case, I've got a proposition for you," Lofty declared.

"Hey, listen, I've read about your type –"

"About golf," said Lofty, heading off yet another rather predictable quip. "You mentioned on Saturday that you were trying to get into the Subscribers' Challenge. Well, me and a couple of mates have entered it, but one guy has dropped out at pretty short notice. Broke his ankle."

Clearly this lying habit was catching, although at least a broken ankle was a more plausible and less embarrassing reason than haemorrhoids. Why hadn't I thought of that?

"So I was wondering if you might like to join our team?" Lofty concluded.

"Are you havin' me on?" gasped Dodgy in surprise. "'*Course* I'll play! First prize is a trip to Augusta, ain't it? Even one of me ex-wives couldn't stop me! Where do I sign?"

Clearly delighted at having closed the deal so consummately, Lofty decided that this would be as good a time as any to introduce me to Dodgy.

"Now that you're on the team, I suppose you'd better start meeting the others. As luck would have it, one of them is sitting inside, just over there. My favourite brother-in-law, Speedy."

"Favourite brother-in-law? What are yer? Poofters?"

I hadn't even formally met him yet, but it was already clear to me that this Dodgy character had about as much class as your average football hooligan. What's more, he didn't seem to give a toss what anyone thought of him. Not only did he shamelessly fart in public, he was also quite happy to throw blatantly homophobic comments around even though he barely knew us. It's not that I minded a bit of banter, but so far Dodgy seemed rather too crass for my liking.

A moment of doubt clouded what should have been wild celebrations at eventually putting our team together. Had we done the right thing by offering him a berth? It seemed, though, that we'd already crossed the Rubicon on that one, so I quickly stood up and stepped outside.

"Hi, I'm Speedy. And by the way, I'm actually his *only* brother-in-law," I added, only half-jokingly. I wanted to make it clear to Dodgy that his blatant uncouthness was not entirely appreciated.

"Simon Rogers. Call me Dodgy," he replied and shook my hand

firmly. "Nice ter meet yer. As long as yer promise me yer not homos!"

So much for my subtle hint.

"I guess you just don't understand close family relationships," I retorted, retaining my serious undertone.

"Close family relationships? Sounds like incest ter me!"

I decided to quit before I lost patience with him. He certainly was 'dodgy', of that there was no doubt, but at least he can't be worse than Rivlin, I thought to myself.

Had I known just *how* dodgy he would turn out to be, I might have recruited Rivlin after all.

9

Lofty and I had mixed feelings after Dodgy left. We undertook a brief post mortem.

"I'm not sure it was the right thing now," said Lofty. "He seems like a bit of a, well, a bit of a charlatan. He's totally charmless. I wouldn't put it past him to cheat either."

"Hmm, well, I suppose it's okay as long as he doesn't get caught," I replied, tongue in cheek. "But seriously, let's not worry about that now. How good do you reckon he is?"

"Well, he said he's a seventeen handicap, but that he can break eighty, didn't he? Sounds like a bit of a bandit to say the least."

"I agree. I actually reckon we have a perfect team though. We've got my two-handicapper. He should be rock solid. Then we've got you – a twenty-three handicap that's deadly with the putter. Now we've got a seventeen handicap who sounds like he can play to a nine. That leaves me – a nine handicap that can play to a seventeen!" I wasn't sure if I was joking or not. Lofty didn't laugh anyway. "If I can keep my game together then we've got a great chance!"

"I still reckon we've got to keep this Dodgy chap on a tight rein. I really don't think he has much regard for the rules. He practically admitted that he cheats."

"Like I said, let's worry about that later. Remember, Big G's going to arrange a match for us? We can have a quiet word with Dodgy then."

"Big G? Why is he called that?"

"Apparently he was very tall as a kid, although from what I can gather it might be a reference to his bank balance."

"Really? Is he loaded?"

"Apparently so. At the party somebody mentioned something about him being so rich he didn't have to work. Like I told you, he's a member at Steenberg. You don't get in there for nothing."

"Well, all that matters is that we've got our team," concluded Lofty. "It's a bit of an eclectic mix, but at least we can play in the damn competition now. Let's get this practice match organised as soon as possible."

"I was waiting for Big G to call, but now that you've told Dodgy that it's already arranged, I suppose I'd better chase him up, hadn't I? But are you sure you don't want to run it past Abigail first? She might not be that crazy about you suddenly playing golf so often."

"Listen," Lofty insisted, "I am the boss in our house. I wear the trousers. If I want to play golf, I'll play golf, okay?"

"Okay, sure," I said, slightly taken aback at this new self-confidence.

"But just hold off on it for a few hours," he said with a wink, "whilst I speak to Abigail and ask her if I *want to* or not."

○

I left Lofty's and arrived at work before seven o' clock, giving me plenty of time to register our newly created team on the *Golfing Journal* website without any inquisitive colleagues asking questions. After all that panicking, we were officially in – a full two hours before the deadline. Talk about cutting it close.

A fairly mundane day's consulting followed, the highlight of which was daydreaming about playing at Steenberg at last. I also imagined us winning the Subscribers challenge, marching off the final green in first place with Bingley's director's coming in last. I left work in a good mood.

As I arrived home, I picked up a text message from Lofty which read: 'Abigail has made up "my" mind. Apparently I do want to play on Saturday. Cheers, Lofty.'

I was pretty excited as I walked through the door.

"Hi everyone!" I said enthusiastically.

"Dad!" shouted Danny, charging up and giving me one of his rugby tackle hugs.

"Oooopphhh. Aaawww, agony!" I said, feigning pain. "You're tackling hard these days!" I wondered how much longer it would be before I stopped having to pretend, and his tackles *really* hurt me. Not long, I figured.

Jamie wandered over more sedately and gave me a big squeeze. Then I saw Buster barrelling down the hallway and seconds later I was knocked sideways for the second time in quick succession. He proceeded to give me a comprehensive face wash.

"I suppose I'll get a turn eventually?" came Shelley's voice. "Mind you, I'm not so sure I want to kiss you after all that."

I went over and gave her a slightly more delicate kiss and a big hug.

"How was your day?"

"Pretty good thanks. And guess what? We've actually got our four-ball sorted!"

"Wow! Really? That's wonderful!"

"Yeah, Lofty did a great job of recruiting that Cockney bloke at the shop and it sounds like he can play a bit too. He's a bit of an uncouth yob, but to be honest anything is better than Rivlin!"

"That's fantastic, darling. I told you it would work out didn't I? Is he going to join you for your practice match?"

"Funny you should ask. I haven't heard from Big G yet. I told Lofty that I'd follow up with him, but I don't want to seem too pushy. It's only Monday after all. What do you think?"

"It's not a bad idea to remind him. He might have forgotten. Why not call him? Invite him down to Westlake after work one evening for a quick practice, and then you can casually ask him if he's booked a match yet? Just be nice and subtle."

"Hey, that's a great idea! One huge dollop of subtlety coming up!"

For 'subtlety', read 'cowardice': I chickened out of phoning him and decided to send a text message instead.

'Hi Big G. I just wondered if you want to come to Westlake and hit a few balls with me one evening this week before our practice match. Have you managed to get a tee time yet? Speedy.'

Perhaps not the most subtle ever, but I hoped it would work. To my surprise, I got a reply within a couple of minutes.

'Have booked a tee time for 08:15 on Sat. Practice sounds good, but why not meet at Steenberg? How does Wednesday at 16:30 sound?'

This was getting better by the minute! I hastily replied and accepted his invitation. Steenberg here I come! I couldn't wait.

○

The next couple of days went *very* slowly, like they tend to do when you're a management consultant waiting for your first visit to Steenberg. But eventually the clock ticked around to four o'clock on Wednesday afternoon. Not for the first time in my life, I practically flew out of the office. About twenty minutes later, I arrived at the impressive Steenberg Golf Club.

I stopped to sign in at the security gate, then coasted up the driveway towards the car park, admiring the glorious landscape as I did so. It was already obvious that the place was one notch above my home club, Westlake. The clubhouse was huge and imposing, and the fairways looked immaculate. I paused briefly as I drove past the eighteenth green. It was magnificent, like a beautiful sea-green carpet. I wanted to put on a pair of slippers and walk across it, but instead I drove into the half-empty car park and pulled to a halt. I climbed out and looked around, taking in the atmosphere. I couldn't wait to play here, although that would have to wait a couple of days. Mind you, even hitting balls on the range here would probably be an experience in itself.

Just then, a gleaming BMW came into view. As it drew closer I recognised the driver's broad smile – Big G. He pulled up next to me and climbed out. He was dressed immaculately in the latest gear, not unlike a real tour player. I imagined that his golf wouldn't be too far off either.

"Good afternoon, young man!" he said enthusiastically. "Are you ready, willing and able?"

"I'm fine with the first two, but not sure about the last one."

I had to admit that I was a little nervous about even hitting practice shots with a two-handicapper. I realised that I'd never actually played with anyone who was better than my current nine handicap, so I was in fact the best player that I'd ever played with! That was a scary thought. And though Big G was theoretically only seven shots better than me, any golfer will tell you that there is a vast difference between a two and a nine handicap.

"Come on, let's go down to the range and smack a few balls, shall we?" said Big G.

We wandered out to the practice range. Just like everything else at Steenberg, the range was in superb condition. It had beautifully manicured grass with a series of Astroturf hitting mats sculpted in seamlessly. Complimentary practice balls were laid out, arranged in perfect pyramids. There was only one other person on the range. At Westlake, the Town Council had decimated the driving range by building a road across it, which meant you couldn't hit your driver there anymore for fear of pelting the passing motorists. They should have renamed it 'the seven-iron range'.

We grabbed ourselves a bay and I lent my bag against the wooden bag-holder-thingy. I reckoned it was probably made from eighteenth-century French oak or something. At Westlake you either just stood your bag up next to you, or dumped it on the ground, being careful to avoid the goose shit.

"Let's just hit a few half-shots to loosen the old joints," said Big G as he started to warm up. He took out a club and started to swing it back and forth. Even this looked better than my proper golf swing. I mimicked him and after a minute or two started to feel looser.

"Let's see what it's like when we put a ball in the way," he said eventually.

He was nonchalance personified as he dragged a ball into place and effortlessly stroked it down the range. It was no more than a half swing like he'd said, but you could tell by the sound that he'd hit it perfectly.

"Hmm. Very nice," I remarked.

"Thanks. How about you show me what you've got? It's not too late for me to pull out, you know!" he joked.

"No sweat," I said, trying to exude calmness.

I had mixed emotions as I put a ball in place and got ready to hit. I felt really nervous for a start, but then I felt really stupid for feeling so nervous. Not ideal.

I recalled a story that I had read about Jim Furyk during his first year on the tour. He'd gone to practice before a tournament and had set up right next to seasoned veteran Lanny Wadkins. Nerves had got the better of him, and he chunked his first two shots, spraying Wadkins with a face full of dirt in the process. If it could happen to Jim Furyk, it could happen to me. I started to feel a bit more nervous.

"Okay Speedy, get a grip," I whispered as I performed my usual routine. As I prepared to let the shot go, I told myself silently, "Don't hit it fat. Don't hit it fat. Don't hit it fat."

I hit it fat.

I looked up at Big G who just raised an eyebrow quizzically then looked down and brushed the muck off his pants. At least it hadn't hit him in the face.

"Fuck," I said quietly, at which point Big G collapsed laughing.

"Nine handicap, are you? Are you sure it's not twenty-nine?"

"Very amusing. It was just nerves. Now that's out of my system I'll be fine. Watch this."

I prepared myself again, this time taking a huge breath of air and exhaling fully before I hit.

"*Good luck!*" shouted Big G as I got to the top of my backswing

I couldn't stop my swing and cold-topped the ball all the way along the ground. Now Big G was in hysterics.

"You bastard! What are you trying to do to me?" I screamed, before collapsing in laughter myself.

"Okay, okay. I'm sorry. I couldn't resist it! Just relax now and hit a smooth shot. You won't even know I'm here."

Reluctantly I yanked another ball into place and got ready to hit.

I walked behind my ball and took two practice swings …
I picked a spot and lined it up …
I addressed the ball …
I waggled the club twice …
I stood there for a few seconds as if frozen …
Then I finally pulled the trigger and smacked the ball …
At last! A beauty, right out of the screws.

"Suck on that, sports lover!" I shouted. "I told you I could do it!"

"An extremely mature shot! The best I've seen today!" said Big G.

With our joints well and truly loosened, Big G and I continued to hit balls. We paused every now and then to compliment each other on a good shot, although in his case I might as well have complimented *every* shot. They were all near-perfect. I was amazed at how purely he struck his irons, but that was nothing compared to what happened when he pulled out the driver. He absolutely murdered it every time, arrow straight and at least thirty yards longer than mine.

After about twenty minutes, Big G put his club down and removed his glove.

"Shall we just have a short break? Best not to overdo it."

I followed suit dutifully.

"So I never did get to find out about the rest of your team. Who are they?" he said.

No need to dodge the question this time. We had a full team now.

"One of them is my brother-in-law, Lofty, and the other is one of his customers. I don't actually know the guy all that well. His name's Dodgy."

"Lofty and Dodgy? Sounds like a comedy act!"

"You're probably not far wrong. I haven't seen Dodgy play, but Lofty's game can be a bit comical. I'm hoping he's going to get more time to practice now that he's changed jobs."

"Where does he work?" asked Big G.

"He's running a coffee shop in town. Just took it over a week or two ago. It's a bit of a career change for him actually – he used to work at African Tobacco. We both did, actually. I left there a few years ago though."

I was feeling very relaxed, in sharp contrast to the first time we'd chatted at the party and I'd tied myself in knots with my unconvincing lies, so I wasn't prepared for what Big G said next.

"African Tobacco? Really? That's interesting. An old acquaintance of mine works there. You might know him – Derek Bingley."

I froze. Big G knew Bingley? That was all I needed! Just when the plan had come together I find out that our new recruit is buddies with our worst enemy, the very man we are trying to exact revenge upon!

I wasn't even remotely ready to start discussing Bingley, the Director's Cup, Lofty's capitulation or Lofty's subsequent sacking, let alone the sick revenge plot that we'd formulated. So instead of inventing another ridiculous tall story, I decided to change tactics. I remembered the old poem 'A Yorkshireman's Advice to his Son', and took a leaf out of that book: *hear all, see all, say nowt*. In other words, keep my trap shut, at least on the topic of

Bingley. A change of subject was in order.

"Derek Bingley? Yeah, I think so. I wasn't there that long though. I'm working for Rivlin & Lloyd now, the management consultants."

"Oh really? A mate of mine at Investec has worked with them."

We carried on talking and I managed to keep us away from the subject of African Tobacco and Bingley. I'd successfully thrown him off the scent for now, but was far from comfortable for the rest of our practice session. After hitting a few more balls in relative silence, I made a weak excuse about having to get back before the kids went to bed, then confirmed that we'd meet at eight o' clock on the Saturday morning for the warm up match. I'd enjoyed the practice session, but Big G's comment about Bingley was a real spanner in the works.

○

For the next couple of days I fretted about what to do, and eventually on Friday afternoon after work I decided that the time had come to enlist the help of my own personal agony aunt. I explained my discomfort to Shelley.

"Now I don't know what to do. Big G and Bingley are old mates, but Big G doesn't know that our sole aim in life is to kick Bingley's ass in the competition. It's a lose-lose situation."

"Well maybe not," said Shelley calmly. "Big G referred to him as an 'acquaintance', didn't he? That could just mean that they vaguely know each other. In fact, from what I know about Bingley I doubt that he has *any* friends. I'm sure that someone as pleasant as Big G wouldn't actually be mates with him."

She had a point.

"Anyway, you admitted that you got your self into a right pickle by trying to lie to him at that party, so why not be honest for a change? Just tell him that you and Lofty both worked with Bingley and that neither of you like him. You don't have to admit that it's a devious revenge plot. Just tell him that you really want to win the competition. Even you can get that right, can't you?"

"I guess so. But when should I tell him? We're playing tomorrow and I don't really want to have such a delicate conversation in front of the others."

"Why not arrange to meet him there a bit earlier? Say that you want to get in a bit of last minute practice or something?"

"Good idea. I'll tell him that I want him to critique my swing. I'm sure that will do the trick."

Yet again, I chickened out of calling him, but a couple of quick text messages later and it was all sorted out. I arranged to meet him at 07:30 the next morning.

Shelley and I had a fairly quiet evening over a couple of glasses of wine and then I decided to get an early night. Our warm-up match would tee off in less than twelve hours. I left Shelley watching some hideous reality TV show.

Before I got into bed I decided to lay out my golfing attire – another habit that I had developed to save time in the mornings. I opened my wardrobe and sighed, remembering something which had happened a few weeks earlier. I'd made a terrible error of judgement.

Shelley had only ever played golf once, and that had ended in disaster. After a slightly errant tee shot, she couldn't find her ball and drove the buggy back up to the tee. That would have been all well and good, had she not driven it straight over the rise and almost into a cavernous bunker. It ended up with its front wheels dangling into the trap, and it took four people to drag it out again.

Despite this unfortunate incident she was usually fairly tolerant of my golf, at least when I was actually out there playing. She was less understanding when I watched it on TV though. To her, the very notion of hitting a little white ball around a field seemed slightly pointless, so sitting in front of TV until the wee small hours, watching *other people* doing it was a monumental waste of time.

I decided that I might get away with it a little more easily if I educated her in the nuances of the game, so I persuaded her to watch a tournament with me. She wasn't keen, but I asked her to suspend disbelief and give it a try. Eventually she agreed, but from that point on it went downhill. *Seriously* downhill.

It's not that she hadn't enjoyed it. Far from it. The problem was with the *part* of it that she enjoyed. She had been much more intrigued with the players' dress sense than with their ball striking. She'd drooled over the nattily attired Poulter, Parnevik, Fowler et al, waxing lyrical about their trendy apparel.

"Wow, what a stunning outfit!"

"Look at his shirt. It's beautiful!"

Then the hammer blow: "Speedy, why don't you dress like that?"

As you can imagine, I was somewhat skeptical. Shelley, however, was inspired and decided to take it to another level. The next day she'd trotted off to the shops and bought me a selection of the latest golf shirts in the most outrageous colours.

Lemon.

Avocado.

Grape.

Walnut.

Butternut.

Salmon.

I wasn't sure whether she'd been to a golf shop or a delicatessen.

So now, as I stood in front of the wardrobe, I had to choose an outfit from this lot. I stared at the shirts hanging there in front of me. It looked like an explosion in a paint factory. Even if I managed to find something to match, I was sure that I'd look ridiculous.

Nonetheless, I thought I would at least give it a go, and spent the next fifteen minutes mixing and mis-matching the shirts with various pants and caps. None of them looked right and some looked downright absurd, even to me.

"How am I going to choose from this lot?" I pleaded in the general direction of the wardrobe.

Eventually I conceded that I had to grasp the nettle: final decision time.

I decided to wear all black. Even though the next day was forecast to be boiling hot, Shelley's answer to the technicolour dream coat would have to wait.

Shelley had always joked about this habit of mine. In recent years, she had suggested that the black cap emphasised my greying hair a little too much, but I didn't care. I told her that it looked quite distinguished and that I resembled George Clooney. From the ears up, anyway.

I laid out my kit, jumped into bed and tried to conjure up some positive images. I always did this the night before a game, just to get myself in the right frame of mind. I had tried a few different visualisations in my time, but I generally came back to the same one: Gary Player. I always tried to visualise being him, adopting his 'never say die' attitude and coming from behind to win in thrilling fashion. I figured that this would stand me in good stead if the match was close. I closed my eyes and tried to picture myself in his shoes, grinding away determinedly and never giving up.

After visualising myself shooting a back nine of thirty, winning by a single stroke and hoisting an imaginary trophy, I decided that I'd better get some sleep. I put in my ear plugs and rolled over.

After I'd finally dozed off, I had a different kind of dream. Instead of a positive visualisation, it was more of a nightmare about the Directors' Cup match with Bingley. It was like one of those dreams where you try to run, but you just don't go anywhere. In this version, Lofty didn't capitulate like he had in real life and it was left to me to make a one-foot putt to win. But no matter how hard I tried to hit it, the ball wouldn't reach the hole. I must have replayed the scene about a hundred times and not once did the ball get there.

What seemed like seconds later, I was woken by a big sloppy tongue licking me like crazy. To my disappointment, it wasn't Shelley.

"Buster! Bloody hell!" I said, fighting off the dog. He might have been small, but he was bloody strong.

I rolled over and looked at my alarm clock. The red LED gradually came into focus: 07:15. I'd forgotten to set my alarm.

"Holy crap! I'm supposed to be there in less than fifteen minutes!"

I jumped out of bed, trying not to wake Shelley. I then performed my usual routine at double speed, grabbed a banana and jumped into the car. Luckily I had already put my golf clubs in the car the night before, because there was no time to be battling with those now.

I was still out of breath when I arrived at Steenberg. I checked in with Security — relieved that they had my name listed — and drove too fast towards the clubhouse.

I looked at my watch: 07:32. I'd just about made it. Not bad considering I'd only got out of bed less than twenty minutes earlier. Maybe Speedy was an appropriate nickname after all.

I looked around as I walked across the car park, taking in the atmosphere. I cast my eyes over the eighteenth green and imagined myself striding up to tap in a three-inch putt that would win us the Subscribers' Challenge. This time, unlike in my dream, the putt did drop. I pictured Bingley in tears as it did so.

Bingley! That reminded me! I was supposed to be explaining the whole Bingley situation to Big G, and he'd be arriving any minute. I'd been in such a rush that I hadn't had the chance to think about it. I had no idea how I was going to broach the subject. I needed to prepare myself.

At that very moment though, Big G swung around the corner in his silver BMW. He drove into the car park and pulled up right next to me. I wasn't going to have a chance to rehearse after all.

"Good morning, young man!" he said enthusiastically. "Bang on time I see."

If only he'd known.

"Yup. They don't call me Speedy for nothing!" I replied, deciding not to tell him how I'd nearly overslept.

"Come on. Let's check in. We can get a quick cup of coffee, then go and belt a few balls whilst we wait for the others. If you still want a few tips from me, that is?"

"You bet I do," I replied, still wondering how I was going to tackle Bingley-gate.

I followed him into the pro-shop where we were greeted by a well-dressed assistant.

"Good morning, Mr Gardner, sir," said the assistant.

A bit more formal than Westlake, I thought. The traditional greeting there was "Howzit, Speedy!"

"Ah, good morning, George. I think we're off at 08:15. I have three guests today. Here's one; the other two will be here just now."

Before I could ask him to explain exactly how long 'just now' was, Big G turned to me and said, "Why don't you go through there and grab us both a cup of coffee, Speedy? I'll just take care of things here."

I guessed that 'take care of things' meant 'pay everyone's green fees'. From a purely monetary perspective, I didn't mind one little bit if he paid. I mean, if someone came up to you and said, "Would you like four hundred bucks?" you'd be a fool to say no, wouldn't you?

I walked through into the palatial breakfast area and over to the coffee machine.

I was used to the basic 'coffee pot on a hot plate' system that they had at Westlake. Basic it may have been but, like most things at Westlake, it worked. Even I was able to operate it. This machine on the other hand looked like something out of Star Wars. I almost thought about stealing it for Lofty, although I had no clue how to use it.

As I fiddled with the buttons, I began to rehearse my speech quietly to myself.

"Well, Big G, when you said you knew Bingley, you didn't mean that you actually like *him, did you? Just asking."*

Not quite.

"So, Big G, did I tell you why Lofty and I hate Bingley so much?"

Nope.

"Okay, Big G, I'll come clean. We're only doing this so we can laugh at Bingley's face when he loses. He's shafted both Lofty and me, and we despise the bastard. Would you like sugar?"

It needed some work.

Just then, Big G came through. Luckily he hadn't heard me talking to myself. I wasn't ready to deliver my speech so decided to clear up the issue of the green fees instead.

"Hadn't I better go and pay?" I offered weakly. It was decidedly unconvincing. My ability to lie had not improved. I could feel my neck getting warm. The seedling of a full-scale blush.

"No worries, it's done. Today's game's on the house," he confirmed.

A very small part of me wanted to argue, but I felt it would look a bit ungrateful. Besides which, had I done so, that blush would have kicked off like a forest fire.

"That's very kind of you. Thanks," I said instead, trying to sound as surprised as possible.

As I got ready to give my version of the Gettysburg Address, I felt like a kid ready to dive off the high board for the first time. I was just too nervous to take the plunge. Luckily, Big G obliged with more small talk..

"I see that you're struggling with the coffee machine a bit. Don't worry, it's tricky. I'll sort it out."

As he poured the coffee, I decided it was now or never and gave myself a final ultimatum: I had to jump. Three, two, one -

"Big G, there was something I wanted to tell you. A kind of confession I suppose." It could hardly be described as 'taking the plunge', but it was a start.

"A confession? Sounds interesting. Do tell," he replied with a smile.

"Erm, it's about us and this competition and Derek Bingley." I held my breath as I waited for his response.

"Derek Bingley?" said Big G, suddenly more serious. "What about him?"

"Well, Lofty and I both used to work at African Tobacco, like I told you. It's just that, well, neither of us, erm, care for Bingley too much. It's a bit of a long story," I said, trying desperately not to say too much.

"Really? I see. How come?" said Big G inquisitively.

"Well, he kind of, I mean, well, he ..." I dried up.

"He what?" asked Big G insistently.

"He ... he *shafted us*!" I declared finally.

Just then our conversation was interrupted by a rough London growl.

"Bloody hell, you are a homo, ain't yer? It's bad enough with yer 'close family relationship'. No-one's shafting me mate! I might be on yer team, but as far as I'm concerned it's strictly about golf!"

10

Unsurprisingly, Big G looked slightly stunned as Dodgy entered the breakfast room, followed closely by Lofty. It seemed that my little confession would have to wait for now, so I decided that it would be prudent to do some introductions instead. Despite Dodgy's never-ending crudeness, I really hoped that we would all get along okay.

"Hi guys. Meet our genial host, Big G. This is Lofty, and, erm, Dodgy. I should explain about Dodgy's little outburst – he doesn't get out much. Spends too much time with computers I'm afraid. Perhaps our classy surroundings will rub off on him today," I told Big G, hoping that Dodgy might take the hint as everyone shook hands.

Before any kind of embarrassing silence could ensue, I quickly spoke up again. "I hope this isn't too early for you, Dodgy?"

"No problem fer me. I only need four hours' sleep. I'm practically an insomniac. Anyway, I've just got two questions: which tee are we goin' off, and what's the course record?"

"Low or high?" I replied. "I think you're right, you might threaten it!"

"We're off the first tee," smiled Big G in his usual sensible fashion. "As for the course record, why don't we go and hit a few balls? We'll get a good idea of which of the records you're most likely to break!"

Having enjoyed probably the best coffee I'd ever tasted, we wandered out to the practice range, Big G leading the way.

I breathed in the warm morning air and looked at the sunrise. I could get used to this, I thought to myself as I lengthened my stride and caught up with Big G.

"Hey, sorry about Dodgy's entrance earlier," I said. "I should have warned you. He's a bit of a rough diamond, but he's an old friend of Lofty's as well as a loyal customer."

Another white lie. Never mind, by now I had my place reserved in Hell anyway.

I waited for Big G to say, "Hah! You lying twat! You're at it again, aren't you? It's written all over your face! You expect me to believe *that*?", but he just smiled. Why wasn't Shelley as gullible?

"Apparently he's quite a handy player," I continued. "Or so Lofty told me."

"I'm sure he's a lovely chap deep down," he grinned, polite as ever. "Anyway, if he helps us win, who cares?"

Hmmm. My sentiments exactly. Maybe we could excuse Dodgy's total lack of manners after all.

I did a few warm-up stretches and got ready to hit some shots. I rolled a ball into place, pulled out a nine-iron and went through my usual routine. Usually I try not to rush or, more importantly, be rushed. I know I'm slow, but whenever I feel pressure to speed up, I play worse. It hadn't got to the point where anyone had *really* objected, so I stayed with it. In fact, if I was ever playing against Lofty – who was a quicker player – I would sometimes deliberately slow down just to annoy him.

But this time I did try to do things a little bit quicker. I was worried that my 'thoroughness' would annoy Big G when we teed of for real. He wasn't just your average plonker hacking around on the course. He had a two handicap. He was one of the elite and once again I felt slightly pressurised by the thought of playing next to him, even though we weren't actually on the course yet. Maybe the whole revenge thing with Bingley was messing with my head.

The net result of all that was that I chunked my first shot badly.

"Danny de Vito!" came a voice. I looked round to see Dodgy standing behind me.

"Beg pardon?" I was a bit embarrassed, not to mention annoyed.

What the hell was Dodgy talking about now?

"I said 'Danny de Vito'. Yer shot – short, fat and ugly!"

"Very funny," I said politely and then mumbled "a bit like you" under my breath. I didn't want to be distracted by Dodgy's heckling, so I did a few more stretches until Dodgy became firmly ensconced in his own bay.

I hit the next few shots more 'thoroughly'. I decided that I would rather play slowly and well than quickly and poorly; my golfing philosophy in a nutshell really. Today was not a good time to change my method. I hit another half dozen balls and gradually found my rhythm. The ball started coming out of the middle of the club.

"Nice ball!" called Big G, watching from the side.

"Thanks," I said, "I'm just trying to get my tempo right."

Big G walked a bit closer. "I'll just watch you hit a few more if that's okay?"

"Great. It wouldn't hurt to get a couple of tips from the master."

"If he turns up I'm sure we can ask him. Until then, you're stuck with me," he said with a grin.

I could feel Big G's eyes on me as I lined up my next shot, but I hit it right out of the clinkers. It was a corker, even if I do say so myself. I turned round to Big G. "What's the verdict?" I asked, relieved that I had not made a total fool of myself.

"Looks pretty good to me. You look a little tense – maybe just relax a bit more. And don't try to be too quick. You've got a slow tempo. Don't try and change it. Keep a comfortable rhythm. Otherwise the swing looks good and you're hitting it pretty pure."

Being praised for good ball striking by a two-handicapper was quite something. I couldn't have been more proud if Ian Poulter had sidled up and said, "Wow, Speedy! Love the threads!"

I proceeded to hit more balls, moving up through the bag to my six-iron, my hybrid and finally my driver. I was hitting it pretty well.

Presently, I looked across to see how the others were getting on. Big G was busy monitoring Lofty and seemed to be saying a bit more than merely "Nice shot". Lofty was looking more like a manic gardener than a golfer, laying a sizeable sod over pretty much every shot he hit. Big G stopped him and demonstrated a proper swing, concentrating on the ball strike.

"Just make sure you come into the ball from the inside," he said. "Like this."

There was a 'thwack' as he clipped the ball effortlessly off the turf, then a 'fizz' as the ball zipped away. I don't think I'd ever seen anyone hit the ball as purely in my life. Big G then showed Lofty how his club should come into the ball, gently moving the club head through the right path for him. Lofty addressed another ball, took aim and let the shot go. It didn't quite have the same thwack or fizz that Big G had produced, but I hadn't seen Lofty strike a better ball in a long time.

"Wow!" said Lofty. "That works!"

"Great! We'll have you playing off single figures before you know it!"

Meanwhile, Dodgy was busy in a world of his own. He was frantically beating ball after ball like a school teacher caning a rebellious child. I watched as he continued his merciless assault, pausing only to drag on his cigarette, not even noticing that he was being watched.

I realised that he really could play. He was hitting what looked like an old two-wood. A real wood, made of genuine, bona fide wood. He had a compact-but-brisk swing with no wasted effort. And he struck the ball very, very well. More importantly, each shot was a carbon copy of the last one. Bosh, bosh, bosh. He hit one after the other down the middle with a five-yard draw.

Dodgy had created a makeshift ashtray from an old matchbox

and, every half a dozen shots or so, he would pick up his cigarette and have a long drag. Occasionally he would congratulate himself on his shot with some comment or other:

"That bastard stayed hit!"

"Blimey! I wouldn't mind a box of *those* fer Christmas!"

"Ah, the trusty old brassie! Never lets me down!"

Having seemingly fixed Lofty's swing, Big G stood discreetly behind Dodgy and observed. Dodgy didn't even break stride – he just carried on relentlessly, almost as if he was trying to break some sort of world record for most balls hit in a day.

Big G watched him hit a few shots and then walked over to me.

"Aren't you going to give him a tip?" I said.

"No point. He's got a simple swing that repeats perfectly. I wouldn't be surprised if he can shoot well below his handicap if he hits it like that. Assuming he can putt that is."

About fifteen minutes later, I found out the answer to that question. Dodgy *could* putt. Like a demon. We had all gone over to stroke a few balls on the putting green and Dodgy was either knocking them in or knocking them close.

Slightly less encouraging was my own putting. Unlike my practice session the previous day, it wasn't good. The greens were quicker than Westlake's and I couldn't seem to get the speed right on my long putts. I missed a bucket load of short ones too. It didn't bode well, but at least it was only a practice game.

As the tee time approached, we walked off the practice green one by one and made sure that everything was ready.

"Why don't we play UK versus SA? A bit of friendly rivalry just to get us into the right frame of mind?" I suggested, making sure I could keep an eye on Dodgy so he didn't do anything to embarrass us in front of Big G.

"Sounds good ter me," he agreed. "I ain't indulged in any decent Saffer-bashin' fer a couple of weeks now."

"That's the spirit, even if it is rather delusional," chuckled Lofty. "Sounds like we'd better have a small wager on this."

"Now yer talking my language," said Dodgy. "How about we play fifty, fifty, one 'undred, fifty the units and fifty the press?"

Lofty looked seriously puzzled and Big G had to come to his rescue. "What he means is that we bet fifty bucks on each nine. Then we have one hundred bucks on the whole match. Then there's the units: one unit for a birdie, one for nearest the pin and one for a sand save. Whoever gets the most units wins fifty bucks. And, finally, the press: if the match finishes early, you bet on the remaining holes for fifty bucks. Simple really."

Lofty looked even more confused.

"Basically," Dodgy summarised, "yer mate Speedy and me are gonna take three 'undred bucks off yer sorry little arse!"

Lofty finally looked like he understood.

"Sorry to disappoint you, but firstly all, you're taking nothing off me and, secondly he's not my mate. He's my brother-in-law."

"Now that," I said, "is fighting talk."

11

We made our way down to the first hole. As we arrived on the tee box I noticed that it was beautifully manicured and looked in better condition than some of the *greens* on some courses that I'd played. In the hazy morning sunshine it looked gorgeous. I couldn't wait to get playing.

"We'll go first," declared Big G purposefully. "I can show you the right line to take, hopefully."

I watched with interest as he pulled an iron – not a driver – from his bag. He then dropped a ball onto the beautiful lush grass – not a tee peg in sight. He took a quick practice swing, which looked as smooth as syrup, and then addressed the ball. One graceful, effortless swish of the club later and the ball disappeared into the distance, boring upwards through the haze and finally dropping to earth about two-hundred and fifty yards away.

"About there, then?" asked Lofty in a stunned voice.

I wanted to shout, "My goodness! Did you guys see that shot?" then drop to my knees and give Big G oral relief. Well, almost. Instead, I managed to contain myself and simply say, "Erm, nice ball. What did you hit?"

"Two-iron," said Big G matter-of-factly. "I prefer to hit an iron off this first tee for safety."

I supposed that hitting a ball two-fifty yards down the middle of the fairway could feasibly be described as safe.

You could have forgiven Lofty for being somewhat overawed, but to give him credit, he managed to hit a fairly straight drive, even if it was at least fifty yards short of Big G's two-iron. Now he could relax and start some well earned chirping.

"Okay, that's us safely on the fairway. Now it's your turn. No pressure, mind you."

"Pressure, schmessure!" replied Dodgy, turning to me. "I'll lead off on the front nine, you can captain the back nine. That way I can blame yer if we lose. Ha!"

He let out a rasping laugh-cough, spat on the floor, teed up his ball, stood behind it and clattered it down the middle of the fairway. You could see the amazement on everyone's faces.

"Take that, yer bloody colonials!" he shouted, before taking a long drag on his cigarette, coughing up some more phlegm and spitting it out next to the tee marker. The only thing missing was rounding things off with a trademark fart.

Now, with all three of my companions having hit the fairway, it was my turn. I hated going last because it exacerbated my slow pace of play. On this occasion it was even worse, as they'd all hit the fairway. Nonetheless, I was determined to carry out my usual routine.

I checked the height of my ball against my driver ...
I walked behind my ball and took two practice swings ...
I picked a spot and lined it up ...
I addressed the ball ...
I waggled the club twice ...
I stood there for a few seconds as if frozen ...
Crack!
I backed off from my drive. Everyone looked at Dodgy.

"Sew a button on *that*!" he shouted proudly. "Sorry gents, I had meself eight pints o' milk stout and a bad curry last night. A real ring stinger it was. It's given me bloody awful wind. I'm gonna struggle ter get *that* out with a cold wash!"

I cringed as I glanced around to try and gauge the general reaction to Dodgy's incessant crudeness and his talking bowels. Was he just too much of a, well, too much of an asshole? I needn't have worried.

"Well, your horn's working – now try your lights!!" Lofty countered, obviously going with the if-you-can't-beat-'em-join-'em approach. I wasn't entirely sure whether Big G was chuckling to himself or just shaking his head in wonderment, but it looked as though he'd decided to accept Dodgy, if only for his golfing abilities.

"For pity's sake, man! Whose side are you on?" I managed, trying to contain my laughter. "I take long enough as it is!"

I gathered my composure, re-executed my routine and somehow hit a good drive down the middle, all whilst desperately hoping that Dodgy wouldn't fart again. My relief was palpable when the ball eventually landed safely.

"Attaboy!" shouted Dodgy. "We've got these Afrikaner bastards by the bollocks already!"

The next notable, and embarrassing, incident occurred on the fourth hole. Fortunately it was quite far away from the clubhouse and the course was relatively empty so there were no other golfers around to witness it. I lined up my drive as usual, but Dodgy let rip with another fart that registered about fifteen on the Richter Scale, only this time it was halfway through my downswing. I tried in vain to abort, but – alas – it was too late. I topped the ball about ten yards forward.

Worse was yet to come. Once the hysteria had subsided, Big G had some bad news. "Sorry, old chap. You didn't reach the ladies' tee. You do know the penalty for that, don't you?"

I was well aware of this particularly cruel golfing tradition: if your tee shot didn't make the ladies' tee you had to play the rest of the hole with your dick hanging out.

I protested vociferously. They couldn't make me do that in our first practice match! And at Steenberg of all places! But they wouldn't budge, and after further protestations, out came the old tallywacker and on I played. The weather was still rather chilly, the net result of which was not ideal – I had more wrinkles than inches. But in the end I had the last laugh. I somehow managed to muscle a three-wood down the fairway, belt an iron onto the green and then hole a twenty-footer for an improbable and slightly humiliating par.

"I think yer should play the rest of the round like that," chirped Dodgy as I tucked myself back in.

"That's a very generous offer, but I think I'll decline, thanks," I grinned, realising that our team felt like it was coming together pretty well after all.

There was only one other mildly controversial incident. On the thirteenth hole, Dodgy hit his ball towards the trees. He went after it alone and when the rest of us got there we found him with the ball in his hand, taking a drop.

"Molehill! Pesky little blighters. My garden's covered in the bloody things as well."

I looked over at Big G and noticed a rather obvious look of disapproval. Lofty and I exchanged glances and raised our eyebrows, but both decided not to say anything. In the end it didn't matter because Dodgy made a hash of the hole for once, but I realised that we had a potential loose cannon in our team.

In comparison, the rest of the round unfolded uneventfully and fairly predictably. Big G played with relaxed grace, making several birdies, just a couple of bogeys and the rest pars. Dodgy behaved like a lout and played almost entirely without grace, but displayed an uncanny ability to get the ball in the hole. Lofty played fine, but every time he had to chip, it ended in a LOIBIP – 'Loss of Interest, Ball in Pocket'.

And then there was me. I played okay, if a little nervously, but my putting was a concern. I still couldn't seem to get the speed of the greens right, either leaving my putts short or racing them miles past. To make matters worse, towards the end of the round my swing started to fall apart a bit too. I was leaking the ball right and I couldn't seem to correct it.

The match itself was very close, with neither team ever taking more than a one hole lead. One up, all square, one down, all square. A real ding-dong affair. I reflected on our team and congratulated myself on getting a potentially great mix of players together. I reckoned we had a great chance at the Subscribers' Challenge.

Dodgy's banter was one of the main features of the day. It was entertaining, if at times a little intense. He basically had a comment to make after almost every shot, especially his own.

"What a shot! Bloody hell, I'm good!"

"How the bloody hell did *that* miss?"

"Half way fer girls! Throw yer bloody purse at it, Mildred!"

"Ooooh! There's some meat left on that bone!"

"I've been in so many bunkers today I shouldda brought me bucket and bleedin' spade!"

"Christ on a bike! Me ball must be afraid of the dark!"

And so it had gone on for most of the round.

As we walked off the seventeenth green, the match was all square. Dodgy had just hit his approach to five feet and holed the putt for birdie, but Lofty made a fifteen-foot par putt on to halve it because he stroked on the hole.

"Yer spawny bastard!" said Dodgy. "Twenty-three handicap, my arse! Yer should be givin' *me* strokes!"

We walked to the final hole, a shortish par five, downhill but into the South-Easter. Dodgy hit a low, chasing tee shot on the tiger-line, drawing down the left-hand side of the fairway.

"That's me worm burner. Long and low like a barmaid's tits," he announced.

Big G hit his two-iron on a similar line, but higher and further, and then Lofty hit an okay drive – not very long and a bit right, but safe. I'd hung back to update the scorecard, so played last. By my standards it was a disappointing drive, not out of the middle at all. It went to roughly the same place as Lofty's. Normally I hit my ball thirty or forty yards further than him and a lot straighter, so I was a bit displeased.

"Well, at least it's safe," I muttered as the four of us set off up the fairway. As we walked, we naturally split up as Lofty and I walked to the right and Dodgy and Big G headed left.

"We've got quite a decent team, haven't we?" I said proudly. "I think we might just be opening a can of Whup-Ass on Mr Derek Bingley in two weeks' time!"

"I agree. But we should probably arrange at least one more practice match before the tournament. I think I need a bit more experience of competition play. We can't risk letting him beat us."

"You're right about that. Dodgy and I will have to give you a chance of revenge after we've spanked your asses today!"

"I guess we'll find out in the next minute or two, won't we?" said Lofty provocatively.

"I love a challenge."

With water on the right and the wind picking up quickly, the green was out of range for everyone so we all decided to play short with our second shots. We all hit nice lay-ups to leave a short iron into the green.

Now came the all-important approach shots. Lofty's ball was just off the fairway into the light rough. It wasn't a terrible lie, but it was just bad enough to make the shot too hard for him. He couldn't hit it cleanly, and whilst he just about got it over the stream that guarded the front of the green, he left it about ten yards short of the putting surface. Advantage to England!

My ball was only a few yards further down, but crucially it was just on the fairway. I had a hundred and twenty-five yards into the breeze. It was almost exactly the same shot I'd had on the final hole of the Directors' Cup: a simple nine-iron. The distance was the same. The slope of the fairway was the same. The landscape was even similar. But I was worried that I had lost my swing. My last three or four shots had all gone short and right. Exactly where the pond lurked. I really needed to focus on hitting a good one this time.

As I pulled out the club, I had a strong sense of déjà vu. It was so similar to that shot I'd had in the Directors' Cup that it was scary. I tried to imagine that I was back there, immersed in that moment a couple of weeks earlier where I had stiffed my nine-iron to less than two feet. As always, I went through my routine.

Two practice swings …
Pick a spot and line it up …
Address the ball …
Waggle the club twice …
Stand frozen for a few seconds …
And, finally, pull the trigger.

It really *was* déjà vu. Okay, so I didn't hit it inside two feet, but three feet wasn't exactly bad.

12

"*Geddin the hole!*" screamed Dodgy at the top of his lungs as the ball fizzed to a standstill.

I have never really understood why people shout this when the hole is still over a hundred yards away. They sometimes even shout it when players are teeing off on a par five! I just wish that they would be more realistic and shout, "Pitch on the green and leave a makeable putt!" or "Land in the middle of the fairway!"

"Yer bloody beauty!" yelled Dodgy from across the fairway, breaking into a football hooligan chant. "Enger-land, Enger-land, Enger-land!"

"Great shot," said Lofty before adding, "you bastard!"

There's something about hitting a quality golf shot. If you've ever played golf, you'll know what I mean. If you haven't, then you'll have to take my word for it. I can't adequately describe it, other than to say that it felt bloody great. I felt a surge of adrenalin go through me. I wanted to be able to bottle the feeling so I could reproduce it at any moment. Like when we needed a birdie to beat Bingley in the Subscribers' Challenge, for instance.

Dodgy duly hit his shot onto the green, but he was at least thirty feet away.

"Doesn't matter. I wasn't tryin' with that one. We've got 'em by the short and curlies, partner!" he declared.

Unfortunately he had reckoned without Big G. He was much nearer the green – about seventy-five yards away – and this sort of shot was meat and drink to him. He seemed to caress the ball onto the putting surface, where it took two skips and then checked up as if he had it on a string. It stopped about six inches from the pin. Gary McCord would have called it a three-quarter-knock-down-baby-trap-draw-punch-wedge. To use more familiar golfing vernacular, it was a gimme.

"Yer bastard! That's just not bloody fair!" cried Dodgy.

It looked like the match would be halved after all. Whilst I was disappointed, I was also delighted that we had Big G in our team. This would be his fourth birdie of the day and by my reckoning he would shoot one under par. Pretty handy.

Lofty made a fairly decent fist of his shot – sensibly choosing to putt instead of chipping, and lagging it up to about six feet. But he couldn't hole out and made bogey. Dodgy putted to about a foot and tapped it in. He then picked up Big G's marker.

"Okay, yer can have that one. Just don't tell anyone that I gave yer a six-incher, if yer know what I mean," he said, thrusting his pelvis back and forth. Then he turned to me. "Right, partner, this ter halve the match. Just knock it firmly into the back of the cup."

Out of nowhere, I suddenly felt uncomfortable. Why had Dodgy said that? He might as well have said, "You've missed a couple of short ones today so don't miss this." It got inside my head and I couldn't get it out.

I addressed the putt in my usual fashion, trying to stick to my routine, but the thought was still there. I drew back the putter and made my stroke.

The ball didn't even touch the hole.

There was a collective gasp and then silence. No-one knew what to say. The match didn't mean a great deal, but everyone knew what it felt like to miss a three-foot putt to halve a match, no matter how much of a social affair it was. Without being too melodramatic, it was the sort of miss that could ruin a career. Or lose the Subscribers' Challenge

Eventually Big G came over, put his hand on my shoulder and gently said, "Never mind. You played really well. It happens to the best of us."

Dodgy was rather more direct. "Christ al-bloody-mighty! Yer let the bastards outta jail there. Yer buyin' the bloody drinks fer that!"

I was crushed, but Dodgy's rather tactless admonishment actually lightened me up.

"Bollocks! Actually guys, I missed on purpose to give the Saffers a victory for once."

"Right, last one ter the bar's a wanker!" shouted Dodgy, and we followed him obediently inside where an attractive young waitress approached us.

"Afternoon, love," Dodgy said lasciviously. "Yer'd better get yer coat."

"I'm sorry?"

"Hurry up and get yer coat – yer've pulled!"

She just looked back in astonishment.

"Come on, Grandpa, it's time for your medication," I said, before manoeuvring Dodgy towards a table.

"Okay, this one's on me," announced Big G. "What's it to be, gents?"

"Hey, just hold on!" I interrupted. "You got the green fees. You can't pay for the drinks as well. Besides, aren't I supposed to pay for the drinks for missing that putt?"

"Sorry, oldest rule in the book. The winners pay for drinks. We have to balance the karma somehow, don't we?"

"Well I read an article yesterday about drinkin' and how bad it is fer yer health," declared Dodgy. "I decided then and there – I'm never bloody readin' again!" He proceeded to double up laughing.

"Okay, you win. But you have to let me get the next round though."

"Deal! Three draughts and a lime and soda it is then."

"Three draughts? That'll sort me out!" chortled Dodgy. "Yer'd better get three straws fer the lime and soda though. I don't want you lot catching herpes off each other! And just ask that waitress if she's changed her mind about the bonk."

Lofty was watching Big G heading to the bar. "Some guys have got it all, haven't they?" he said enviously.

"Don't feel bad," Dodgy replied immediately. "I know I'm handsome, charismatic and brilliant at golf, but actually I'm not *that* rich and me dick's only ten inches long."

"Shall I tell him or do you want to?" I asked Lofty. "Erm, Dodgy, I think he might have been talking about Big G. Just a thought?"

"Awww, you blokes are just jealous."

The banter was interrupted by the piercing ring of Lofty's cellphone.

"Crap, it's the missus," he said. "But at least it gives me an excuse to get away from this lout! Excuse me a second, guys."

He got up and walked away from the table to answer the call. As he did so, Big G came back to the table, looking disdainfully at Lofty talking on his cellphone. Obviously it wasn't acceptable to take calls in the hallowed confines of the clubhouse.

"They could chuck him out for that. He's going to have me expelled from my club," he said, only half jokingly.

"Don't worry. We'll reserve a spot for you at Westlake – they're a very sociable bunch. I'm sure they'll have you," I reassured him.

Lofty duly trudged back to the table. "Wives! You can't escape them, can you?"

"Beware the call of the lesser-spotted Ferkaryer bird," warned Dodgy darkly.

"The call of the *what*?"

"The bloody Ferkaryer bird. The phone rings, yer answer it and then this voice screeches '*Where the fuck-are-yer?*'"

"Ferk – are – yer! Ha! That's perfect timing!" I grinned. "I got an email yesterday asking me to submit a team name for the Subscribers' Challenge. I think you just christened us! We can be the 'Ferkaryer Four'!"

"I'm not bothered what we call ourselves as long as we kick Bingley's butt," Lofty said without thinking.

I stopped grinning. I hadn't had the chance to warn Lofty that Big G knew Bingley. As I'd missed the opportunity to explain everything to Big G before the match, I was suddenly nervous that we were in for an awkward conversation.

"Bingley? Who's Bingley?" asked Dodgy, slurping his beer. I really hoped that Lofty wasn't going to climb onto his soap box.

Some hope. That was all the encouragement that Lofty needed. Off he went on a serious rant, whilst all I could do was sit there and cringe.

"He's my former boss. A right piece of work. I'd worked at that bloody company for years and he bloody screwed me over. I hate the bastard. Well, we both do, don't we Speedy? He flippin' shafted us both. I should have seen it coming, what with his reputation. No-one trusts him. Speedy warned me, but I didn't listen. That's what got us into this competition in the first place – we're going to sort the bastard out this time. I can't wait to see the look on his face when we finally –"

"Lofty, Lofty, stop. Please stop," I implored. Lofty cut short his diatribe and looked at me indignantly.

"What? What have I said now?"

"Lofty listen. In fact, *everyone* listen. I had hoped that we could avoid this but I think it's time for me to put the cards on the table."

Dodgy leaned forward. "I'm all ears."

"That makes a change," chirped Lofty. "You're usually all mouth!"

"Quiet," I told them both. "I've got a story to tell."

I took a deep breath and looked at Big G who had remained silent.

"As I was trying to tell Big G this morning before we got rudely interrupted, there's a bit of history between us and Bingley. And this history is basically the reason that we entered the competition. Let me explain."

I recited the entire story one more time, trying my best to gloss over Lofty's capitulation, whilst at the same time making clear that Bingley had made a decent job of buggering up both my career and Lofty's.

"Wow," said Dodgy. "That's gotta suck."

"Yeah, we thought the same, so we decided to try and get our own back. That's basically why we've entered the Subscribers' Challenge: we know Bingley is mad keen to win it. So we entered, just to get our revenge.

"But that's not the end of it. Now there seems to be an added complication. What *you* didn't know," I said, turning my attention to Lofty, "is that Big G and Bingley are actually old friends. I wish I'd had chance to tell you. That kind of complicates things a little."

"Ah," whispered Lofty, looking rather sheepish. "It does rather, doesn't it?"

I turned back to Big G and carried on. "Obviously that's not our only motivation. There is the added bonus of a trip to Augusta, of course. But I think it's better that this whole revenge thing is out in the open. It's basically what I was trying to tell you before the match, just when Dodgy made his entrance. Anyway, there you are; I've said it!"

I held my breath and waited for his reaction. When it finally came, it wasn't what I expected.

"Well, I have to say that I'm not entirely surprised. What Bingley did sounds like par for the course. Pardon the pun."

"Huh? I thought you and Bingley were buddies?"

Big G looked a bit self-conscious. "Erm, not really. We're not friends, that's for certain. Not even 'old friends'. It would be more accurate to say that the two of us have a bit of a 'history' too." Big G mimed the quote marks with his fingers.

"How do you mean?" It was my turn to be intrigued. I wasn't letting him off the hook now. To all intents and purposes I'd shown him mine. Now he should show me his.

"I guess it's my turn to make a confession now, isn't it," he sighed.

"What?" interrupted Dodgy. "Yer not a ravin' —"

"Dodgy button it, will you!" I said abruptly. I didn't want his never ending chirping to get in the way now. "Carry on Big G."

"Okay, fair enough. Goodness, where to start?" Now it was Big G's turn to take a deep breath. "When I was a student, I dated his daughter. It was fairly serious I suppose – for eighteen-year-olds. But Bingley didn't approve. I don't think he really liked me. Just before I went to university, he basically made us split up. He kind of made threats. I was young and I didn't know how to handle it. So I did what he wanted and broke up with her."

"Crumbs. What a bastard! Why would he do that?"

"Who knows? I'm sure she and I wouldn't have stayed together anyway, but my biggest regret is that I let him threaten me and get away with it."

"Sounds like you're in the same camp as Lofty. I think he feels a bit daft too, don't you, Lofty?"

Lofty produced another sheepish grin.

"So would you perhaps be keen for a bit of revenge yourself then?" I went on.

"Let's just say that I wouldn't mind sticking it up him, if you'll pardon the expression."

"Stickin' it up him?" interjected Dodgy. "You *are* a ravin' -"

"Dodgy, will you bloody well knock it off!" I said, impatiently. "Why not make a serious comment for once? Haven't you got anything sensible to say?"

"Well, yeah, actually I do. I've got a question."

"Really? Okay, go ahead."

"Whose round is it? I'm bloody gaspin' fer another drink," said Dodgy, before guzzling down the last of his beer.

It seemed that Dodgy was the only one who was unfazed by the

revelations about Bingley.
As it turned out, that couldn't have been further from the truth.

13

After we had finished our drinks we went our separate ways, but only after Dodgy had forced Big G to book a game for the following weekend.

"Yer bloody Saffers aren't gettin' away with this. I want a rematch next week – same time, same place, different result. And don't yer bloody well gift-wrap it fer 'em this time," he said with a glance in my direction.

"Okay, no problem," Big G interjected. "We'll go a bit easy on you next time. We'll miss a few putts on purpose; concede a few four-footers for you. Deliberately lose. That sort of thing."

I looked at Lofty, who looked back knowingly. "Don't even go there," I told Big G who suddenly realised what he'd said.

"Ooops. Sorry, Lofty. Many a true word spoken in jest, eh?"

"Don't worry, I'm over it now. Or at least I will be once the Ferkaryer Four have thrashed Bingley in the Subscribers' Challenge."

"Here, here! I'll book for Sunday."

○

"Hi, love. How did it go?" enquired Shelley as I arrived home.

"Good news and bad news. The good news is that we all seem to get on okay and we all played fine, apart from Big G who played like a god. He gave us a few tips too, which was great. Looks like we've gelled pretty well. We've even got a name now."

"I thought you had a name – 'Awesome Foursome', wasn't it?"

"Technically, yeah, I suppose it was. But we invented a better one." I wrote it down on a piece of paper and showed it to her proudly.

"Fer-kar-yer Four," Shelley read out slowly. "Ferkaryer Four?"

"When I've been at the course for six hours and you wonder

where I am, you call and say 'Where the –'"

"Ferk-are-yer! I get it. Very amusing. What was the bad news?"

"I missed a tiddler on the last green to lose the match."

"Oh no! Shame, sweetie! But rather miss one now than in the competition, I suppose."

"Hey, speaking of the competition, I came clean to Big G about how we're planning to get one over on Bingley. Not quite the way you advised, but he got the message. And guess what – Big G can't stand him either!"

I told her the story about Big G and Bingley's daughter. "So Big G seems like he's onboard with this whole notion of kicking some Bingley ass. If only I could get my game together, we might have a chance."

"Why don't you ask Big G to help you out? If he's as good as you say, can't he give you some more tips?"

"That's a good idea. I don't know what I'd do without you!"

"Hey, that's not all I'm good at," she said, grabbing my collar and pulling me towards her. "The kids are still at my mum's. What do you say I give you a post-golf workout? I've missed your tiddler too, you know."

"As I said, I don't know what I'd do without you," I sighed and followed her obediently towards the bedroom.

◯

A few minutes later – perhaps a bit quicker than Shelley would have liked – we both lay on the bed panting furiously.

"Phew," I said, "that sure gives another meaning to the expression 'the nineteenth hole', doesn't it?"

"Yeah, but no-one said that you have to play it so much quicker than all of the other holes," she giggled.

I laughed. "Hey, lay off. I'm getting old! Besides I need to conserve my energy for golf!"

"I didn't hear you saying that five minutes – sorry – two and a half minutes ago."

"Okay, write me out a report card and put 'could do better' on it then. I'll try harder tomorrow."

"That's wishful thinking! Who says there will be one tomorrow? Maybe it's best that you focus on golf instead. That reminds me, don't forget to ring Big G and see if you can organise a practice session with him."

"Thanks for the reminder. You kind of took my mind off it for a minute."

"I told you – it was two and a half minutes. Don't be too harsh on yourself!"

Finding some energy, I jumped up off the bed. "I might even see if the other two can come along too. You know, a bit of male bonding."

"Whatever floats your boat," Shelley said as I dialled Big G's number. "I'll still be waiting for you if it doesn't work out."

I winked at her as he answered. "Hey, Big G, it's Speedy."

"Hey! Long time, no see! It's only been, what, a few minutes?"

"Yeah, that's what Shelley said," I replied.

"What are you on about?"

"You know, she kind of, erm, *commiserated* with me when I got home, if you get my drift."

"Congratulations. You got your annual leg over?" He was pretty close to the truth there. "You can't have phoned just to tell me that. You want me to teach you how to make those tricky little three-footers, don't you?"

"Ha ha! Shelley could have said that too. Funnily enough though, you're not far off the mark. I actually wondered if you want to go and hit some balls this week. I feel that my swing was a bit all over the place at the end there – apart from my brilliant final approach that is. Anyway, I'd really like you to have a proper look at it. I know that I'm technically the opposition until we get to the Subscribers' Challenge, but I'm sure you can tell me what

I'm doing wrong."

"No problem at all. We can go over to Steenberg and do it there. My normal rate is three hundred bucks an hour, but I'll give you a discount of, ooh, let's say one hundred per cent? How's that?"

"Sold! When would be good for you?"

"Well I seem to be free for the *whole of next week*! When would you like to do it?"

"I think I can get off work at about four o'clock on Monday. How about we meet at Steenberg at half past?"

"Perfect. Four-thirty it is."

"Is it okay if the others come too? I haven't asked them yet, but I'm sure it would help us all to practice a bit."

"Of course. The more the merrier. I don't think Dodgy needs any tuition, but it's probably worth having him around for entertainment value."

"Cool. I'll round them up."

I said goodbye to Big G and then immediately called Lofty.

"Hey, ugly! It's your favourite brother-in-law."

"I thought we'd cleared this up? It's *only* brother-in-law, remember? And have some respect when you speak to me. I'm the reigning family golf champ, remember?"

"Yeah, well, you did choose a good partner, didn't you? Anyway, speaking of your golf partner, he and I are meeting the day after tomorrow at half past four at Steenberg to whack a few balls. Do you want to come along? And whilst you're at it, you can invite that reprobate friend of yours if you like."

"That sounds great. Mind you, I wouldn't exactly call him my *friend*," he joked.

We didn't know it yet, but Lofty had just spoken yet more of those pesky true words in jest.

14

Some days seem to go quicker than usual, apparently gone in a couple of hours. Some seem to take, well, a day. Others drag on and on. It feels like they take weeks. Then there was Monday 14th March, a routine day at the office, waiting for the much-needed practice session that would follow. That day took *forever*.

After what seemed like a bazillion millennia, the clock finally ticked round to four o'clock. At bloody last. It had been worse than watching a Huddersfield Town home game.

I said goodbye to my colleagues and practically sprinted out of the door. I couldn't wait to get to Steenberg and furiously belt some golf balls. The traffic was light, but I was raring to go and drove impatiently to the course. Eventually, after about five centuries, I arrived at the gate. Security took about fifteen thousand years to sign me in, before I finally drove briskly to the car park where time seemed to start behaving normally again.

I climbed out of my car and admired the scenery all over again. It really was a beautiful place. As I turned to walk over to the putting green, another car arrived. Big G pulled up in his Beemer and opened his window.

"Go and practice some three-footers – I'll see you in a minute," he called out.

I smiled. Although it was my full swing which seemed to have gone south, Big G was closer to the truth than he realised. After replaying that last hole in my head so many times since Saturday, I was now a bit nervous about my putting too. It was normally quite a strong feature of my game, but I'd lost some confidence with that infamous missed tiddler. So I did as he'd suggested and started practicing some short putts. Presently, he strode up.

"Good afternoon, young man," he beamed. "I was only kidding about the three-footers, you know."

"No, you were right. I *do* need to practice them. 'Drive for show, putt for dough' and all that. I can't risk us losing a *real* match in those circumstances."

"Don't kid yourself. Saturday *was* a real match. And victory tasted *soooo* good!"

Our banter was interrupted by the squeal of tyres as Dodgy's old BMW came careering around the corner. As he passed us, he stuck his head out of the window and shouted "*Arseholes!*" at the top of his voice.

"He's a real class act, isn't he?" I said despairingly.

"He's okay. A bit of a rough diamond, but he means well. And as for his handicap – seventeen? Yeah, right! Total bandit. He might as well wear a sombrero. But for once, I don't care. As long as he helps us beat that so-and-so Bingley and win the Subscribers' Challenge, I'll be happy."

Before we could begin some enthusiastic Bingley bashing, Dodgy came marching towards us.

"*Come on, yer bloody tossers*! Let's go and pound some drivers. Puttin's fer girls!"

With that we ambled over to the range, Dodgy leading the way. He didn't even warm up. He lit a cigarette, grabbed a bay and started thrashing away with his driver like a metronome on steroids. He had started hitting balls before we'd even put our bags down. As before, he was content to plough a lone furrow.

However, this time he stopped after about ten shots and turned round to Big G who was still doing some stretching. "Wadda yer reckon, Leadbetter? Yer got any advice fer me?"

"Would you take any notice?" asked Big G, surprised that Dodgy had asked.

"Of course, man!" said Dodgy indignantly. "I'm like Brian Clough, me."

Big G looked puzzled.

"If someone disagrees with me, we sit down round a table and talk about it for twenty minutes. Then we decide I was right!" Dodgy explained before unleashing a rasping laugh-cough.

"I see," said Big G, looking a bit nonplussed. "Well, hit a couple more balls for me and let's have a look."

Dodgy obliged, putting down his cigarette, teeing up a ball, then coaxing a ten-yard draw, right down the middle.

"I have to say, it's not pretty," said Big G. He was right. Dodgy's swing was not a thing of beauty – an abbreviated turn of the shoulders, followed by a clumsy-looking lurch forward. "But on the other hand, it's very effective."

He was right about that too. "Perhaps just try and swing right through to the finish – you tend to stop a bit abruptly. Otherwise, I really wouldn't fiddle with it much at all. Although maybe you could put that fag out and try to control your musical backside?"

"Just make sure yer don't stand downwind!" Dodgy said proudly. "Thanks fer the tip."

Big G strode over towards me briskly. He watched me hit a few balls.

"We know he can hit irons," called Dodgy. "Maybe yer were right in the first place, Big G. Go back to the green and teach the plonker ter putt, why don't yer? If he misses a three-footer in the Subscribers' Challenge I'll never forgive him!"

"You carry on over there with the gentleman's persuader, old man. We'll start with the professional's clinic over here, if that's okay with you," Big G told him before turning back to me. "Right, Tiger, let's see that syrupy swing of yours."

Unfortunately his optimism was misplaced. Syrupy it was not. I hit lots of balls and he gave lots of advice, but I just couldn't hit the ball properly. I couldn't seem to get my rhythm right. The gradual collapse of my swing that had started on Saturday was in full swing, so to speak. I was officially crap.

After about half an hour, I'd had enough. I couldn't have hit a barn door at ten paces.

"Okay, that's me done. I'm sure this will make me a player in the long run. At least I'm using up all my bad shots on the range."

"That's the spirit. Positive thinking. Remember – we've got some butt to kick in less than two weeks," offered Big G.

"Yeah, true. But there are some issues to sort out before then."

"Issues?"

"I'm gonna get my game together, then Dodgy and I are gonna kick *your* asses on Sunday. Those issues."

"I know I said to think positive," he smiled, "but please! Keep it real!"

Before I left, we decided that we should make this post-work practice a regular thing, so agreed to meet again on the Tuesday, Wednesday and Thursday evenings and then have a rest on Friday and Saturday before our rematch. The wives were going to love us.

Sadly for me, I failed to keep it real. If anything, I got worse.

If Monday was bad, Tuesday was worse, Wednesday was worst and I'm not sure there is a word to describe what Thursday was. 'Shite', I suppose. By then I was hitting the ball about as badly as I ever had and was almost contemplating pulling out of the whole thing.

On Friday I went into the office not thinking about work. My mind was consumed with thoughts of my crappy golf swing. We didn't have any more practice sessions left before the rematch and, technically speaking, my game was up to shit. I needed a miracle before Sunday if I was going to play well. I was well and truly in the golfing doldrums and needed to sort it out – quickly. Sunday's rematch was one thing, but more importantly the first round of the competition was only a week away.

I couldn't concentrate on work and at about three o'clock I'd had it. "Desperate times call for desperate measures," I murmured as I made the call.

"Hey, Big G, it's Speedy."

"Ah, what an unexpected pleasure. I thought you'd be sick of me after this week."

"On the contrary," I told him, "Is there any chance –"

"See you there at four o'clock," he said and hung up.

"POETS day. I'm outta here," I announced to myself.

"POETS day?" said my desk neighbour. I think he'd got used to my regular self-chatter.

"'Yeah – Piss Off Early; Tomorrow's Saturday'. Have a good one!" I replied and twenty-three minutes later I arrived at Steenberg.

"Right, let's see you hit one or two shots," Big G said as we arrived at the range.

I located my nine-iron. I'd read that Sam Snead used to always start his practice sessions with a nine-iron, so I did the same. Call it clutching at straws, but I had to try anything and everything to break this curse.

I did a few stretches, grabbed my club and dropped my first ball onto the mat.

I walked behind the ball and took two practice swings …

I picked a spot and lined it up …

I addressed the ball …

I waggled the club twice …

I stood there for a few seconds as if frozen …

I hit the ball straight in the teeth.

It stung my hands like crazy. The ball scuttled along the ground like a scolded dog.

"Bloody hell!" I spat. "That was crap!"

My swing may have been ropey all week, but I was still embarrassed at how rubbish my first shot had been.

"That was just first tee nerves. Hit a few more for me. And relax," said Big G calmly.

But it wasn't the first tee. It was the practice range. And it wasn't nerves either. It was what is technically known as the triple S –

'Shite Swing Syndrome'.

I hit another ball. It was a carbon copy of the previous one. Maybe I could have put the first one down to nerves, but after a second one I knew something more fundamental was wrong. I hit a few more shots. None of them were very good. Now I was getting annoyed. I was desperate to hit one good shot. I put another ball down. This time I really focussed. I went through my routine and let the shot go.

It was the worst of the bloody lot.

"Okay, okay! Stop!" said Big G. "I can't bear it anymore!"

I turned round and held out my hands in despair. "You and me both. What am I doing wrong? Please help or we'll have to go to the bar and get shit-faced instead!" I felt foolish and frustrated.

"We're gonna have to get a bit technical, I'm afraid."

"Bring it on. I'm so desperate I'll take anything right now."

"There are two things—"

"Only two? I'm stunned!"

"Well, two *main* things. But we can fix them easily. Firstly, you're taking the clubface back closed, mainly because you're too tense. You're gripping it like a bloody vice. You need to relax and let your left arm rotate as you go back."

He demonstrated the movement. "That will allow the clubface to roll open properly. The other thing is that you're rushing the downswing. It's probably just the tension in your body again. That's the main problem. Just take it to here and let your left shoulder touch your chin. Then pause for a fraction of a second before you unwind – slowly. And stay relaxed."

It sounded like a lot of information to cope with all at once.

"Okay, do it for real, clever trousers," I said, trying to buy myself more time to take it all in.

Big G grabbed a club and showed me the two moves in slow-mo. "Rotate it back, pause at the top, then unwind through it."

He hit a ball just as he had demonstrated. It was a perfect strike.

The ball fizzed away as if he had shot it out of a rifle.

"Wow!"

"Now *you* show *me* how it's done. Just stay relaxed and grip it softly."

"Yeah, that's what I said to Shelley," I quipped as I practiced the moves a couple of times.

This time, when I addressed the ball, I abandoned my usual routine for once. I just concentrated on staying relaxed and executing the instructions I had been given. I looked at the target, then made my swing.

The ball took off like an Exocet missile, hardly deviating an inch and even checking up as it landed.

"What a shot!" I gasped.

"Even if you do say so yourself?" laughed Big G.

"Oh, yeah, sorry about that. I used to be egotistical, but now I'm perfect."

"I don't know about that, but your shot was just about perfect. Arrow-straight and, if I'm not mistaken, with a healthy dose of backspin with a range ball. Pretty handy."

A surge of pride gushed through my body. This was even better than Ian Poulter complimenting me on my dress sense.

"That's it really," continued Big G. "Just relax, rotate your left arm and then pause before you swing down. You'll get more consistent and maybe find a bit more power too."

I continued to hit balls for the next half hour or so, moving through the bag, employing the same technique every time. It worked beautifully, even with my driver. I didn't want to stop, just in case I lost the feeling. My swing had finally clicked.

I was suddenly confident of a UK win on Sunday and, what's more, I was confident that we could take out Bingley in the Subscribers' Challenge.

One week to go. I couldn't wait.

15

Even before he had opened it, the letter looked ominous. It had the words 'South African Revenue Services' emblazoned across the front. A letter from the taxman was seldom good news. He nervously turned the envelope over and slid his finger under the flap. Tentatively, he removed the letter. He checked again that it was addressed to him, just to be sure. He read the first paragraph out loud to himself:

"We enclose herewith your tax return indicating our estimation for the forthcoming tax period. Please sign the form and send it, together with your payment of R140,102.37 made out to South African Revenue Services, to the above address. Kindly be advised that a penalty may be imposed on late payments in addition to interest at 13% per annum."

Lofty's whole body went numb.

16

On my way back from Steenberg I felt good. My swing had finally come right. It looked like I was going to peak at the right time. If I'd been walking home, I would have had a spring in my step. When I was in a mood like this, *nothing* could bring me down.

Then my phone rang. It was Lofty. On second thoughts, maybe *he* could. Bad news was coming. I could feel it.

"Speedy, something has come up. I've … I've had a bit of a catastrophe today. It's kind of messed with my head."

Lofty had a knack for making a drama out of a crisis, but I had to admit that the way he said it worried me this time. "Sounds ominous. What kind of catastrophe?"

"It's not life threatening, but it's not great either. Revenue Services wants R140,000 from me. Now."

"*What!* A hundred and forty grand? Are they mad?" I swerved to the side of the road and switched the engine off. Even I couldn't handle this conversation while driving.

"Maybe," said Lofty mournfully, "but they're serious too. I phoned them and there doesn't seem to be any way around it. Something about failing to register as a provisional tax payer when I became self-employed. So now they've billed me for a whole year's tax in advance. I have to pay it before I've even earned any money. I either do it now or risk a further fine or even jail. It's hectic."

"Hectic is right. What're you gonna do?"

"Well, I haven't been to church for about thirty-nine years, so praying is probably out. I spoke to my bank manager instead, but that hasn't helped much either."

"What did he say?"

"He said he wants to go back to the old system where *they* keep *my* money," said Lofty, ruefully. "The cupboard is bare, so to speak. Now I'm fresh out of ideas. What's worse, so is Abigail. Anyway, I just wanted to let you know that I'm obviously going to have to drop out of the Subscribers' Challenge."

My good mood was officially over.

"I can't very well swan off to a golf match with this hanging over me, can I?" Lofty continued as I struggled to keep up with the depressing news coming through my phone. "Apart from anything else, it wouldn't go down well with the wife. It's got huge implications for us."

I made one final attempt to calm Lofty down. "Look, I realise that it seems desperate, but let's not do anything precipitous."

"Huh? That's a Shelley word, isn't it?"

"Don't do anything hasty. You can't pull out of the match yet. We've got time to sort it out. Don't worry." I tried to sound convincing.

"Sorry, Speedy, unless they decide it's all been a terrible mistake, Sunday's game will be my last for a long, long time."

O

"What? A hundred and forty grand?" Shelley said in astonishment when I got home. "Holy cow, he'll have to sell a lot of coffees to cover that."

"Definitely more than a few cappuccinos, yes. And there's more. He also says that he's pulling out of the Subscribers' Challenge. Obviously I can see that he's got a really big problem to deal with, but the more I think about it, the more I lose sympathy for him. After everything we've been through, I'm more than a little annoyed at the fact that he is going to just bail out like this. What are we gonna tell the other two guys? They're both dead keen. I can't bear to let them down – or lose out on this last chance to screw Bingley. Big G's put in so much effort organising games and practice sessions at Steenberg too."

"Wait a minute," said Shelley excitedly. "Maybe that's an idea!"

"What is?"

"Big G! He's loaded, isn't he? Why not ask him for help? You know – a loan. I know it's a bit cheeky, but I'm sure Lofty could pay him back eventually. You said yourself that they would rebate the fine."

"You must be mad! We can't do that! We've just met the guy. It's too, well, too forward. We hardly know him, do we?"

"Why not do it in a round-about kind of way instead? Be subtle again."

"Meaning what exactly?"

"Pretend you are asking him for information about tax laws or something. He might just offer the money himself – he's been so generous already. Try something along the lines of 'Hi, Big G, it's Speedy. I need to ask your advice on something …'"

O

"Hi, Big G, it's Speedy. I need to ask your advice on something …" It was first thing on Saturday morning and, as usual, I was doing exactly what my wife had suggested.

"Sure, man, no *problemo*. Always glad to help if I can."

"It *is* a *problemo* unfortunately. Quite a big bloody *problemo* actually," I said hesitantly. "Do you know anything about tax?"

"A little bit. Mostly ways to avoid paying it!" he laughed.

"Well, that's kind of what we're wanting," I replied, feeling a little braver.

"Oh? Who's this 'we'?"

"Yeah, erm, it's a friend of mine," I said, suddenly wondering if I should avoid mentioning Lofty's name. It's not like I'd asked his permission to talk about his financial affairs with a guy we'd both only just met. On the other hand, Big G was far more likely to offer to bail my 'friend' out if he knew it was Lofty. I decided to risk it.

"Let's just call him, ooh, I don't know, erm, Lofty. Just a fictitious name, you understand?"

"Aha," said Big G thoughtfully. "I think I'm with you."

"Really, Big G," I gushed, knowing I was beyond the point of no return, "I shouldn't be telling you this. He doesn't actually want anyone to know about it. He's mortified."

"It's okay, I won't squeal. What does this fictitious character called Lofty need to know?"

I filled Big G in on Lofty's letter from the tax man. "The *problemo*," I concluded, "is that he doesn't have a hundred and forty grand lying around."

"Jeepers! One forty? I'm not surprised. That *is* a bit stiff!"

For the next twenty minutes, I asked Big G whether there was any way Lofty could get around the regulations and he asked me all sorts of questions about the situation and Lofty's personal details. We tried our best to answer each other, but at no stage did he ever give any indication that he might help Lofty out with the money. It wasn't exactly the outcome that I had hoped for.

Finally he made a suggestion. "Why not meet me at Steenberg later? I'd like to see a copy of Lofty's letter and then maybe you can buy me a beer?"

I was tired. It was a Saturday and I'd been planning a quiet afternoon and an early night. We had a golf match early the next morning and I'd been at the golf course every night the previous week. Now I was being asked to ferret out Lofty's tax details and go drinking. It would probably end up being a long, depressing session and I'd arrive home late and sloshed. Shelley would never stand for it. I couldn't do it. I simply couldn't.

"Okay, see you there. I'll give you a call once I've got the letter."

Shelley was going to kill me.

I quickly got on with the next move: obtaining Lofty's tax letter. I didn't want to be too obvious about asking for it, because I didn't want Lofty to find out that I'd been speaking to Big G.

Fortunately, I had a cunning way around it: go to his shop for a cup of coffee. If I made him think I was just supporting his business, he'd lower his guard and wouldn't be suspicious. Once I got my coffee, I'd simply ask him for a quick look at the letter. Pretend that I might have some ideas. I knew he'd have it with him where he could stare morosely at it in between serving customers.

I spent the morning doing household chores and looking after the kids to make things up to Shelley. She went easier on me than I had expected – after all, I was helping *her* brother out.

Mid-afternoon I arrived at the coffee shop and ordered a cup of Americano. Then I prepared myself for my latest act of deception.

"Mmmmm, great coffee," I said unconvincingly. "By the way, have you got that tax letter on you?" Tact had never been a particular strength of mine.

"Sure, it's in my bag here," said Lofty obligingly. "Have you got some brilliantly cunning plan to get me off the fine?"

"Not exactly." I tried to keep the guilt out of my voice and made a note to give Satan a call to reserve a nice spot in Hell. "I'm just trying to make sure I haven't missed something. Want to read all the fine print. Do you mind if I take a copy of it to read over at home?"

"Sure, go ahead." He hadn't smelt a rat. I was obviously better at this espionage stuff than I'd thought.

"You can lay me down on the floor and shag me senseless if it helps get me out of paying the fine," Lofty smiled weakly.

"Very tempting, but I'll settle for just the photocopy for now, if that's okay?"

"Suit yourself, but don't say I didn't offer."

I finished my coffee and then headed into Lofty's office at the back of the shop. He had a pretty nice set-up – computer, phone and quite a fancy little printer/fax/copier/scanner that he'd bought to try and make the operation a bit more modern. I copied the letter and put it into my jacket pocket.

As I did so, I heard the door of the coffee shop open and then slam shut.

"Good grief, it's blowin' like bloody hell out there! What a bloody wind!"

Dodgy. At least he would lighten the mood a touch. I needed cheering up.

"That's funny," I called out, "that's what we always say when *you* arrive."

"Hey! Speedster! I'm a bit surprised ter see yer here," exclaimed Dodgy as I emerged from the back office. "I thought yer'd be doing a hard day's consulting ter make up fer all the time yer've spent at the golf club this week."

"Are you mad? It's bad enough being a consultant, I'm not going to work weekends too. Do I look that stupid to you?"

Dodgy raised an eyebrow. "Do I *have* ter answer that?"

"Erm, no. Don't. If you must know, I just felt like a cup of the best coffee in town."

"What the hell yer doin' in here then?"

"Very funny," said Lofty, trying to get Dodgy to settle into a corner far away from his other customers. "Anyway, he's come to help me sort out a tax problem."

"Tax? Isn't that some dosh yer have ter pay ter the government or somethin'? Can't say I've ever bothered with it personally."

"You might end up in the same situation as me then," said Lofty. Surprisingly, it looked like he was going to share his predicament with Dodgy. I hoped he wasn't expecting a shoulder to cry on – Dodgy was far more likely to use the information as fuel for his next round of jokes instead.

"The bastards have hit me with a hundred and forty grand," added Lofty.

"Christ on a bike! That's more than I earn in a good week!"

Then he realised that Lofty wasn't laughing and quickly became more serious. "Ooops, sorry, mate," he said, "that's not good. I'm not even sure *I'm* dodgy enough ter be able ter squirm outta that one."

Speaking of squirming out of things, it was time for me to go and take Lofty's letter to Big G.

"Okay, guys, got to leave you to it, I'm afraid," I said. "I've got things to do."

"Where you going on a Saturday afternoon then?" Dodgy asked.

"Erm ... to the dentist," I answered hurriedly. Fortunately this little white lie was slightly more convincing than some of my previous efforts.

"Strewth! The dentist! Rather you than me! I bloody loath 'em! Yer know what I always do when I visit my dentist? I grasp him firmly by the bollocks and say 'we're not going to hurt each other, are we?'"

As Dodgy doubled up laughing, two stunning twenty-something beauties walked into the coffee shop. Dodgy noticed them as he came up for air, and couldn't take his eyes off them. "Off yer go then, more fer the rest of us!"

"Let me get you a cork for your backside then," whispered Lofty, picking up a couple of menus, "otherwise you'll ruin it for both of us!"

"Good luck," I said. "At least this might take your mind off your tax trouble."

I got up, smiled at the two ladies, savoured a few lewd thoughts and headed to the car. I wasted no time in calling Big G.

"I've got it!" I told him excitedly.

"Got what? The clap? The Holy Grail?"

"No, man, Lofty's tax letter."

"Great. Are you on your way to Steenberg yet?"

"Yup, just set off from Lofty's."

"Okay. Race you there."

○

When I got home – luckily not too late – Shelley was preparing supper. Again. She had already fed the kids, but I did my bit and got them ready for bed. I didn't have much in the way of good news so the least I could do was spare her the nightly bedtime ordeal. I read the boys a quick story and kissed them goodnight before heading to the table. I poured Shelley a much needed glass of wine.

"Did you get what you wanted?" she asked.

"More or less. I got the letter and I've given it to Big G already. That's why I'm late. I'm sorry."

"It's okay, just keep the wine coming. What did he say?"

"Not much, as it happens. I gave it to him and he said he'd 'look into it'. That was it. No mention of a loan even though I did my best to push him in that direction. I guess the plan didn't really work. We might still be out of the competition."

"I'm sure you guys will come up with something between you," she said in her ever-optimistic tone. "You've just got to get your revenge on Bingley. It wouldn't be fair otherwise."

"You're right about that," I agreed, "but I'm not entirely sure that the world is fair."

We duly finished the bottle of wine and, three minutes after my head hit the pillow, I was spark out.

○

It would have been appropriate if that Sunday had been Valentine's Day: the rematch was a massacre. Dodgy and I handed them the proverbial dog licence: a seven-and-six pasting.

There were two main reasons for this comprehensive shallacking. The first reason was that I played above myself. My new swing was working perfectly and the rest of my game wasn't too shabby either. No missed tiddlers and I holed a few pretty long putts as well. The second reason was Lofty. His game was shabby. Very shabby. Bloody awfully, abysmally shabby. Shite, in fact. And he made no secret of the fact that his tax fine was weighing heavily on his mind.

We had a few beers after the match, but Lofty's doldrums were contagious and the atmosphere was subdued. Although I'd convinced him not to go public with it yet, he'd already made up his mind to pull out of the competition. When the subject of further practice sessions was raised, I persuaded Big G and Dodgy that it would be less pressurised if we all did a bit of sneaky practice on our own rather than meeting as a team. I knew that Lofty had no intention of practicing and was pretty convinced that he wouldn't even be playing in the competition.

○

All week I was on tenterhooks. I got nervous every time the phone rang, wondering if it would be Lofty calling to confirm his withdrawal. And as each day passed, I got more worried. What if he did stay in, but then played horribly like he did in our rematch? It seemed like a catch-22.

Friday finally came around. Only one day until the Subscribers' Challenge. I watched the clock all day at work, wondering how long I could wait before I called the organisers to pull out. As the last hours of the day dragged by, I sat at my desk and stared at my computer like I'd been doing for most of the day. Most of the week, actually. I wanted to go home and have a beer.

It seemed like I spent every Friday worrying these days. First it was Lofty getting fired. We'd gotten over that. Then it was going to a party I didn't want to go to, although I suppose that worked out okay. The week after that I was nervous that Dodgy was going to upset everyone at our first practice match, and last week it had been my golf swing. Now it was Lofty's financial meltdown and our imminent withdrawal from the competition. This time it didn't look like there would be a happy ending.

I wondered if I should call Lofty, but decided against it. I knew he wouldn't change his mind. The selfish bastard hadn't even apologised. I tried to take my mind off it and once more imagined sinking a nice beer. As I thought about the cool, crisp taste of an ice-cold Guinness, I was startled by the shrill ring of my cellphone. I anxiously checked the display: Lofty.

Surely he wasn't phoning to apologise now? It really was too late for that. I braced myself and answered the call, still not entirely sure how I was going to react.

"Lofty," I said disconsolately.

Before I got chance to say anything else, he cut in.

"Speedy! You remember that tax fine?"

Remember that tax fine? Was he nuts? Of *course* I remembered the bloody tax fine! I'd been thinking about precious little else all week.

"Tax fine? I *think* so, yeah. Don't tell me someone has mysteriously paid it off for you?" I said as sarcastically as possible, hoping against hope that it would somehow prove to be true.

"Nope," said Lofty, "even better. They've cancelled the bloody thing! I don't have to pay a cent!"

"*Cancelled the fine???* Are you sure?"

"A hundred per cent!" he crowed triumphantly. "I got a call from them just now. I've literally just put down the phone. They said they'd looked at it again and had decided to waive the fine. I feel like I've just won the lottery!"

"So do I! Quite apart from your problems, I thought I was going to lose a team member and that we'd have to pull out of the competition! But why have they changed their minds?"

"Search me," said Lofty, almost hyperventilating. "I didn't ask. I don't care. All I did was ask them to confirm it in writing. They said that the letter's in the post."

"Unbelievable. That's marvellous. I assume you're back in the team now?"

"You'd better believe it! Wild horses and tax men wouldn't stop me now!"

"Great stuff! But hold on. Are you sure you don't want to reconsider?"

"Huh? How do you mean?"

"You're playing like a wanker, aren't you?!" I retorted. "Wouldn't we be better off without you?"

I hoped that my little jape wouldn't come true, but in truth I didn't care. Our dream was still alive.

17

Saturday, 26th March. The first round of the Subscribers' Challenge. It had arrived at last.

I set off – dressed all in black as usual – on the now familiar journey to Steenberg in a relieved state of mind. I was more relaxed than I had been all week. Lofty was still in the team after all. And what's more, he wouldn't have all that worry weighing him down. I just hoped that he would play better than he had last week.

We'd arranged to meet at ten o'clock. As I pulled up I checked my watch: 09:57. Hmm, pretty good again, I thought. I sat in my car for a moment, switched off the radio and just looked out over the beautifully manicured course. I felt a little surge of adrenaline in my stomach as I once again imagined myself holing the winning putt. Then I had a stronger feeling – one of revenge – when I pictured the look on Derek Bingley's face as we shook hands.

"Commiserations, old chap!" I said out loud, trying to visualise the scene as clearly as I could.

I climbed out of the car and hauled my gear out of the boot. I changed into my golf shoes, loaded my bag onto my trolley and pulled out a ball, a glove, two tee pegs – one short, one long – my lucky 'Guinness' ball marker and one of those funny little pitch mark repairers. Oh, and a pencil. Now I was ready.

My thoughts turned to the state of my golf game. I hadn't practiced much during the week, so I hoped that my miracle cure from the previous week would still work and that no new gremlins had worked their evil little way into my swing. I took a deep breath, then strolled over to the range.

Surprisingly, Big G was already there, gracefully easing perfectly hit shots into the distance.

Geddin the Hole!

"Hey, what are you doing here so early?" I asked.

"Came here to hit a few balls," said Big G. "I knew that once you arrived I'd be spending all my time fixing your bloody swing again!"

"Hey, don't joke. I'm bloody nervous about that. It had better hang together today or we're in trouble. Anyway, enough about my problems. I've got good news."

"You've learned to putt?"

"Very funny. It's actually even better than that. They cancelled Lofty's tax fine! He's off the hook!"

Big G's expression didn't change. He just looked back at me and raised an eyebrow astutely. "I know," he said quietly.

It took a moment for this to register with me. "Huh? How could you know?"

Big G held my gaze for a few seconds and raised his eyebrow a notch further, waiting for the penny to drop. Eventually, when his eyebrow could go no higher, he broke the silence. "Remember me saying that I would make some calls?"

I nodded.

"I made them."

"What? You …" Eventually I started to cotton on, and all I could manage was, "How?"

"Let's just say that I know people in low places, shall we?" said Big G. "I have contacts in the revenue service. They send out fines like that from time to time, but it's not too difficult to get them quashed if you know who to speak to. They were probably going to pay him back eventually anyway."

"Wow!" I said. "Are you going to tell Lofty?"

"Nah, let's just leave it. He still doesn't know that you told me, does he? He thinks that I only found out from him at the practice match. Besides, it would be like telling the kids that Father Christmas isn't real. He'll be much happier if we keep it secret."

"Yeah, you're right," I said. "Anyway, come on, let's celebrate.

Let's take our excitement out on some poor, defenceless golf balls."

"Not so fast!" came an unmistakable voice. "We've gotta have at least four cups of coffee before we start. I've had no sleep. I need some caffeine. *Now!*"

"Good morning, Mr Rogers. Heavy night, was it?"

"Yer could say that. I was with yer wife, yer mum and yer sister –" he began.

"Come on then," I interrupted. "Let's get that coffee and wait for Lofty."

Lofty was at the coffee station when we got there, looking well-rested and full of the joys of spring. We toasted his fantastic news with Steenberg's finest mocha java, and then it was time to begin our final practice session.

"Right. Before we warm up, how about we talk tactics?" suggested Big G.

"Careful," I said. "You'll confuse Lofty. He thinks tactics are a type of mint. Anyway, before that, I've got something for you all."

"That's very kind," chirped Dodgy immediately, "but I never screw on the first date."

"I'm relieved. Then I'd like to present you all with one of these instead." I delved into my bag and pulled out four golf caps. They all had a logo emblazoned on the front – a golf ball, surrounded by the words 'Ferkaryer Four'. Each person's cap had their name printed on the back. I'd designed them myself and was pretty proud of the result.

"There you go, your very own Ferkaryer Four souvenir caps!"

"Wow! These are great!" said Big G enthusiastically.

"Just like the Ryder Cup!" grinned Lofty.

"Bloody marvellous!" enthused Dodgy.

I was chuffed. I'd got the male bonding thing right.

We all donned our new caps in unison. I felt like one of the three musketeers, except that there were four of us. I'd always secretly wanted to be D'Artagnan …

"Okay, now that we're a proper team, shall we discuss our strategy?" I offered.

"Yeah, good idea," said Dodgy. "Let's all shoot four under par, then we can go and get absolutely wankered in the bar! After that we can each pull a big-titted twenty-year-old tart and spend the evenin' havin' red hot monkey sex. Any more questions?"

I ignored him. "What do you think, Big G? Do we need any tactics or should we just play?"

"In my experience, it's at least worth finding out which holes we stroke on, so that we can do a bit of planning and avoid blowing it. We might need every point we can get."

He and I scrutinised the card and made a few pencil marks while Lofty looked on, bemused. Dodgy scanned the room for young women and, when he couldn't see any, farted loudly.

"Come on, yer bunch of girlies. I prefer the old 'clobber it, find it, clobber it again' approach. Obviously that gives *you* a problem after step one," he said, looking at Lofty, "but even then I'm not sure I'm into all this bloody planning."

"Nah, me neither," agreed Lofty, ignoring Dodgy's jibe. "I'm just going to go out there and try and shoot the best score that I can."

"That's the spirit, Loft. What do yer reckon yer capable of? Yer know, realistically?"

"Well I'm not all that familiar with the course yet, so if I can shoot in the low nineties I'd be happy. To break ninety would be a real bonus. How about you?"

"Let's see. I'd like to par the first, birdie the second, eagle the third, then eagle the rest of the par fours, double-eagle all the par fives and ace all the par threes!"

"No, come on! Stop mucking around!"

"Well you started it!" guffawed Dodgy.

At that point, Big G and I gave up on the idea of serious discussions and we all headed for the door. Halfway across the room, I realised that I'd left something behind.

"Ooops. I've forgotten the scorecard. Don't wait for me, I'll see you out there," I said as I went back to fetch it from the table. As I turned back to catch up with the others, I saw Big G stepping back to let someone else through the door. I felt my stomach tighten as I saw a familiar face.

Derek Bingley.

Big G looked away from him as he passed. He didn't seem to want to acknowledge the man either. Obviously he was still slightly uneasy about dealing with Bingley, even after all these years. He almost looked scared. Lofty was too busy bantering with Dodgy to even realise what was happening, but they were fortunately both hidden behind Big G's broad shoulders, and Bingley missed an opportunity to lay into Lofty and put him off his game. I was relieved that he didn't notice me either.

"He's the last person I want to speak to right now," I whispered to myself.

I hung back and watched Bingley as he strode arrogantly into the room. He marched over to the other side of the room and attempted to get a cup of coffee from the fancy machine.

"Waitress?" he shouted impatiently. "Get over here! This wretched machine won't do what it's supposed to do! Sort it out – I haven't got all day!"

A terrified looking girl scurried across to pour the creep his coffee while I took the gap and slipped outside. I made my way after the others towards the range, pausing for a minute just to calm down a little. The sight of Bingley had sent my pulse rate up a notch.

When I got to the practice range, the rest of the Ferkaryer Four were already hitting shots. Big G was striping it majestically, down the middle every time. Dodgy was clobbering it inelegantly, nowhere near as far, but also straight. Lofty was hitting it surprisingly sweetly. Not totally straight and not that far, but his bad ones were still okay.

That left me. I was hoping to find that my new swing thoughts had remained in my memory bank. I found a bay and took out a nine-iron – just like Sam Snead used to – and I lined up my first ball.

I hit it straight in the teeth. Not very Snead-esque at all.

"Bloody hell!" I said, to no-one in particular. "I hate this bloody game!"

"Don't worry," said Big G reassuringly. "Just get warmed up. Stay loose. Remember those swing keys we talked about – rotate back and pause at the top. It will come right." Wisely, he left me alone – he didn't want to confuse me, which wouldn't have taken much effort at that point. I was worried that I'd regressed all the way back to where I'd been two weeks ago and it was not a good place to be.

After hitting the next few balls like a thirty-six handicapper, I sat down to refocus. I tried to think of something that would work. I reminded myself of Big G's advice. I reminded myself of how my swing felt when he'd fixed it for me that day. Finally, I told myself to keep my eyes on the ball.

I stood up and placed a ball down on the turf …

I walked behind the ball and took two practice swings …

I picked a spot and lined it up …

I addressed the ball …

I waggled the club twice …

I stood there for a few seconds as if frozen, this time staring at the ball for all I was worth …

I finally pulled the trigger and smacked the ball, keeping my eyes on it until it had gone.

I'd hit better shots in my life, but I couldn't remember exactly when. The ball shot off the clubface and into the distance, as straight as a length of frozen rope.

I looked over at Big G, who had a grin all over his face. "It's clicked," I said.

"You bet!" replied Big G, flashing his ice-white teeth.

I continued hitting great shots – very modestly – for a few more minutes and was finally feeling like we were all on good form at the same time, when it all suddenly changed again.

We had decided to practice the short game and it didn't take long for the first seeds of doubt to surface. Not with me, but with Lofty. His chipping was a disaster. He hit ninety per cent of his shots fat. Those were his good ones. It was like watching someone trying to weed their garden.

"Good grief!" he said after about a dozen mis-hit shots. "I'm gonna have to pull out of this match to save myself further embarrassment. Either that, or play under an assumed name."

"Hey, haven't I seen you on TV?" interjected Big G. "You're that famous motivational speaker, aren't you? Author of that book *Positive Thinking*?"

"Yeah, just call me Norman Vincent Peale."

"Norman who?"

"Aw, just go and Google him, why don't you? Second most prominent positive thinker in the world after yours truly. Anyway, it doesn't matter. I'm just gonna hit every green so I don't have to chip."

"Okay," I interrupted, "and when you've come back from La-La Land, we'll see about winning the Subscribers' Challenge, shall we?"

That would prove to be easier said than done.

○

The format of the Subscribers' Challenge was pretty standard. We would play the Stableford points system (one point for a bogey, two for a par, three for a birdie and so on), with two scores to count from each four-ball. A marshal would follow each team to ensure that there was no jiggery-pokery, otherwise known as cheating. The top two teams in today's Western Cape leg of the competition would play in the national final at Erinvale the following weekend.

At 12:58 the starter called us to the tee.

"On the tenth tee, the one o'clock fourball: the Ferkaryer Four."

Every team had to submit a name, but I reckoned we had the best one by a mile. We all chuckled to ourselves, but we also knew that a good team name wasn't going to win us the competition.

"Gardner, Holmes, Rogers and Jacobs," the starter continued.

I felt a tingle go down my spine. It was only the first round of what, in the grand scheme of things, was a relatively unimportant competition that was only for club golfers – even if it did have such a sweet prize. But for me it felt like my very own US Masters. Furthermore, it represented revenge. Sweet revenge.

We teed off in order of handicap, lowest first. Unlike our practice matches we'd be playing the back nine first. The tenth hole at Steenberg, which would be our first, is quite long for amateurs like us. It's stroke five – the fifth hardest hole – and measures about four hundred yards, and that day it would play even longer as it was into the wind. Despite this, I figured that Big G would hit an iron on the opening hole as usual.

He strode up to the tee box and, sure enough, out came the two-iron. Just as before, he dropped the ball on the turf – no tee peg – took a smooth practice swing and addressed the ball. Then he absolutely marmelised it, straight down the middle of the fairway. There was no applause, but there were several audible gasps from the few people who were watching.

I watched in admiration as his ball disappeared into the distance, straining my eyes until it eventually came back down to earth. Then I suddenly realised it was my shot next. That wasn't all I realised either; I was also bloody nervous. Nonetheless, I resolved to perform my usual routine – with the new swing thoughts built in, of course.

I teed up my ball and checked its height against my driver …
I walked behind the ball and took two practice swings …
I picked a spot and lined it up …
I addressed the ball …
I waggled the club twice …
I stood there for a few seconds as if frozen, staring at the ball …
Then I finally pulled the trigger …
Crack!

I smacked the ball right up its backside, making sure I kept watching the same spot until the ball had gone. Belatedly, I looked up. Phew! A good one. In fact a very good one, centre right. No gasps as such, but a couple of people murmured "Shot" under their breath.

"*Yur da man*! Brilliant shot, old mate. We'll make a bloody golfer of yer yet!" said Dodgy as he bulldozed onto the tee box with a cigarette dangling from the corner of his mouth. He executed his own routine, which contrasted sharply with mine. If I was the tortoise, he was the hare. On steroids. Ball on the tee, fag on the ground, a hitch of the pants, then *wallop*! A perfect five-yard draw down the middle. There were a few calls of "Good shot", but these were drowned out as Dodgy noisily dropped his guts. It was as if he was celebrating his drive.

"Thank you, thank you, yer just too kind," he said, passing Lofty who was walking onto the tee. "And let's hear it fer me slightly-less-talented partner too."

Although Lofty seemed a little embarrassed, it didn't seem to affect him too much. He hit a very respectable tee shot down the right half of the fairway. You could always tell when Lofty had hit a decent drive: he would immediately begin a frantic search for his tee peg. It was as if he was thinking, "Okay, I got the ball away fine. Now, those tees are ten bucks for a packet so I'd better not lose one." A golfer's version of Maslow's hierarchy of needs.

"Fer Gawd's sake, leave it," said Dodgy. "Maybe someone will hand it in fer yer. Come on, we've got a bloody competition ter win."

With that, the Ferkaryer Four marched purposefully down the fairway to meet their destiny.

18

I had already contemplated what would constitute a good score. In an ideal world, we would get at least four points per hole, plus some fives and sixes. We might even get the odd seven if we were lucky. It was crucial for the four of us to avoid having simultaneous bad holes. When one player struggled, at least two of the others had to play well to compensate. Technically speaking, that was called dovetailing. Factoring all that in, a good score would be over ninety points. It would probably take something in the mid-nineties to win, but I tried to stop thinking about it too much as we approached our balls.

Unsurprisingly, Lofty had hit the shortest drive; about two hundred yards and just on the fairway. That still left him with the thick end of two hundred to go which was quite a long way for him.

Under normal circumstances, he would probably have pulled out his three-wood, tried to hit it too hard and made a right mess of it. I wanted to warn him not to risk it, but I felt that perhaps it was better to let him just get on with his game. In the end I didn't have to worry: Big G took matters into his own hands.

"Okay, Lofty. I'm going to try and help you around the course today," he said. "I think it will help us a lot if we can get your strategy right. You might be able to bag us some decent points. Just tell me if I get in your face too much though."

"No, that's great. I need all the help I can get!"

"Okay, good. Now let's have a look. You've left yourself just under two hundred, and the green is well-protected. There's a bunker on the left, a stream on the right and more trouble if you go long. It's basically a career shot to get there. You should lay up instead. Leave yourself about seventy or eighty yards, a full lob wedge. That means you've gotta hit this next one about one-twenty. So you need an eight or a nine."

Lofty stood there, transfixed. It had never occurred to him that golf could be this well planned.

"Let's hit the nine, just to err on the short side," Big G concluded. "You mustn't leave yourself a half shot. Are you with me?"

"Okay, coach, you've got it. Whatever you say," said Lofty obediently. "Nine-iron it is."

I don't think he had a clue what Big G was talking about, but the words 'hit the nine' seemed to have seeped through into his brain somehow. He pulled out the club and took his stance, then – astonishingly – hit a lovely shot down the middle of the fairway. Just as Big G had planned.

"Great shot! You didn't force it," said Big G approvingly.

I was impressed. Not only with Lofty's shot, but also with the way Big G had worked it all out for him. I realised that one of Lofty's main problems was course management. Maybe if I'd spent less time teasing him and more time giving him guidance during all our games together, his game might have progressed more quickly. Big G's coaching could end up saving him a bunch of shots.

I had hardly had a chance to start walking again when I heard a loud *thwack*! as Dodgy played his second shot, from a spot about ten yards closer to the green. The ball shot forward on a low trajectory, hardly getting more than ten feet above the ground, and finally trundled up and onto the green.

"Well, that should be there or thereabouts," he said matter-of-factly.

"Nice shot," I called. "What did you hit?"

"The trusty one-iron," replied Dodgy. "Never lets me down."

A seventeen handicap and he could hit a one-iron on the green from nearly two hundred yards? This guy was taking the Mickey. "Bandit!" I grinned.

"Hey, gringo! *Handale! Handale! Hariba! Hariba!*" he yelled back at me in a high-pitched Mexican accent.

Big G and I both then found the green. I pushed mine rather too far right, leaving myself a long putt, but he hit a beauty to within eight feet. Things got even better when Lofty flipped his lob wedge to about fifteen feet, again just as Big G had envisaged. As we walked towards the green, I tried not to get ahead of myself, but as our four balls came into focus, sitting there on the green, I couldn't help thinking what a solid start we'd made.

Then I silently berated myself for celebrating too soon. I should be doing what the pro's do. Stay in the moment. Not get ahead of myself. Focus my mind on the next shot. Don't start sucking each others' dicks yet. All those good things.

I strode onto the green with renewed focus for what was quite a tricky putt – all of fifty feet and very quick if it went past the hole. I really didn't want to race it off the green. I took my stance, settled myself and let the putt go.

I had been too cautious. It was well short, only just inside Big G's marker. I still had at least six feet to go.

"That's okay," said Big G, supportively. "Maybe you should try and putt out. You can give me a look at the line from there. See if you can get us the par."

It made sense so I agreed, but my putt was again tentative and it pulled up just short. Two great shots and then a three-putt. Damn!

"Don't worry. You get a stroke. It's still two points. And we've all still got chances. At least you've got us on the board."

That much was true, but I was still disappointed with my effort.

Dodgy was up next. He had a twenty-footer. In contrast to my painstaking method, he just had one quick look at the hole and then made his stroke. The ball cosied up to the hole beautifully, dying just a few inches short.

"I'll take that fer par," he smiled, tapping the ball into the hole with the back of his putter.

"And you get a stroke there too," said Big G. "That's three points. Well played."

My three-putt wouldn't matter so much now, especially if Big G made birdie.

About ten seconds later, he did just that. Another three points.

"Yessssss!!!" enthused Lofty. "Great putt!"

"Why, thank you," replied Big G modestly, "but we're not done yet. You're gonna make yours now. This hole is a double stroker for you. If you can make this putt it's worth four points."

Even though Lofty was a decent putter, Big G carried on with the advice. He clearly felt that Lofty played better with a bit of guidance.

"Did you see how my one just started to die at the end? It wants to break left a touch, so either take a bit more break or just hit it a bit firmer. I think maybe you should go inside right and firm. There are no prizes for being short. We've already got two three-pointers in the bag."

Although clearly bemused by the technicalities, Lofty stood over the putt and prepared himself. I willed him to make a better job of it than I had.

He did. The ball clattered into the back of the hole, jumped a couple of inches in the air, and dropped obediently into the cup.

"*Oh yeah! Oh yeah!*" chanted Dodgy, placing his hands on the top of his club and gyrating his hips in some kind of bizarre pole-dancing routine. "We bagged seven points! We bagged seven points!"

We all laughed, but for me it was through slightly gritted teeth. Yes, we had bagged a seven-pointer which was a great start. Great for the team. But I had three-putted and hadn't contributed. One hole; one three-putt. Not a great start for me.

"Get over yourself," I muttered under my breath as I walked to the next tee. "That's your bad hole. We still made seven. Put it behind you and get scoring."

On the next hole, a short par four, that's exactly what I did. I hit a sensible three wood off the tee, then a scrumptious wedge to about ten feet. Setting off towards the green, putter in hand, I practically ordered myself to make a positive stroke. As I stood over the ball I reminded myself one last time, saying "Knock it in" just before I let the putt go.

It was never anywhere but the centre of the cup.

Birdie. Three points. What's more, my putting woes seemed to be behind me now.

Big G could only make par – Hah! Only a par and I *birdied* it! – and Lofty made a LOIBIP after going in the bunker and failing to get out in three attempts. But Dodgy came to the party again with another par – net birdie – and we had another six points. Thirteen points after two holes. At this rate we could almost book our places in the final already.

Our good play continued over the rest of our front nine. We didn't get six or seven points on every hole, but – as Big G had requested – we dovetailed brilliantly. Whenever someone had a bad hole, someone else would play it well. At least two of us contributed on every hole and our solitary bad hole was the tough fifteenth where we made only two points. Otherwise, though, we played superbly.

Dodgy was particularly inspired, making only one blob – golf-speak for failing to score any points on the hole – and taking an impressive total of only forty strokes in the process. Four over par. Not bad for a seventeen handicap.

That all added up to a very healthy forty-eight points for our team at half-way. I headed for the leader board and was thrilled to see that only one other team had scored more than forty-five. But I got a chill down my neck when I read who it was: African Tobacco Directors. They were on forty-seven, just one behind us.

We ordered a quick sandwich each and wolfed them down voraciously. I am a very fast eater, in contrast to my normally slow and meticulous nature, and gobbled mine down even quicker than the others did. I wanted to see if the tee was clear so I left the guys to it and walked over towards the tee box. Bingley's team was playing directly ahead of us and they hadn't even started their back nine. We were okay for time. No need to rush.

I then noticed something else: a rumbling in my stomach. It was what I commonly refer to as a Robocrap: that strange feeling in the lower intestinal tract, which leaves you in no doubt that you've only got 'twenty seconds to comply'. I headed for the restrooms briskly.

As I sat on the throne – chatting to myself and minding my own business, so to speak – I heard two people arguing heatedly outside in the corridor. Always keen to gloat over a competitor's problems, I cupped my ears in an effort to make out what they were saying, but the voices were too faint behind two closed doors.

But then one of them walked into the restroom and I could hear every word: "I've told yer, arsehole, I've had it with yer. Yer can threaten me all yer bloody like, but the deal's off!"

The unmistakable voice of Dodgy.

19

I waited inside the crapper until Dodgy left. Yes, I had to break the world record for holding ones breath, but I certainly couldn't let him see me. I needed time to figure out what on earth he could have meant. I did not have a good feeling about it at all.

When I eventually appeared on the tee box, the others were already there.

"Where've yer been?" a flustered-looking Dodgy asked.

"Just went to check my handicap. I forgot to do it before we started and I wanted to make sure it hadn't changed. Didn't wanna get D-Q'd."

"Keeping this team all in one place is like herding cats," Lofty complained. "First you go wandering off and then Dodgy chooses the last possible moment to go and relieve his nerves. He must be about two kilos lighter after being away that long – although at least he smells better now. Let's get the show on the road please, ladies!

"How about we put fifty points on the board this time?" Big G agreed. "Then we can book our tickets to the final."

Our second nine was almost as impressive as our first, and when we walked off the penultimate green, we had amassed forty-two points. We now had ninety points with one hole to play.

Dodgy in particular played amazingly and with a determination that I had not seen before. This just made me more curious. What had happened outside the restroom? There was definitely something dodgy about it. Pun intended.

Then I reminded myself that we still had one more hole to play. The mystery of Dodgy and his latest deal would have to wait; there was another more pressing mystery. How many points would we need in order to qualify? By a rare stroke of good fortune, this particular mystery was revealed rather more easily than I expected.

From the green we had to walk across a narrow road which came out a few yards in front of the final tee box. As the rest of my team headed off, I lagged behind to update our scorecard. A moment later, as I set off to catch up, I heard some familiar African Tobacco voices. I froze instinctively. I didn't want to encounter Bingley just before I played my final tee shot. He would try and rile me, no doubt.

I inched back behind the thick bushes that flanked the road and listened intently. Bingley and Hammond were standing about ten feet away, just on the other side of the road, behind some more bushes. They hadn't seen me, but I could see them as I peered through the foliage.

More to the point, I could hear them too. They were studying Bingley's cellphone. "Brilliant news, Hammond, look. We're leading with ninety-six. Everyone else has finished, and the next best score is only ninety-four. Those muppets behind us only have ninety. I just got a message from their marshal. They surely can't overtake us now, but even if they do we're bound to finish second at worst. Your diabolical play hasn't cost us after all! We've done it! We're through! Ha ha!"

Not for the first time in his life, the devious bastard had been cheating. He had obviously primed the marshals to send him text messages updating him on the other scores. He would have known exactly where his team stood throughout the game. It hadn't guaranteed that they'd qualify, of course, but it would probably have been a very handy advantage all the same.

One thing was for sure: it was bloody illegal.

"The cheating son of a bitch!" I said through gritted teeth.

As soon as the coast was clear, I rushed over to the tee box where my partners were waiting.

"Guys, you're not gonna believe this. Bingley has been getting scores from the marshals! He knew what the other teams had scored and he's worked out that they're bound to go through."

"That mother-f –" began Dodgy.

"Wait," interrupted Big G. "We can use this. What did he say, Speedy? What did he say the points were?"

I repeated the scores I'd heard.

"Right. We're the last group. That means ninety-five will clinch second place, doesn't it?" Dodgy and I nodded slowly, but Lofty looked confused. Big G spelt it out for him: "Bingley's mob have ninety-six. Everyone else has finished and the best total is ninety-four. If we get five points here, we've done it."

He was right. Although Bingley had been up to his old tricks, this time he'd actually helped us.

"What if it's a count-back?" Dodgy asked.

"What the hell is a count-back?" said Lofty, showing his lack of competition experience again.

Big G explained patiently. "If it's a tie, whoever has the most points on the toughest hole wins. Stroke one here is the fifteenth," he said, consulting the scorecard, "and that's the only darned hole that we've messed up. They're bound to have got more than us there. We'd lose. Ninety-four won't be enough."

We now knew what we had to do. Five points and we'd qualify for the final. Anything less and we'd be going home. For good.

"Gentlemen," announced Big G, "we've just got to play the best damn golf of our lives. No pressure, mind you."

"Okay, let's get down to business," I said, looking at Big G and trying to sound confident. "It's stroke ten. Dodgy and Lofty stroke, but we don't."

"Let's bloody go and make this happen!" shouted Dodgy determinedly. He really was fired up.

The hole was a fairly long par four, uphill and far from straightforward. It was an especially tough tee shot. There was a vineyard on the left and a huge bunker all the way up the right. Further right was a row of trees and then out-of-bounds. The

Geddin the Hole!

green was also well-protected, with a large bunker to the left, out of bounds right and more trouble behind the green. In a word, challenging.

Big G would lead off as usual. I suddenly felt really nervous for the first time as I watched him tee up his ball. He had his driver in his hand. I didn't know why, but I had another of those bad feelings.

Justifiably so, as it turned out. Big G hit his only really bad shot of the day – a wild, snap hook that never had a chance. As Lee Trevino said, "You can talk to a slice, but a hook won't listen". This one was about as good a listener as my boss, Mr Rivlin, the self-proclaimed sounding board. I watched in desperation as the ball disappeared over the bushes and into the vineyard. Big G hung his head. No-one said anything until Dodgy eventually broke the silence.

"That was a Captain Kirk, I'm sorry ter say," said Dodgy.

"A what?"

"Captain Kirk: it's gone where no man has gone before. Yer in the crap, Biggus. Come on, fellas. The big guy's carried us the whole way round. We can't let him down now!"

By Dodgy's standards, that was quite a poignant moment. A rallying cry straight from the heart. Sadly it didn't have the desired effect on me.

Perhaps I felt that I had to make up for Big G's horror show, but I also went with my driver. I never quite settled and took an 'anyway' – as in, I didn't feel right, but I hit it anyway. Always a mistake. Maybe no man had gone there before Big G had, but now I'd gone there too. My shot was a virtual replica of his: high, wide and not very handsome, over the bushes and into the grapes.

Now we were in trouble. Two out of two out of bounds and only Dodgy and Lofty left to play. We were rapidly running out of options. My heart skipped a beat as Dodgy barged his way onto the tee, that look of determination still in his eye.

"That son of a bitch Bingley is not gonna beat us," he muttered to himself. "Never."

I wondered why he had suddenly started caring so much about Bingley now. He had only ever shown any interest in the trip to Augusta. But that was not at the forefront of my mind in those stressful moments. All I could think about was Dodgy hitting the fairway.

To my great relief, he obliged. That metronomic little draw, straight down the middle.

"*Come on!*" Dodgy cried, doing a fairly passable impression of Stuart Pearce after *that* penalty for England against Spain in Euro 1996. We took a moment to congratulate him before the relief turned to anxiety again: it was Lofty's turn.

He had to make a score here. My heart skipped a few more beats. I tried to work out how we were going to get our five points. Big G and I were surely out of the hole, but Lofty and Dodgy both stroked. If either of them could make par, that would be three points. If the other got a bogey to go with it for two points, that would be five for the hole. So it was simple: a par and a bogey to qualify.

At this stage I don't suppose any hole would have been easy, but the green was particularly tricky, with a big ridge across it and trouble all around. Bogey would be a good score at the best of times, let alone right now. I couldn't bear to watch.

I peeped through my fingers to see Lofty pulling his driver from his bag. I wanted to stop him. I wanted to say, "No, you fool, hit three-wood!" but I'd just clobbered my own drive out of bounds and didn't think I had the right to start shouting the odds.

Lofty looked nervous, but he composed himself. To everyone's relief, he got his drive away. But it wasn't great – a pronounced fade towards the bunker on the right. We held our breath as the ball sailed further and further right. Time stood still as it disappeared into the trees, before we heard the distinct thump of ball on timber. Then we breathed a collective sigh of relief as the ball reappeared, dropping down, in play. We prayed that he'd get lucky and have a clear shot for his second.

Big G and I both hit another drive each, but both went too far right this time, and into the trees in the same direction that Lofty had gone. This time, though, neither ball emerged. Three off the tee and still in serious trouble. We'd have to get down in two from there to even score a point. Even that probably wouldn't be enough. As we set off down the fairway, I walked up alongside Big G.

"Well, I suppose you had to hit one bad shot today," I offered sympathetically.

"Yeah, but the driver was a bad choice. Should've hit the two-iron. Anyway, now I've probably got to play coach. Looks like we're going to need five points out of these two guys."

Before Big G and I looked for our balls, it would be Lofty's turn to hit his second. We walked over and found his ball. The good news was that he had an unhindered swing. The bad news was that he had no shot to the green. He was totally blocked by the overhanging branches. In one sense that made it easier – he had to chip out and play for bogey. Big G didn't even have to advise him. "I've got to chip out sideways, haven't I?" he asked rhetorically.

"That's it," said Big G positively. "Bunt it down there." He pointed across the fairway. "Just make sure you get it over the bunker," he added, just in case Lofty wasn't nervous enough.

Lofty took his time with his shot – allowing himself several practice swings – then eventually did what was asked of him, punching the ball out over the bunker about forty yards down the fairway. He still had a fair distance to go, but at least he was on the short stuff.

"Perfect!" I said, knowing that the job was not yet even half done.

Dodgy, meanwhile, didn't seem to need any coaching. He strode purposefully up to his ball and chose his club with little hesitation. He hit a good shot, but with the out of bounds looming large, he was slightly too cautious. The ball landed on the green, but was about thirty feet left of the hole. Not exactly birdie territory, but at least it was an almost definite par.

For Big G and me it was more bad news. I hadn't had the same good fortune as Lofty and my ball had gone out of bounds again. I was officially out of the hole.

Big G didn't fare much better. His ball had landed in a terrible spot and he could only hack it a few yards forward. Although he got it onto the fairway with his next attempt, he was still well short of the green. By now he'd played five, meaning that he couldn't score any points. Disconsolately, he pocketed his ball.

As Big G and I were now both toast, everything really did depend on Dodgy and Lofty. We got to Lofty's ball. He had about a hundred and twenty yards left.

Big G resumed his coaching duties. "Alright, Lofty, Speedy and I are goners, so we need you here. Don't flirt with the out of bounds. Just play to the middle of the green, not towards the pin. Exactly where Dodgy's landed will be fine. Get it on the green, two-putt it and make your bogey. Then let's get outta here and pack our bags for the final."

Lofty looked over at me with a terrified expression on his face.

"Come on, Lofty, you can do it!" I said reassuringly, wishing that I really believed that. I think I was more nervous than he was.

"Lofty, I've just got two things ter say," Dodgy contributed. "Firstly, yer've got one-twenty ter go, and secondly, yer the greatest! Now come on! Let's do this!"

Dodgy was turning out to be a bit of a dark horse in the motivational speaking department. Either that or a serial bullshitter.

Lofty pulled out his club and addressed the ball. I was so nervous that I thought my heart was going to jump right out of my chest.

With minimal hesitation, he let the shot go. It was a decent strike, but in his eagerness to avoid the out of bounds he pulled it well left, towards the bunker. We couldn't tell if it had landed in it or not. Wherever it was, he had to get it up-and-down.

When we got to the ball, it was good news of sorts as it wasn't in the bunker. The bad news was that it was *behind* the bunker, which was actually worse, especially for Lofty whose chipping had been lousy all day. All of his life, in fact.

Dodgy suddenly decided to take charge. "Okay, guys, executive decision. I'll putt first. If I make it, Lofty can afford ter take six. He can play his next one sideways and then two-putt."

It made sense. If Dodgy made his birdie it would be worth four points. Lofty could then afford to make a double-bogey six. He'd only make one point, but we'd still make the required five points on the hole. He could play to the right of the bunker and back towards the front of the green. He'd have to aim away from the hole, but – more crucially – he'd be playing away from the out of bounds that lurked beyond. In theory he could even have used his putter. If he took that line he could leave himself about forty feet, from where he could almost definitely two-putt and make his six.

It was a good theory, but as with many good theories, it fell apart at the first hurdle. Dodgy hit a good putt – a great putt, in fact – but it just burned the hole and stayed above ground.

"*Bollocks!*" he spat as he tapped in for par.

I knew what he meant. Now our elaborate plan B had to be shelved. Lofty had to get down in two which meant chipping over the sand towards the hole.

"At least I've got a lot of green to work with," declared Lofty thoughtfully.

I did a double-take. I wanted to check whether Phil Mickleson had suddenly turned up, reverted to a right-handed stance, donned a Lofty mask and joined our team.

He hadn't. It was indeed Lofty.

A lot of green to work with??? Was he nuts? True, there was about fifty feet of green between him and the hole, but realistically the amount of green he had 'to work with' was irrelevant. He had to get the ball up quickly to clear the bunker, but still stop it before it shot off the other side of the green and possibly even out of bounds. For him, it was a nearly impossible shot. You have to remember that this was Lofty, a guy who had all the chipping skills of a water buffalo.

Sure, Phil Mickleson would have been able to play this shot in his sleep. Big G would have made a decent fist of it. Even I could probably have pulled it off and got the ball somewhere on the green. But Lofty wasn't Phil, he wasn't Big G and he wasn't even me. He was Lofty: the man who couldn't chip.

Big G decided that the time for lessons was over. "Make a nice positive stroke," he said, and left the rest to Lofty.

"Just keep your head still," I blurted, then I crossed my fingers on both hands, half covered my eyes and waited.

Lofty got himself ready. He must have taken five or six practice swings before settling over the ball. This was it.

Swish!

There was a sickening *clunk* as he hit the ball right in the teeth. I uncovered my eyes just in time to see the ball shoot forward into the face of the bunker, then hop in the air, go over the lip and just pop out the other side before coming to rest just short of the green.

Bollocks indeed. He was lucky that it didn't stay in the sand. He still hadn't made the green and was fifty feet short of the hole. There was no chance of him holing it from there.

I was gutted.

As we trudged to the back of the green to put our bags down, I noticed a familiar face in the watching crowd.

Bingley.

He sidled over until he was standing only a few feet away. "Never mind, old chap," he whispered. "Better luck next year. We'll be thinking of you when we win the final."

Our dream was over. I felt like crying.

O

I dragged myself through the front door with a look of pure dejection on my face. Shelley didn't need to be a genius to guess what had happened.

"Oh no, darling," she said softly. "You didn't get through, did you?"

I just kept looking down, shaking my head.

"Darling. What a shame."

"Lofty just had to get up-and-down and we would've done it. I told him that he just had to keep his bloody head still. He bladed the bloody thing through the bunker. It didn't even reach the green! He didn't get it within fifty bloody feet!"

"He must be devastated, especially after that drama with his tax bill. He'll be really down. Do you think I should phone him to commiserate?"

"What the heck for?" I screamed, my face splitting into a huge grin. "He's right here! He bloody holed the putt! We did it!"

I ran over to hug Shelley, followed closely by Lofty, Dodgy and Big G who all charged into the house and gave us both a huge team hug. Big G hardly knew Shelley and Dodgy had never even met her, but that didn't stop them. Seconds later we were joined by Buster who proceeded to jump all over us and lick everything in sight. Not a bad philosophy in itself, really.

Yes, we'd actually done it. Lofty might not have been able to chip – but, boy, he could putt. He putted the ball from the fringe and blow me if he boxed it. Seriously. Blow me. Please. The moment it had left his putter, the ball was never anywhere else but in the hole.

Lofty made the obligatory phone call to Abigail, but Big G reluctantly made his apologies. He wanted to stay but he'd made a prior arrangement to meet someone about a property deal or something. The rest of us settled in for a hard night's celebration at my place. It was a long, drunken night. When we eventually turned it in, Lofty took the spare room, and Dodgy crashed in the lounge with Buster. They seemed to be kindred spirits after all. Everyone woke up with blinding headaches, but it had been worth it. We were in the final.

As Lofty would say, however, every silver lining has a cloud. This one was a cumulonimbus: Bingley and his team of directors had, of course, taken the other place.

We would be meeting again in the final at Erinvale.

20

"Hi-diddly-dee, a golfer's life fer me," sang Dodgy gaily as he climbed out of his car the next morning. He still had a bit of a headache and felt a bit queasy. Good thing the police hadn't stopped him on his way back. He might still have been over the limit.

Suddenly he felt a hard *thwack* across the back of his neck. The shock made his knees buckle and he fell forwards heavily onto the gravel.

"Uggh," he groaned. "Who the hell –"

"Never you mind who the hell. You need to worry about *what* the hell. Like what the hell is gonna happen to you now that you've messed my boss around."

"Yer boss?" Dodgy managed as he clambered to his knees. He looked up to see two huge men standing over him. The slightly larger, uglier one was doing the talking. The other one held a baseball bat in his bear-like paw.

"That's right. You two had a deal, remember? You didn't fulfil your side of the bargain, so we're here to teach you a lesson. You're not going to be able to hold a golf club this weekend, let alone win a competition."

Dodgy's mind was racing. He had to think of something quickly. "Listen, let's talk about it. You do me a favour, I'll do you one – we both know how these things go down. How much is he payin' yer?"

"Why don't we stick to things that *are* your business? Or do you wanna argue with me and make this even uglier?" said the thug, stepping even closer.

"No, course not. It's just that, well, whatever it is, I can match it if you fellas leave me alone. I've got dosh …" He *didn't* have dosh, but he'd worry about that later.

"Do I look stupid?"

It was tempting.

"No, 'course you don't," Dodgy lied. "Yer smart, that's obvious. Which is why I don't think yer'd turn down twenty grand. Each. Just tell the boss that yer beat the crap outta me and we all walk away happy."

The two hired monkeys looked at each other. It seemed that he had picked the right number.

"It ain't just the money," Thug One growled eventually. "I'd be happy to rearrange your face for free, but if you make it twenty-five a piece, then I might just have a convenient lapse of memory. Just 'cos I'm a nice guy."

"Deal," Dodgy said hurriedly. "I don't have it handy right now though. I'll get yer the cash by next Monday." He needed to buy himself some time.

"That's, erm, eight days' time," the thug counted on his fingers.

"Yeah, eight days," said Dodgy, resisting the urge to compliment him on his outstanding mathematical ability. "I'll have it by then."

"Fine. You've got yourself a deal. Enjoy the match on Saturday, won't you? And just in case you get forgetful, here's a reminder."

He grabbed hold of Dodgy's shirt and brought his hand up under his ribs.

Dodgy heard a loud crack pierce the air. A split second later, everything went black.

21

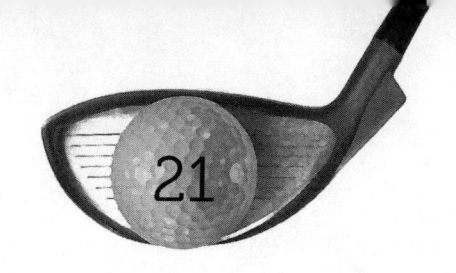

I was the last one to get out of bed the next morning. Shelley had gone to bed and left us to our celebrations the previous night. She'd risen early and made some breakfast for the others before they set off for home. They'd all promised to get going at first light, although Shelley had had to throw Dodgy out when Lofty had left. I'd been allowed a much-needed lie-in.

Eventually, at about nine o'clock, Shelley came in and woke me up.

"Morning, sleepy-head," she said. "Up you get. What do you fancy for breakfast?"

"Phew. How about a couple of lightly sautéed Alka-Seltzers?"

"Coming right up. How about a nice greasy bacon roll for main course?"

"Now you're speaking my language."

Over breakfast, I relived the golf match one more time. My memory of the events was slightly muddled, no doubt due to the twenty or so beers I'd consumed afterwards, but Shelley humoured me, bless her.

"It was unbelievable. On the eighteenth Big G and I both carved our tee shots out of bounds. It was all up to Lofty and Dodgy. When Lofty messed up his chip I thought we were sunk, but the little bugger walked up and knocked it in the hole. You should have been there. It was like the Ryder Cup!"

"I'm so proud of you," said Shelley. She'd heard this story about a hundred times, but still acted as if it was the first time. "All of you. You did so well. Now you've just got to go out and do it one more time next week. It'll be awesome if you pull it off."

"If we play like we did yesterday we'll have a great chance. Especially Dodgy. I think he shot about six or seven over par. For a seventeen handicap! That's unreal. He was so focussed and he –"

I stopped suddenly as another piece of the jigsaw from the

previous day slotted back into place. It was starting to feel like a Tarantino film. "Oh my goodness! I'd forgotten about that!"

"About what?" said Shelley, clearly baffled by my sudden realisation.

I told her about Dodgy's altercation which I'd overheard from the toilet. "I didn't get a chance to ask him about it. I didn't want to say anything in front of the others and then I got caught up in the excitement of winning and forgot. I should give him a call or something, shouldn't I? There could be something fishy going on. Maybe he's in a bit of bother."

I was interrupted by the telephone. My immediate thought was that it was Dodgy. I braced myself and reluctantly answered.

"Hi, Speedy, it's Lofty."

"Lofty!" I said with relief. "What an unexpected pleasure! The hero of the hour, no less!"

"How do you fancy going to hit a few balls? I feel inspired for one thing and, what's more, I need to get out of the house to clear my head, if you know what I mean. Gym would be *too* hectic, but I think a few perfectly struck iron shots might just chase the hangover away."

"Sounds like a plan. Let me just check …" I glanced over at Shelley, who had a knowing look on her face.

"Okay, what's this plan?" she said, wearing her best long-suffering wife expression.

"Lofty is demanding that I meet him at Westlake to try and, well, you know, shake off the hangover."

"You mean a bucket of golf balls, then a couple of beers?"

"We were thinking more in terms of cups of coffee than beers, but that's the general idea, yeah."

"Alright then. Tell him you've got a free pass. I'll take the kids round to my mum's for a couple of hours. It might be the last time though," she said begrudgingly.

"Thanks, love. And why don't you take Buster with you? Maybe he can eat her bloody Yorkshire terrier for lunch."

I wasted no time. I told Lofty to be there in thirty minutes and set off so quickly I left my cellphone on the kitchen table. When I got to Westlake, Lofty was already there, unpacking his stuff.

"Ah, the man of the moment. Looks like you've rediscovered your passion for golf?"

"You can say that again," said Lofty. "What a putt! All of sixty feet! Never looked like missing!"

I decided not to mention the horrendous chip that preceded this wonderful putt, nor the fact that the length of said putt seemed to have increased by roughly ten feet since the day before. I figured that he was entitled to bask in his success after the stresses of the past month.

"Yeah, well, let's not get carried away quite yet. We've got the big one next weekend. That miracle putt will mean sod all if we lose in the final, especially if Bingley wins. Maybe we should go and practice chipping," I went on, unable to resist a little dig, "so that next time you leave yourself a *six*-footer instead of a *sixty*-footer? Just a thought."

"Yeah, yeah. Mock all you like. I happen to have a plan up my sleeve to fix that, actually. Just you wait and see."

"Ha ha! It had better be a good one. I can't wait to hear it!"

With that we went over to the practice area and hit shots for a while, not really worrying too much about it. This was just to unwind and clear out the cobwebs.

"So let's see this plan to fix your chipping," I said eventually. "I'm bored of just beating balls with the driver."

"You can't, my plan's only happening later. Besides, mindlessly beating balls works for Dodgy, doesn't it?"

"Hey! Dodgy! That reminds me! Yesterday at the competition I heard him arguing with someone about a deal. It's been bugging me."

"A deal? When? I never heard anything."

"You wouldn't have. It was in the toilet at halfway. He was having a big fat row with someone. I didn't hear much, but he said something about a deal being off. It sounded, well, dodgy. He might be in trouble. He sounded pretty pissed off."

"Hmmm. Maybe we should call him. What do you reckon?"

"Shelley always says it's better to get things out in the open and she's usually right. I think we should call him right now."

"Okay, but you'll have to do it. My cellphone's on the blink. Kind of took it for a swim," said Lofty furtively. He was always either breaking or losing things.

"My word, you're useless. I suppose I'll have to save the day again," I said, reaching for my phone. But after a few minutes of fruitless searching and cursing, I realised that I didn't have it. "Damn it! I must have left it at home."

"What was that about saving the day?" mocked Lofty.

"Yeah, alright," I said, sheepishly. "Never mind. Let's get out of here. I'll call him when I get home and get to the bottom of this. It's starting to concern me."

"Yeah, okay. I've got to go shopping now anyway."

"Oh no, is Abigail gonna drag you round the mall?"

"Erm, no, actually. As a matter of fact, I'm going alone."

"Really? The man who has everything? Whatever could you need?"

"You'll see soon enough"

"I see. The mysterious ace up your sleeve? Well, I suppose you might as well have a secret, everyone else seems to have one."

When I arrived back at the house, Shelley was already back from her mum's. I didn't even have to ask her if she'd seen my phone; she presented it to me as I walked through the door.

"You got a phone call just after you left. It sounded pretty important. Here, I even took the message down."

"That sounds ominous," I said as she handed me the piece of paper. I looked at the note. "Co-incidental too," I added. I

Geddin the Hole!

flopped down on the couch and made the call. It was answered within seconds.

"Speedy! Thank gawd!" said Dodgy in his unmistakable gravely voice.

"Mr Rogers! I heard that you phoned. How are you?"

"Bloody awful, thanks fer askin'. If yer've ever been zapped with a bloody electronic tazer gun then yer'd know. The bastards put a million volts through me! I was in bloody agony. Anyway listen, we need ter talk, mate. I've got a confession ter make. It's been eatin' me up!"

"Not more drama? What's on the menu exactly?" I said, not letting on that I'd tasted the hors d'oeuvre of his half-time argument already. From what he'd said about being zapped, it seemed that a huge main course was to follow. I was intrigued to say the least.

"I'm not sure how ter tell yer this. I had a bit of a run-in with someone at the match yesterday ..."

His confession petered out limply, so I decided to help him along a little. "Let *me* make a confession. I heard you arguing. I was in the bog at the time."

"Shit," he said quietly and I realised he must be in big trouble – he didn't seem to even realise his pun. "You heard us? Then yer know?"

"Not really. I heard you telling someone that the deal was off, but that was all. I didn't hear the part about *what* deal exactly. And I didn't know about this business with the tazer gun either. But anyway, you were saying?"

"Look, Speedy, this is a real nightmare. I guess I'd better come clean fer once in me life, hadn't I? It's about Bingley. We know each other. It was him that I was arguin' with."

Not Bingley *again*! What was it this time?

"*You know Bingley?*" I said in disbelief. "*How?*"

"I have done fer donkey's years. I'm afraid that he ain't just the

Marketin' Director at African Tobacco. He's what's known in the trade as a corrupt son-of-a-bitch. He's done loads of dodgy deals. All sorts of stuff. He's practically a gangster. That's how we crossed paths."

"Bloody hell," I murmured, struggling to take all this in.

"That's not all, Speedy. Look, I'm sorry mate…" He paused and I could almost hear him trying to pluck up the courage to confess.

"Carry on," I implored.

"The day before I met yer in the coffee shop, Bingley contacted me and offered ter pay me if I joined yer team. Yer'd turned down his offer of a place on his team and he wanted me ter get yer chucked out."

"He *what?*"

"I was a plant. He said he'd make it worth me while if I got onto yer team and got caught cheating ter make 'em disqualify yer. I wanted the cash. I agreed. I didn't care."

"You bastard –" I began.

"No, wait! Once I met you blokes and heard the story about Lofty gettin' fired, I changed my mind. I wanted ter be on the good guy's side fer once. I decided ter back out. Honest! I told him ter stick the dosh up his arse. Then yesterday he collared me again. Tried ter get me ter throw the game on the back nine. Threatened me. But I told him again ter stick it where the sun don't shine. That's the part yer heard."

I couldn't believe this.

"But that's only the half of it," Dodgy went on.

"There's *more?*"

"Way more. I thought he was just makin' an idle threat, but I was wrong. Today, when I drove home from your place, I got jumped by these two knuckleheads. He'd only gone and hired some henchmen. They roughed me up a bit and zapped me with that tazer, but I stuck ter me guns. I said I ain't throwing no golf game fer no-one, least of all him."

"So why are you confessing all this now? Have you suddenly found religion?"

"Erm, not exactly. There was a price; I agreed ter pay 'em off."

"I see. How much?"

"Twenty-five large."

"*What?* Twenty-five *thousand?*"

"That's right," he said. "Each."

"Oh, my giddy aunt! Are you serious?"

"'Fraid so. And I don't have two brass farthings ter rub tergether."

Now I faced a serious dilemma. I had no real reason to believe him, let alone help him. I'd only met the man three weeks previously, for heaven's sake, and even that turned out to be a set-up. On the other hand, however, we needed him in our team if we were going to win the Subscribers' Challenge. The rules were very clear on that: team members could not be changed during the competition. It was a case of 'all for one and one for all', and the same applied to the Augusta trip for the winners.

Could we risk bailing him out so we could get our own back on Bingley? What if this was another scam? What was there to stop Dodgy betraying us anyway and getting us disqualified next time?

The events of the past month flashed in front of my eyes again until, finally, I made up my mind.

"We'd better go and talk to Big G."

22

Lofty had had enough. He was going to sort it out, once and for all, so off he headed with gusto – and Abigail's credit card – determined to triumph over this particular adversity. He stepped tentatively inside, making sure that no-one saw him. The truth would come out eventually, he knew that, but he certainly didn't want to get caught actually making the purchase. That would be unbearably humiliating.

Skulking around, he tried to avoid the hordes of over-zealous salesmen. Why was it that, when he needed help, the salesmen were all in Narnia, but now that he wanted to be left alone, they were all over him like a badger chewing his ankle?

It had taken a long time to reach this point.

He had considered taking lessons instead, but that was really expensive. What's more, the very idea reminded him of school, standing outside the headmaster's office, unbuttoning his trousers and waiting for that pain in the nether regions. It also reminded him of getting the cane. Either way, it brought him out in a cold sweat.

He could feel his resolve wavering, so paused to remind himself of the importance of conquering his biggest affliction. Facing his Waterloo, as it were. All he had to do was find what he needed, pay for it and get out of there.

He read the signs as he walked round…. 'Drivers' ….. 'Fairway woods' … 'Putters' ….. 'Wedges' ….. Then he saw it. His heart skipped a beat as he walked tentatively towards the sign. Emblazoned in big, bold, blue letters was the word *'Jiggers'*.

That weird little golf club, like a lofted putter, that was designed for people with a pathological inability to execute any form of chip shot whatsoever. It had finally come to this. Lofty eyeballed the jiggers with mixed feelings. They looked hideous. He needed one, but could he stand the embarrassment?

A cheerful voice suddenly broke the silence. "Hello, sir! Looking at the jiggers, I see?"

Lofty looked up to find a gormless-looking salesman grinning at him. "Ah, you noticed. Thanks," he said with as much irony as he could muster.

The salesman didn't bat an eyelid. He dived straight into a well-rehearsed and extremely tactless sales pitch. "These are great clubs for people who can't chip. Do you struggle with your chipping, sir?"

Lofty could feel his ears reddening. "Look, could I ask you a favour? Actually, two favours?"

"Sure, sir. Go right ahead."

"Firstly, could you please tell me which of these is the cheapest?"

"Sure, sir. On a bit of a tight budget, are we? Wife got you a bit under the thumb, sir? Ha ha ha!" On the Beaufort annoyance scale, this guy was hitting gale force. He carried on, oblivious, at the top of his voice. "Here's the cheapest one, sir. Three ninety-nine. Free head-cover too. Great bargain. And what was the other thing, sir?"

"Ah, yes. Would you kindly *bugger off and leave me alone*???"

Lofty had mixed feelings as he left the shop four hundred bucks lighter. He was slightly ashamed to have lost his cool like that, but in a way it was quite exhilarating to have told someone to bugger off in public.

He also still felt a bit embarrassed. The guys would slaughter him for this. But he'd had no choice. He couldn't chip and he had to do something before the final. He couldn't rely on holing fifty- or even sixty-foot putts. That putt in the qualifier had been a one-off.

23

I arranged to meet Big G and Dodgy at Steenberg after work on Monday to sort out the drama with Dodgy and Bingley. I knew that Dodgy's only chance was for Big G to lend him the money, unless Big G knew some bigger, uglier thugs who he could call on. I doubted it. Tax office managers, maybe. Brutal, violent henchmen? Not likely.

I'd told Big G to arrive half an hour earlier than Dodgy, so that I could brief him on the situation first. My plan was to present the bare facts and hope that he would come up with the idea of lending Dodgy the money himself. I'd learned from the Lofty tax debacle that being subtle sometimes had a better outcome than just asking outright, even if I wasn't very good at it.

"Let's go inside and get a coffee," I said earnestly as Big G and I met in the car park. "I'll explain in there."

We poured ourselves coffee and sat down at a table in the corner. I took a deep breath and began yet another long story. I was beginning to feel like Hans Christian Anderson.

"I'll cut to the chase. It's about Dodgy. I know I implied that Lofty knew him from the coffee shop, but the truth is that we haven't actually known him long. In fact, we only met him the day *after* I met you. We didn't have a fourth player so, when we found out that he played golf, we invited him onto the team. It seemed like a happy co-incidence. But it turns out that he didn't just meet us by chance. It was set up."

"Set up? How do you mean?"

"Our friend Bingley engineered it. He planted Dodgy in our team. Dodgy was supposed to cheat and get us disqualified."

"*What?* How did you find that out?"

I explained the whole story about Bingley and his thugs as Big G listened in shocked silence. "Now Dodgy's made a deal with them," I concluded.

"I suppose that figures. Is it a dodgy one?" asked Big G, only half joking.

"Of course. He said that he'd pay them off if they'd leave him alone, but therein lies the problem: he's made a ten-dollar bet with only five dollars in his pocket, so to speak. And he's not Lee Trevino either. He needs to somehow get out of this fix if he's going to stay in our team, and we're only a team as long as he's in it. So we have a choice: we can either throw him under the bus or think of a way to help him out."

"Phew!" breathed Big G. "That's not exactly what I expected. I knew Bingley was a nasty character but this is a whole side of him I knew nothing about back then when he shoved me around. Wow."

"It appears that shoving people around is what he does best. We've got to decide whether we're gonna try and find a way to help Dodgy out of this mess or not. This time it might be a bit trickier than speaking to someone in the tax office. What do you reckon?"

"How much is he in for?"

"Fifty big ones."

"Jeepers, he doesn't do anything by halves, does he?"

"In for a penny, in for a pound I guess," I said, trying to lighten the mood a bit.

"Look, it's not the money," Big G went on. "I could loan him the money. We'd have to make him sign something to make sure I get it back, but it sounds like he won't need too much convincing on that front."

I found myself distracted slightly as I wondered how it would feel to be able to make huge financial decisions like that so quickly. Pretty good, probably.

"It's more a case of whether we believe him or not," Big G continued. "How do you know he's not double bluffing? He might still shaft us anyway."

"He might, but on the other hand we can't even enter without him, can we?"

"Yeah, I suppose not. I guess it depends how much we want to play this thing."

I could answer that question. More than anything I'd ever wanted. *Ever.* But, much as I wanted to say so, I wanted Big G to make the call. It was his money that we were risking. I waited in silence.

"I want to talk to him face to face. Once I've looked him in the eyes I'll be able to make my final call."

"Here's your chance," I told him as Dodgy walked in, looking extremely guilty.

"Hello, chaps," he said quietly. "Is it safe fer me ter come closer?"

"For now, yes," I said without a hint of a smile.

Dodgy obliged. My stern tone wasn't lost on him.

"So are you ready to fill Big G in on this whole situation?" I asked, deliberately catching him unawares. I didn't want to make life easy for him.

"Oh," said Dodgy in surprise. "I thought yer'd have told him already."

I shook my head. I was going to make him sing for his supper alright. Besides which, it wouldn't hurt to hear him explain one more time.

"Okay," Dodgy began, "it's like this ..." and he proceeded to tell the story over again, pretty much as he'd told it to me the first time. At least he was consistent. Big G and I just sat and listened, paying particular attention to Dodgy's demeanour and mannerisms. Was he lying? Was this just a more elaborate scam? We had to be sure.

"So I kind of panicked. I offered ter pay 'em off twenty-five grand apiece if they promised ter leave me alone. They bought it.

Trouble is, I don't have fifty grand lyin' around. I have ter give it to 'em by next Monday."

Big G looked over at me.

"That's the case for the defence," I concluded. "Or is it the prosecution? Anyway, no further questions, your honour."

"I'll tell you what," he said slowly. "I trust you, Dodgy. Now there's a contradiction in terms! You didn't know that Speedy was in there when you were arguing with Bingley, yet you still told Bingley to stuff it. It sounds genuine to me. On the other hand, I don't like risks. So how about this? I'm guessing these thugs are expecting their cash whether we win or lose on Saturday. We'll play the final and if you deliberately lose us the game, we'll throw you to the lions. The thugs can have you."

Dodgy winced visibly.

"On the other hand, if you *don't* get us disqualified, whether we win or lose I'll transfer the cash to you on Monday morning. You'll have to sign some paperwork committing to a repayment schedule, but I'm guessing that won't be a problem?"

"'Course not. No sweat! Thank yer, Big G, thank yer. Yer've got yerself a deal!" said Dodgy, relief written all over his face. In truth, he didn't have much choice. He shook hands enthusiastically with us both.

"Look, Dodgy, we're choosing to trust you," I said seriously. "We need you in the team – and not just because the rules say you have to be there. You practically got us through that last round and we need you to play even better on Saturday. If you need inspiration, just visualise Bingley's face when we beat him."

"Bloody right! That's all the motivation I need!" grinned Dodgy. Then he spat violently on the beautifully tiled floor.

Big G and I looked at each other. We could trust him alright.

O

Our first practice for the week was on Tuesday at four o'clock.

Everyone arrived early for a change; the recent revelations seemed to have sharpened our focus somewhat. Fortunately, once he got over the initial shock, Lofty had been comfortable with Big G's solution to the situation and we could all greet each other cordially, have a quick stretch, then set about our business of smacking balls down the range. The Dodgy-Bingley situation didn't have to be mentioned.

After about twenty minutes of hitting balls, interspersed with coaching from Big G, I had a thought. "Hey, guys," I announced, "why don't we go and do some chipping? We need to tighten up our short game before next week." I emphasised the words 'we' and 'our', whilst glancing over at Lofty.

"Good idea," agreed Big G. "Let's have a little contest, just to sharpen our competitive edge. Whoever gets it closest wins twenty bucks from the others?"

"Sounds like a plan," Lofty said confidently, surprising us all, and he led the way to the practice green where we waited patiently for Big G's instructions.

"Right, let's start with something simple," he said. "Just a little chip-and-run to that flag there. Let me demonstrate."

He dropped a ball down by his feet and pulled out a club. He took a couple of practice swings and then *swish*! He clipped the ball clean as a whistle. It skipped onto the green before checking up obediently on the third bounce and stopping about two feet away from the hole.

"Sweet as a nut, but is it good enough?" commented Dodgy who didn't wait for an invitation to play his shot. Instead, he walked up to the place from which Big G had played and dropped a ball down. "Age before beauty," he said, looking at Lofty and me.

He didn't even take a practice swing. He just bunted the ball onto the green with about one per cent of the finesse that Big G had displayed. Yet the ball trundled up towards the hole and stopped just inside Big G's.

"Yer see," he said, taking a long drag on his cigarette, "yer don't have ter be fancy. Yer just have ter get the bloody thing up ter the hole." Then he lifted his leg and farted loudly. "Take that too," he said proudly.

When Lofty and I had stopped laughing, we looked at each other, unsure who would play next.

"Okay, I'll go," I said eventually. "Put some pressure on you again. You play better that way, remember?"

I dropped my ball down and took a couple of practice swings. I reminded myself to commit to the shot. The last thing I wanted to do was chunk a shot with the other three just waiting to tease me, even if it was only for twenty bucks. Eventually I played the shot – and made a clean strike. The ball skidded towards the hole, but I'd been a shade too firm. It went past by about four feet. Not a bad shot, but I wouldn't be taking home the prize. The only thing more certain in my mind was that Lofty wouldn't be taking it home either.

"Okay, Lofty, get inside Dodgy's to win," said Big G.

"Just don't think too much about that one you played last week," I grinned. "Or perhaps you want to just hand over your twenty bucks now?"

Lofty hesitated and then pulled a club from his bag. There was a brief silence.

"What the hell is *that*??" spluttered Dodgy. "A bloody mashie niblick??"

I burst out laughing. "He's only gone and bought a jigger! A bloody jigger! Those are for seniors! Women seniors at that!"

"Alright, boys, have your laughs," replied Lofty bravely – and we obliged. "Very amusing, I'm sure, but you won't be saying that in a minute. Just watch this."

He dropped his ball down and took a few practice swings as we tried desperately to suppress our giggles. He addressed the ball and then clipped it onto the green.

Then we stopped laughing. The ball rolled out beautifully towards the hole. For a second it looked like it would go in, but at the last moment it just drifted left and lipped out. It came to rest about two inches away.

"Take that, suckers! I'm back!"

Lofty quickly offered high-fives to the rest of us and we all responded with vigour. Then he reminded us of the bet, which drew a more muted response. But, all in all, it was good news. Okay, we were all twenty bucks poorer, but – finally – Lofty could actually chip! Technically it was jigging, but we didn't care. We carried on chipping – and jigging – for the rest of the practice.

I was enjoying myself. Another few sessions like this and we would be unstoppable.

○

We met every evening that week at four o'clock and practiced for an hour. No-one mentioned Dodgy's deal with Bingley. We just practiced.

Big G played coach, making subtle and not-so-subtle fixes to our swings as required. As usual, he mostly left Dodgy to his own devices. We had more chipping and putting contests and plenty of money changed hands. We got to know each other even better and, if I dare say it, we developed a very strong bond as a team. A pure, one hundred per cent heterosexual bond, you understand.

It was Dodgy who came up with the great suggestion of pooling all the winnings from our bets to buy drinks at the weekend. If we won, we'd celebrate; if we lost, we'd drown our sorrows. I hoped that we weren't tempting fate.

After Thursday evening's session I received an email from the organiser of the competition. It had further details of the day's events, including confirmation of tee times. As I read it, I noticed one very interesting paragraph. It basically re-emphasised that they couldn't afford to allow any cheating. This time, instead of sending a marshal round with each group, they had split each four-ball up into pairs, then matched them with a pair from another team.

I wondered if they had gotten wind of Bingley's text message strategy in the previous match. At least he wouldn't be using it this time. I checked the starting times, then phoned Big G to discuss our strategy.

"Who do you think should play with whom?"

Big G paused for a moment. "I suggest that we stick with the UK–SA format. "That way I can coach Lofty a bit and if, heaven forbid, we have to play with Bingley, I can try and keep him from being intimidated."

"Great," I said. "That sounds fine. So who should go out first then?"

"We will. See if we can get some points on the board. You can bring up the rear. Just think: the fate of the Ferkaryer Four might be resting on your shoulders as you step onto the eighteenth green!" he said and I could tell that he was grinning.

As it turned out, he wasn't far wrong.

24

I managed to get through Friday without going insane. Just.

Shelley and I went to bed early, but I battled to get to sleep. Images of rolling green fairways and golf balls bounced around my head until I felt like a pinball machine. In due course I must have nodded off, pictures of golf courses still lingering in my tired mind.

Before I knew it, my alarm went off and I was awake. I slid out of bed and went through my familiar morning routine. Shelley had agreed to take the boys out for the morning to give me some space to prepare myself and, by the time I got as far as the kitchen, they'd left. Sweet.

I knew that Shelley had put up with a huge amount of disruption as a result of the crazy hours I'd put into golf during the past five weeks. I made a mental note to pick up my washing at least twice in the days ahead to show my appreciation. I owed her – and Danny and Jamie – big time. Better make this last day of freedom count.

I had a decent breakfast and did some stretching which, unfortunately, got Buster wildly overexcited. He joined in gleefully, doing his best to knock me off my feet every time I bent over to touch my toes. Seemed I owed heaps of love and attention to someone else in the family once this was all over.

Finally, freshly showered and slobber-free, I donned my distinctive black gear.

Our tee-off time was set for 12:45, but we wanted to arrive early and had arranged that I would be picked up at ten o'clock. We'd decided to travel together in Big G's car. To be more precise, it was just *one* of his cars: a monstrous SUV that he kept for special occasions. I have some *shoes* that I keep for best …

Driving together would give us a chance to do some final

bonding and talk tactics. The only risk was Dodgy's malodorous farting. We had agreed to take it in turns to be on standby, ready to wind down the windows.

Soon enough, ten o'clock arrived and, before the doorbell even rang, I heard Dodgy's unmistakable voice yelling down the driveway, "Come on yer plonker, move yer ass! We've got a bloody tournament to win!"

I checked myself in the mirror one last time. "Come on Speedy," I whispered. "This is the big one!"

I exited through the garage, grabbed my golf gear and approached Big G's car. "Is it safe to get in?" I asked.

"So far, yes," said Lofty through the window, "but if there's any suspicion of intestinal activity from you-know-who, then the windows are all coming down. I'd be on my guard if I were you."

I closed the gate, set the house alarm and loaded my stuff into the SUV's huge boot. Then I jumped in and buckled up.

"Okay, boys, this is it!" I announced excitedly. "Let's go! Big G, start the Ferkaryer-mobile!"

Big G chuckled, then put the newly christened vehicle into gear and set off. This was indeed *it*.

The journey to Erinvale was relaxed and jovial. Inevitably, Dodgy polluted the air several times. The car windows went up and down like a whore's knickers. We teased Lofty about his jigger. Still the subject of Dodgy and Bingley didn't come up, but deep down we all had a little bit of extra determination to win this thing.

As we came off the highway and drove into the winelands, I was taken aback by the beauty of the place. Of course I had witnessed it before when we'd been on the odd family outing, but days and weeks of slogging away in an office had caused the memory to fade somewhat. I hadn't been out this way for a while and each time I came back I was amazed at just how stunning it was.

The mountains rose up imperiously over the vineyards. The late summer sunshine bathed the whole landscape. It was the perfect backdrop for putting the final nail in Bingley's coffin.

And then we were there. We pulled off the road and into the Erinvale estate. It was simply splendid. Majestic houses scattered in between the rolling vineyards. Quite a place.

Big G drove along the meandering road up towards the clubhouse and parked the Ferkaryer-mobile. We piled out and went to get our golf clubs from the back. Before we could get there, however, we were greeted by two smiling young men dressed in elegant Erinvale tunics.

"Good day to you, sirs. May we take your clubs?"

"Gordon Bennet!" exclaimed Dodgy. "Even the bloody criminals are polite round here! Yer'll have ter take me on first," he said, adopting a mock boxing stance and throwing fake jabs. "Hoo! Ha! I'm a bit tasty, me, so watch out! I might look fat, but I can bloody handle meself!"

"Nurse!" Lofty called. "He's escaped again!"

The two nattily attired young men seemed to take no notice of this tomfoolery. They simply hauled the golf clubs out of the car, put them onto two motorised golf carts and drove off in the direction of the clubhouse, maintaining a professional silence all the while.

"We've got yer bloody licence number, so don't try anythin' funny!" called Dodgy after them.

"Keep your voice down, Dodgy," laughed Big G. "This is a classy establishment you know. Or at least it was until you arrived. Anyway, let's get our gear together and go inside to get changed. We can't change in the car park, can we?"

"Speak fer yerself," Dodgy retorted, pretending to pull his shirt off. "There might be some chicks watchin'. I could give them a right treat. It's not every day yer see a perfect one-pack, is it?" He lifted his shirt and exposed his sagging midriff.

"Charming!" I said. "A perfect specimen of brains and brawn, aren't you?"

"Yer'd better believe it!" said Dodgy. "And I'm loaded with both!"

A very lucid vision of Baloo, the bear from *The Jungle Book*, leapt into my mind.

Sporting our all-important Ferkaryer Four caps, we headed off to the clubhouse. It was magnificent, definitely in the same league as Steenberg.

After changing our shoes, Lofty and I went outside and took in more of the atmosphere while Dodgy and Big G made use of the five-star ablution facilities. The putting green was beautiful. It looked like someone had laid down a green velvet carpet. We located our clubs, grabbed our putters and went off to roll the rock.

Shortly afterwards, Dodgy came out of the changing rooms. He had a look of disbelief on his face, and was shaking his head. What was wrong this time? Was it all going to fall apart *now*?

"Dodgy?" said Lofty worriedly. "What's up? You look worried. Has something happened?"

"Yeah, somethin's happened all right. I saw Big G gettin' changed. That's what's happened. I looked round just as he was whipping his trolleys off. Now I know why he's called Big G – he's hung like a bloody stallion!"

A few moments later Big G appeared, to be greeted by huge grins from us. "Dodgy's just explained why Bernadette has a constant smile on her face!"

"Yeah, and why she walks bow-legged too," added Dodgy. "Poor girl."

If there was one thing you could say about Big G, it was that he maintained a cool, calm, suave exterior no matter what the circumstances. But not this time. He blushed beetroot red and didn't know where to look. Eventually he found words. One word, actually.

"Homos," he said quietly.

Once the raucous laughter had died down, we approached the organiser's table to collect our cards. They were pre-printed with our names and the names of the other two players that we would be paired with.

Dodgy and I were paired with Bingley and Hammond. Somehow I had known we would be. Sod's law. In a way I was relieved; at least Lofty wouldn't have to worry about him. But I was nervous too. Would Bingley still have any influence over Dodgy? I sincerely hoped not.

Big G and Lofty would be playing with the other two African Tobacco directors, HR Director Bruce Knight and Finance Director Kenneth Dunt. I didn't really know anything about them other than the fact that Dunt's nickname was Denneth. A clever spoonistic play on words: Kenneth Dunt–Denneth K … You get it, right? But, much as I enjoy them, the day was not about clever nicknames. The day was about winning the Subscribers' Challenge.

Now that we had our scorecards, it was time for some ABF – Absolutely Bloody Final – practice. We hit irons for about fifteen minutes, then went back over to the putting green. I'll give you three guesses who was standing right there. Clue: he's a supercilious prick.

We all paused, then Dodgy took a deep breath. "Right, let the dog see the rabbit," he declared purposefully and we watched as he strode up to Bingley.

"Ah, Bingley, yer sick piece of crap. Just wanted ter confirm somethin'. All bets are off and it's too bloody late fer yer ter do anythin' about it. Goddit? And I'll be in yer group too, so don't try any funny business or I'll break yer bloody nose."

Bingley just looked at him, shocked and speechless, giving Dodgy all the encouragement he needed to go in for the kill.

"And one more thing. Just a little favour I'd like yer ter do fer me." Dodgy paused briefly, edged closer to Bingley, then added with a whisper "Go and screw yourself."

With that he pushed past Bingley and onto the safety of the putting green.

"I guess that answers a few questions," said Big G.

"Yeah, you can say that again. Today is turning out to be a day of revelations. First we find out about your gargantuan trouser trout and now we get confirmation of Dodgy's undying loyalty," I agreed.

"The only revelation I'm interested in is winning this bloody final," said Dodgy. "Come on. Let's go and box a few putts."

We followed Dodgy onto the green as Bingley hurried away in the opposite direction. We then practiced putting for quite a while in relative silence. This is good, I thought. Everyone is concentrating. Was this what sportsmen meant when they talked about being in the zone? I hoped so.

Presently I glanced at my watch. It was only a few minutes until we teed off. They'd be calling us to the tee any minute.

Right on cue the starter's voice boomed out through the tannoy, "Next up on the first tee: Gardner, Jacobs, Knight and Dunt."

We all stopped putting. The Ferkaryer Four looked at each other. This was showtime.

"Okay," said Big G, "that means us. Come on, Lofty. Let's go and make this happen."

We all touched knuckles in a very heterosexual kind of golfer's male bonding ritual. Then Lofty and Big G set off to do battle and I felt a surge of adrenalin. I wanted this so badly.

"You two just go out there and play the best golf of your lives – and get that bloody jigger working!" I called after them.

Dodgy and I resumed our putting practice briefly, but then I stopped and headed over to him. "Let's go and watch them tee off. You know, for moral support. What do you say?"

"Yeah, we could," replied Dodgy, "but we might put 'em off. Don't yer think?"

It was unusual for him to be so considerate.

"If you fart maybe, but otherwise I think we'll be okay. Why don't we just make sure they don't see us until after they've teed off then?"

"Good idea," he agreed.

"Right, I'll just knock this one in."

I dropped the ball down and took aim at a hole that must have been all of fifty feet away. Sixty, using Lofty's scale. I took the putter back and casually stroked the ball towards the hole. About five seconds later the ball clattered into the stick and dropped in.

"Bloody hell!" said Dodgy. "Nice one! That might just be an omen!"

I favoured the contrary glass-half-empty viewpoint. Maybe I'd been paying too much attention to Lofty and his 'power of positive' thinking stuff. "I hope I haven't just wasted one."

I retrieved my ball from the hole, tipped my cap to an imaginary crowd and then set off with Dodgy towards the first tee. As planned, we hung back out of sight. We got there just as Big G was lining up his drive.

"We'd better wait until they've both played, then we can go bonkers," said Dodgy semi-sensibly.

"Good call," I agreed. "If we cheer after Big G's shot then Lofty will crap himself from the pressure."

As we waited, I started to daydream again. How would I be feeling when we arrived on the final green? Would we have a chance to win? Even better, how would I celebrate if I holed the winning putt? My mind started to run away with itself. Dozens of images of famous golfers and their celebrations started flooding into my brain.

Would I just nonchalantly nod my head and tip my cap, rather like the impassive Retief Goosen had done after winning the US Open? I doubted it. I wouldn't be able to keep as calm as Retief.

Mind you, who could? The man has the pulse of a snake.

Would I go totally ballistic instead and do one of those frantic fist-pumps that Tiger Woods has popularised? Would I go for a more discreet version, like the one Seve Ballesteros did at St Andrews in 1984? You remember – the kind of rhythmical, jolly, bouncy, jerking movement that made it look for all the world like he was bashing himself off? Mind you, I wouldn't have blamed him if he had, under those circumstances.

I doubted that too. I might not be able to keep calm like Retief, but I'm not a very demonstrative person either. Besides which, simulating self-abuse in public wasn't really my thing.

Perhaps I'd just cry? Lots of golfers had done that. Woods sobbed uncontrollably in 2007 after winning at Hoylake. Darren Clarke was another – he cried in the 2006 Ryder Cup, despite a very warm and comforting hug from Tom Lehman. Even the normally emotionless Nick Faldo cried after he holed out to beat Curtis Strange at the 1995 Ryder Cup – or maybe he'd just got something in his eye? Probably the most famous weeper ever was Sam Torrance, who burst into tears at two separate Ryder Cups. In fact, at the 1985 event he spent most of the eighteenth hole in floods of tears. Not satisfied with that, he went on to say 'shit' on live television. That was quite cool.

But whilst I certainly am not averse to the odd profanity, blubbing my eyes out in the middle of a golf course isn't exactly my style.

Maybe I'd just lose it and collapse in a heap like Ben Crenshaw did after the 1994 Masters or really push the boat out and fall to the ground, beating my fists like a deranged lunatic in the mode of Costantino Rocca after his famous putt through the Valley of Sin at St Andrews in 1995. Although, to be fair, Crenshaw's mentor had just died and Rocca's putt was longer than most of my drives.

I could always do a simple dance. Something like Sandy Lyle's little wiggle after he'd clinched the 1988 Masters. Although, I have to admit, I wouldn't want to show my horrible sweaty armpits to the world the way that he did. How about copying José Maria Olazábal when he minced across the green like a total ponce after the 1987 Ryder Cup, much to the embarrassment of the whole of Europe? And, yes, I mean the continent, not just the golf team. I didn't fancy that.

Maybe I'd do something a little more subtle, not to mention masculine? That might be better. Just a simple jump in the air perchance, like Phil Mickleson did at Augusta in 2008? No, that would still be too poncy, especially the way he pointed his toes. How about a quick little hop, skip and jump like Nick Price did at the 1992 Open? Nope, it all felt a bit too effeminate for my liking. Dancing, skipping and jumping were out.

I could try performing one hundred high-fives just like Hale Irwin at the 1990 US Open or execute a perfect belly flop into the lake like Paul McGinley at the 2002 Ryder Cup. Perhaps I could orchestrate a massive invasion of the green as the US Ryder Cup team did at Brookline in the 1999 contest. But there would only be a few people around the green for me to high-five, there was no lake to jump into and, in all truth, I wanted to wait until the match was actually finished before we staged our celebrations. I thought of Ian Woosnam being lifted up by his erstwhile caddy, Wobbly, and shouting "Put me down, you daft bugger!". But I didn't have a caddy.

I wondered whether, instead, I could just stand there and shout at the top of my voice. I remember the normally quiet Philip Price screaming his head off (probably using some sort of colloquial Welsh expression like "*Sospan Fach!*") after holing a putt to beat Mickleson in the 2002 Ryder Cup and I could clearly recall lip-reading Faldo when he yelled "Jesus!" after holing out in the semi-darkness to beat Scott Hoch at the Masters 1989.

Thwack!

Geddin the Hole!

I came out of my daydream with a start as Big G bombed his drive down the middle of the fairway. There were some muted grunts of "shot" from the few onlookers. Dodgy somehow managed to stifle his war cry.

Lofty then strode onto the tee, looking unusually focussed. I noticed that he had recently developed a routine. That was a good thing. It showed that he was taking it a bit more seriously. I hoped that it would have a positive effect on his game.

On this occasion he was spot on. After lining up and placing his club carefully behind the ball, Lofty smacked a very presentable drive down the fairway. It was probably a hundred yards short of Big G's drive, but by Lofty's standards it was fine. And it was on the short grass.

"*Geddin the hole!*" screamed Dodgy at full volume. There weren't that many people watching, but they all looked at Dodgy in unison. He just grinned back. Lofty picked up his tee with an expression of pride mixed with embarrassment and set off down the fairway.

"Go on, boys," yelled Dodgy. "We're right behind yer!"

Big G just raised his hand in acknowledgement, but didn't look back.

I now started to feel nervous. Really nervous. It was our turn next. That was nerve-racking enough, but – to make matters worse – Dodgy's little one-man show had drawn attention to us somewhat. The thought of all those eyes staring at me shredded my nerves to bits.

We pulled our bags up to the tee and watched our partners hit their second shots from the fairway ahead. Lofty played first. The green was out of view around the corner so we couldn't see where the ball landed, but we noticed Big G and Lofty perform a quick high-five. That had to be a good sign. Big G then made a syrupy smooth swing as usual. I just knew he'd hit it close.

We watched the group disappear around the corner, then

moments later heard the starter's voice, "Next up on the first tee: Holmes, Rogers, Hammond and Bingley."

I felt a shiver run down my neck: I was first to play. The first hole at Erinvale is renowned as the most intimidating opening shot in the whole of South Africa. A dog leg to the right over a fynbos-edged dam, with two huge trees in the fairway, staring menacingly back at you. If you concentrated, you'd realise that the fairway was perhaps not *that* hard to hit, but with all the potential trouble – not to mention the pressure – it looked awfully small to me.

As I teed up the ball, I could feel everyone's eyes on me just as I'd anticipated.

"Come on Speedy, focus," I muttered as I tried to lose myself in my routine.

I checked the height of my ball against my driver …

I walked behind my ball and took two practice swings …

I picked a spot and lined it up …

I addressed the ball …

I waggled the club twice …

I stood there for a few seconds as if frozen …

Then I finally pulled the trigger and smacked the ball …

Crack!

It was a beauty. Fading past the trees, right down the middle of the fairway.

I breathed a huge sigh of relief. I'd got my first shot away safely

Dodgy now barged his way onto the tee box. The contrast couldn't have been greater. Maybe it was just bravado, but he looked as though he didn't have a care in the world.

He took a drag of his cigarette and casually tossed it on the ground …

He coughed up a nice big gobful of phlegm, then deposited this on the ground not far from his cigarette …

He hitched up his pants, teed up the ball and addressed it …

Then he belted it for all he was worth …

Luckily, this time he didn't fart.

Unsurprisingly, he hit a trademark low draw straight down the middle.

"Bloody great shot!" he called out, oblivious to everyone who was watching. "Come on, Speedy, let's go and bring home the bacon!"

There was relative quiet as Bingley and Hammond prepared to tee off. Neither Dodgy nor I acknowledged Bingley, although I had shaken hands with Hammond and wished him luck. I didn't mean it, but it seemed like the right thing to do. Both of them hit reasonable drives and our Subscribers' Challenge final was underway at last.

The next few hours were probably going to be the most important of my life.

25

Dodgy and I reached our balls and waited to play our approach shots. As Big G walked off the green in the distance, he looked back and gave me a very obvious thumbs-up. He and Lofty had clearly started well. This good start was improved even further when neither Bingley nor Hammond could find the green with their approaches.

Dodgy and I both received a stroke on the hole. Big G's little signal had convinced me that he and Lofty had made some decent points, so I felt that at least one of us should be aggressive and try to make birdie. I suggested this to Dodgy and, unsurprisingly, he was up for it.

"Okay, *il capitano*," said Dodgy. "Birdie comin' up."

With that, he hit a sweet four-iron onto the green, fifteen feet from the pin. He may be cocky, I thought, but he might just make good on his promise. Things got better still when I played a quite superb approach shot to six feet.

To my continued glee, Bingley and Hammond both made double bogeys. Although Dodgy missed his putt, I provided the *coup de grâce* as I rattled in my birdie. We'd made a handy start to say the least.

"Another seventeen of those and we're as good as home," barked Dodgy, making sure that Bingley was in earshot.

Whilst we didn't quite achieve that, things carried on in a similar vein for most of the front nine. I managed to perform a delicate juggling act between playing aggressively and playing safe. As I knocked in another lengthy putt on the ninth hole, I knew that we had posted a good score for the first loop.

"Not a bad front nine, eh?" I called, spotting Big G and running up to him like an excited puppy to its master. The only difference was that I didn't have my tongue out. Well, not very far out anyway.

"Not bad at all. What did you make there?"

"A three-pointer and a two-pointer. What does that give us?"

"Lofty and I both got two, so that's five on that hole. Let me see ..." Big G added up the points, then flashed me a trademark grin.

"Forty-nine!" he announced. "Not bad at all. Especially as the directors only got forty-four. The halfway scores are on that board over there. The next best score seems to be thirty-nine. It's looking like a two-horse race already."

Just then, there was a low buzzing sound. For once it didn't emanate from Dodgy's trousers. It was Big G's cellphone.

"Excuse me a moment, I'd better just see who this is," said Big G politely. He answered the phone and I went inside to find Dodgy and get a quick bite to eat. When I got there, Dodgy and Lofty were enthusing about our great start. When I revealed our points total, they were even more excited.

"Don't get carried away, guys," I interjected. "I know we've done well so far, but the fat lady's not even on stage yet. We've still got work to do."

"Fair enough," said Dodgy, "but yer promised ter give me a blow job if we win, didn't yer? Yer can be me witness, Lofty!"

"Yeucchh! The thought is enough to put anyone off their game. Even me with my newly found chipping skills."

"You mean *jigging* skills," I corrected. "What you do with that club can't be classed as chipping."

"Whatever it's called, I've had three up-and-downs already and I'm not finished yet!"

"You'd better jig your way out to the tenth tee. It looks like the fairway's clear."

I looked out towards the tee box and saw something that caught me by surprise. Big G was sitting on the wall, still talking on his phone. He was looking extremely distressed. Concerned, I waited nearby until Big G finally hung up.

"Hey, Big G, what's up? You don't look wildly happy."

"Yeah, erm, just a bit of unexpected, erm, bad news, I guess. Nothing I can't handle though." He was clearly battling to put on a brave face. "We've got a match to win, remember?"

With that he stood up and trudged towards the tenth tee. All was clearly not right.

That fact became all the more apparent as soon as we started the back nine. Big G's game was a far cry from what it had been on the front nine. Right from the first drive, he looked all over the place. In fact, he looked positively disconsolate as he trudged off the tenth green and I knew it wasn't going to be just one bad hole. More would be coming.

Big G had been our rock. With him playing badly, our score was bound to suffer severely. Something had to be done.

I delved into my mental box of tricks and scratched around. I tried to remember previous matches when I'd handled the pressure and shot the lights out, but the cupboard seemed bare. Then, in a last attempt to find inspiration, I thought of Gary Player.

In the 1978 US Masters, Player had decimated the back nine, coming home in just thirty shots to overtake the fifty-four-hole leader, Hubert Green. He made six birdies in nine holes and won by a single stroke when Green missed a three-footer on the final hole that would have earned him a playoff.

Whilst I wasn't expecting to make six birdies and shoot thirty – especially as I started with a bogey – I knew that I needed to go low. Big G was not himself and it might well affect Lofty who was playing alongside him. Even Dodgy had looked a bit shaky on the tenth hole after watching Big G butcher it. As we walked onto the eleventh tee, I cleared my mind and tried to focus on playing one shot at a time. I know it sounds clichéd, but I also knew that's what the best golfers do. Golfers like Gary Player.

I didn't quite emulate him, but considering I'm only a meagre nine handicap, I didn't do badly. I picked up one birdie against only one bogey, playing holes eleven to seventeen in level par. If I made a par at the last, I would be home in thirty-seven – just one over.

More important than my individual achievement was the fact that the Ferkaryer Four were still in the hunt. Dodgy had played fairly solidly, although not brilliantly, and if Lofty and Big G had managed to pick up a few three- and four-pointers, we'd be right in it. The bad news was that Bingley and Hammond had improved and played very steady golf. If their partners had done the same it would be too close to call.

Every hole at Erinvale was tricky, and the eighteenth was one of the most difficult of the lot. A long dog-leg right of over four hundred yards. The tee shot wasn't especially tough, especially with a slight tail wind, but a cluster of deep pot bunkers lurked dangerously on the right.

For most of the match there had been very little dialogue between ourselves and the directors which was not surprising given our history. Dodgy's confrontation with Bingley had shut the man up completely and it was a blessed relief not to have to deal with his snide comments at every turn. The final hole was no different. We all teed off in silence, all managing to avoid the bunkers.

I was, however, starting to get nervous again. We had to make sure that we finished well. One little mistake might end our dream. It was time for another motivational speech.

"Come on, Dodgy, we've played really well up to now. Let's just hit one more good shot each and we can bring it home."

"No problem, guv'nor, I've got this covered."

The green was huge – sixty yards long – and had a wicked slope with four deep bunkers surrounding it, plus a river beyond. Choosing the right club would be crucial. The hole location was hideous, cut on the front right, just in front of a bunker. It was what's known in the trade as a sucker pin, meaning that only a sucker would aim directly at it. The smart play was to aim between the hole and the left bunkers, and let the ball feed down to the cup. But too far left and you faced a nightmarish bunker shot onto the steeply sloping green.

Bingley was ready to play. He had about a hundred and sixty yards to go. I watched intently as he played a cautious shot, long and left of the hole. It took a dangerous hop forward, but stopped before the back bunker, about thirty feet away from the hole. It would be a tough putt across the slope, but it was a birdie chance nonetheless.

Hammond was next, from about one-fifty. He had the right idea, attempting to fade it in towards the hole, but hit it too far left. The ball missed the green and stayed up in the semi-rough. Another couple of yards to the right and it would have been perfect, but now he'd left himself a scarily fast chip for that elusive birdie. He'd surely be cautious instead and try to make sure of the par.

Now Dodgy was up. He had a similar distance. This was a bread and butter shot for him under normal circumstances. Unfortunately, these circumstances were anything but normal. For once he got nervous and tweaked the ball left. Straight into the bunker at the back left of the green.

"Bollocks!" he shouted and banged the club on the ground.

At last it was me. I had a perfect angle from a hundred and forty yards. I took aim on a spot between the left bunker and the hole.

I walked behind my ball and took two practice swings …

I picked a spot and lined it up …

I addressed the ball …

I waggled the club twice …

I stood there for a few seconds as if frozen …

Then I finally pulled the trigger and smacked the ball.

As I let it go, I sensed that I'd also pulled it a touch, trying to avoid leaking it right. I held my breath as I watched the ball descending.

"Be good, be good," I implored the small white dot.

It wasn't. The ball disappeared into the same bunker that Dodgy's ball had found. If I got a good lie, it would be tough. If not, it would be impossible.

I walked ahead anxiously, my heart pounding. I could have waited for Dodgy, perhaps discussed tactics, but my adrenaline was pumping and I was too restless to wait. I practically sprinted up to the bunker to get a look at my ball. I was sure it would have plugged.

Luckily I was wrong. My ball had landed on the front slope and had rolled into a reasonable lie. Dodgy's had gone further back and had plugged in a downslope. The proverbial fried-egg. It was a nearly impossible shot, and bunker play was possibly the one chink in Dodgy's armour. I guessed that he wouldn't be able to get it close.

This time I was right. Despite a valiant attempt he couldn't get it out. He hit his next one long, straight into the other bunker. Two ugly hacks later he picked it up and pocketed it. It was all up to me now.

I knew I had to take the thing by the scruff of the neck. As I put my bag down and entered the bunker, I looked up to see Big G and Lofty watching me from the sidelines. I tried to visualise a long, syrupy swing taking about an inch of sand, caressing the ball out like a professional with oh-so-soft hands. Gary Player could probably have splashed the ball out to within about a foot with a two-iron. I would be quite happy to hit mine that close with my sand wedge, thank you very much. Realistically, if I got it to within six feet I would have done well.

I looked back towards Big G and Lofty, who had now been joined by Dodgy, and gave them the thumbs up. It just felt like the thing to do. Maybe it was to try and give myself a much-needed confidence boost. One thing was for sure, I was crapping myself.

I sized up the shot. I had to get the ball up quickly and land it on the fringe, just short of the green. I needed to hit it very high and very soft. Easier said than done.

I took my stance and made a couple of practice swings …

I was ultra careful not to ground the club …

I took a moment to settle myself …

One last waggle and I played the shot …

The ball came out exactly right – high and soft, landing just on the fringe, right where I had planned. It rolled onto the putting surface and, for a moment, I thought it was going to stop. But then the little beauty dribbled forward and seemed to pick up speed. It rolled down the green, eventually coming to rest about five feet above the hole. Under the circumstances, it was nothing short of brilliant. Modest, too. Maybe not as good as Mr Player with a two-iron, but pretty darned good.

All that remained was making the putt – a scary five-foot downhiller.

Hammond played next. To my surprise, he played quite a bold chip. As the ball approached the hole it looked as if it might even go in, but at the last minute it veered right, kissed the edge of the hole and stayed above ground, eventually trickling a full eight feet past the hole. He missed the return putt and walked off with a bogey.

Bingley now stood over his thirty-footer. I knew that it was a slippery downhiller and Bingley knew it too. Surely he'd be cautious?

He wasn't. He gave the putt a real go. Luckily for me, he misread the break slightly. It missed right, coming to rest about six feet past the hole. Crucially though, it was on exactly the same line as my ball.

Excellent! Just what I needed. I could go to school – watch Bingley's putt and get an idea of the line.

Then he pulled the rug out from under me once again. He just picked up his ball.

Geddin the Hole!

"I don't think I need that one," he said smarmily. "I do believe we're already in for six points."

I was shattered. Bingley's team must have been cheating again and we hadn't spotted it, even with them right next to us. He must have got a text with the scores from one of his hangers-on – another mug being bullied by him, no doubt. What a wanker!

I avoided eye contact with him and tried to refocus. I wouldn't be going to school after all. Just as well. I never liked school.

I walked backwards to read the line of the putt while I waited for Bingley to get out of the way. I'd noticed that my ball had started to veer ever-so-slightly right as it crawled towards the hole on my last shot. I also knew it was downhill and therefore very quick. It needed to be hit softly and with a touch more break than one would expect.

I crouched down behind the ball and picked a line just outside the left edge of the hole. As I stood back up, I saw Bingley walking towards me. I stood rigidly next to the ball as Bingley sidled up and placed his hand on my shoulder.

"You do know that you have this putt to win, Mr Holmes?" he whispered. "I could make it worth your while if you were to accidentally miss it, you know."

I said nothing and stepped away from him, but my ears started to feel warm as a new thought overwhelmed me. Was it really to win or was he just messing even more with my head?

I fought to regain my composure. I wanted to imagine someone holing a crucial putt and the scene of the 1989 Masters came back into my head: Faldo draining that long putt under the darkening Augusta skies to beat Hoch. That had been a proud moment for me as an Englishman. I closed my eyes and focussed hard on the image.

Then something weird happened. My mental video went into a kind of spontaneous rewind. Faldo and Hoch reversed up the fairway and before I knew it they were on the tenth green. Hoch was standing over his three-foot putt. The very one that would have won him the Masters. He missed and he never contended in a major again.

Not the sort of image I wanted in my head.

Suddenly I doubted myself. Hundreds of images of nervous professionals missing crucial putts flooded into my brain. I remembered Bernhard Langer after he missed that six-footer at Kiawah Island in 1991, his face contorted in anguish as if he'd been taken roughly from behind by a leather-clad biker with a handlebar moustache. Or something. Nobody cares that he won a tournament the following week. He lost the Ryder Cup. Single-handedly.

I pictured Craig Stadler missing an absolute tiddler in the 1985 Ryder Cup, Doug Sanders bending down to remove a blade of grass and then missing the putt at the 1972 Open, Nick Price snapping his putter over his knee before hiding it under the crook of his arm at the 2000 President's Cup. He thinks that nobody noticed, but he's wrong. I did.

I had to erase these destructive pictures from my mind.

As I approached my ball, I closed my eyes tightly and gave myself a final pep talk.

"This is the moment you've been waiting for. Make it count."

I took my stance, then told myself to keep my head still and stare straight down, even after the ball had gone. As I drew back the putter, I said out loud, "This one's for you, Bingley."

I let the putt go.

I heard Dodgy scream, "Geddin the hole!!!!!"

I dared not look.

26

I was still looking down at that spot on the ground as Dodgy charged up to me shouting, "*Yer beauty! Yer bloody beauty!*" followed closely by Big G and Lofty who stampeded onto the green. Apparently I'd holed it. The scenes were reminiscent of the 1999 Ryder Cup. This time, though, the match was actually over. We'd won.

I'd been determined not to peep so I hadn't even seen it, but the ball had somehow found the back of the cup. I didn't care how. I'd done it. The Ferkaryer Four had done it.

Bingley looked ill.

"Well played, Paul," said Dodgy, shaking Hammond by the hand. As he approached the crestfallen Bingley, he leaned over and whispered in his ear. "Take that, yer corrupt sack of shit. I told yer I couldn't be bought."

As Bingley reluctantly shook my hand, he very obviously avoided eye contact. I couldn't resist one final jibe. "Revenge, Mr Bingley," I said, "is a dish best served cold."

For once, he didn't have a reply.

Technically, we weren't supposed to know the result yet, but everyone knew that we'd won. About twenty minutes later it became official. We handed in our card – after careful inspection – and checked all the other scores to make sure that we hadn't miscalculated. Then came the prize giving.

After sitting through fifteen minutes of boring speeches and minor prizes, the Ferkaryer Four finally went up to receive our prize. A trip to Augusta National, home of the US Masters, in just three weeks' time. We'd be following in the footsteps of the greatest names in golfing history. We'd be breathing the same air the gods of golf breathed. As far as we were concerned, we would practically be amateur golf's world champions.

What made it even better for us was that we'd taken it straight from Bingley's hands. Sweet revenge indeed. He'd never made any secret of how badly he wanted to win the Subscribers' Challenge. He'd told so many people that he was going to take it and now he was going to have to face them all with nothing but a runners' up award to show for it. Lofty and I were vindicated. We had achieved everything we had set out to achieve all those weeks ago.

Dodgy, of course, was revelling in the achievement too. He'd nearly ended up in intensive care for the sake of the team, for heaven's sake.

"What a match, chaps. Can yer believe that we stuck it ter Bingley like that? I always said he didn't like it up him. We even carried our bloody talisman fer the whole back nine," he said, pointing unsubtly at Big G.

"Yeah, sorry, guys," said Big G forlornly. "I guess I just lost the plot coming home there. Must have been the pressure." He managed a half-hearted smile.

I knew it had been that phone call. I would have to find a quiet moment to chat to Big G about it – time for me to support him instead of always needing his help. Right now, however, the best thing I could do for him was to join in with the banter and try to take the focus off him.

"Fortunately for us, you came good," I said to Dodgy. "Seems like you're quite a loyal kind of guy after all. I must admit I never doubted it," I added, with a heavy dose of irony.

"Yer too kind. Don't forget it was you that holed the winning putt!"

"You're right and I suppose if you'd known how to play a basic bunker shot, then we wouldn't have needed my heroics, would we?"

"Just a minute," interjected Lofty. "You're forgetting one thing: the mighty jigger. You two didn't see it, but that thing saved the day. I must have gotten up-and-down about, ooh, eighteen times."

"Why not make it nineteen?" said Dodgy. "Get yer bloody drink up-and-down. Skull it and let's get another round in. Might have to make it the last one though. I don't want ter get too sloshed. I've got me eye on that little barmaid over there. I wanna make sure I'm match fit when the big moment comes. Need ter make sure I keep me composure in front of goal, if yer know what I mean. You geezers might just be goin' home without me."

At that moment, the aforementioned barmaid walked past. She was roughly half Dodgy's age.

"Alright, love? Any chance of a quick cuddle?" he leered, trying his best to look attractive.

"Erm, not really. Sorry."

"I suppose a bonk's out of the question then?"

He didn't need to worry about finishing his beer. One second later he was wearing it. The rest of us finished our drinks in more traditional style and – once we had stopped laughing at Dodgy – we were ready to go.

"It was a simple misunderstandin', I tell yer," muttered Dodgy as we got into the SUV. "She was givin' me the eye, I promise. These bloody youngsters today. Bloody prick teasers the lot of 'em. Don't know a good thing when they see it. It's her loss anyway."

"I thought she had impeccable taste. I've never seen a girl finish a beer so quickly either," said Lofty, giggling.

"Yeah, go on, laugh. See if I care. There's plenty more fish in the sea."

The return journey to Cape Town was punctuated by two comfort stops and involved more good-humoured banter. We performed a thorough post mortem on our match, comparing yet more notes about our brilliant play, being sure to throw in much-exaggerated accounts of putts we'd holed or great shots we'd hit.

Big G, however, was subdued. He just drove, making one or two token comments. Fortunately Dodgy and Lofty were too taken up in the moment to realise.

About forty-five minutes later they dropped me off at home. I opened the garage, dumped my golf gear and, instead of trying the old 'oh-crap-we-lost' gag, I ran inside shouting "*Campioneh, Campio-neh, olé, olé, olé!*" at the top of my voice. Buster charged towards me, followed closely by Shelley who was almost as excited.

"I don't believe it!" she cried. "Tell me you're not kidding? Did you do it? Really?"

"You'd better believe it, buster!"

The pun was unintended, but upon hearing his name Buster went even more crackers than usual, if that was possible. He began leaping in the air and grunting like an epileptic warthog.

"I boxed a five-footer on the last hole to win it! And Bingley was standing right there beside the green watching. He looked sick when it went in. It was awesome!"

"Wow! I can't believe you did it! I'm so proud of you. You're actually going to Augusta!"

"Incredible, isn't it? I'll be there in twenty-one days! I can't wait!"

"Hey! I wonder if they have postcards for sale there."

"You don't seriously want me to send you a postcard of a golf course, do you?"

"Of course not," she replied, "but you have to send one to Bingley! You know – 'Weather is here; wish you were beautiful'. That kind of thing."

I could see that she was just as delighted as I was that we'd finally exacted revenge on the biggest bully either of us had ever had the misfortune to meet. Delight turned to excitement and excitement led to the bedroom where Shelley, well, *congratulated* me. Twice.

The victory had been consummated.

"I've just remembered – I have to call Big G," I said to Shelley first thing the next morning. "He got a phone call at halfway. Not sure what it was about, but it seemed to upset him. Must have been pretty hectic, 'cos he played terribly on the back nine."

"For goodness' sake! Not another mystery! I thought we'd had our last with Dodgy. You'd better give him a bell. I'm going to have some breakfast." I needed to be careful. Now that the competition was over Shelley had every right to lose patience with my involvement in the lives of my unpredictable golfing friends.

Big G didn't sound very cheery as he answered my call. "Speedy. Hi," he said quietly.

"Hey, big guy. Just phoning to run through the packing list for Augusta!" I told Big G with false joviality.

"Oh, yeah, that. I hadn't thought that far," said Big G in a detached kind of way. He left me no choice.

"Big G, you've done a lot recently to help all of us out. It's time for me to return the favour. That phone call … I don't want to pry, but it obviously affected you badly. Wanna tell me what it was about?"

There was a moment's silence at the end of the phone. Then Big G spoke. "Okay, I'll come clean," he said in a whisper, "but let me just go outside. I haven't told Bernadette yet. Heaven knows what she's gonna say."

I waited until I heard him close the door behind him. "Not more confessions, surely?"

"You have no idea. Where do I start?" He sighed deeply. "Do you remember that night after the first round of the Subscribers' when I went off for that meeting?"

"Yeah, vaguely. Is that what the phone call was about?"

"Well, yes. Kind of. But there's more. Much more."

"Shit. Do tell."

"Well this lady had contacted me a few days before about a property deal. I didn't know her from a bar of soap, but it seemed legitimate enough. I got there and things were going fine, but then it got a bit, erm, complicated."

"Complicated? In what way?"

"Speedy, she bloody seduced me. I'd had a few drinks and she was damned attractive. I just couldn't stop myself. Then yesterday there was the phone call. It was her. She basically said that she was going to tell Bernadette everything. It was a bloody set up all along."

"A set up?"

"It was Bingley. He damned well hired her to seduce me. Can you believe it? She said that I'd have to throw the game, otherwise she was going to tell Bernadette everything. I couldn't believe it. That's why I crumbled on the back nine. I wasn't trying to muck it up, but just couldn't get my head right."

"Jeepers. I'm not surprised. What are you gonna do?" I was gobsmacked and tried hard not to imagine what would happen to my life if it had happened to me.

"Search me. At some point I'll have to tell Bernadette about it. I'm just not sure how to. I've got so much spinning round in my head right now."

I tried to sound level-headed although, in truth, my head was spinning too. "Tell Bernadette now, before she finds out some other way, like from Bingley or his hired help. Say that it was just a big mistake, or that you were set up or something. Surely she'll understand?"

Not for the first time, my judgement was seriously lacking.

○

After the initial excitement of my victorious announcement at Rivlin & Lloyd, I kept a low profile the following day at work, concentrating mainly on boring but essential admin work. In truth, I wasn't unhappy about that. I only had half a mind on work at the best of times so I didn't fancy doing presentations or writing business proposals today of all days. Admin might be boring, but at least it isn't very taxing.

At about half past three, just as I was thinking about packing up and leaving early, my cellphone rang. I looked at the display eagerly, thinking it might be Big G phoning with a happy ending to yesterday's story, but it wasn't. It was Dodgy. I guessed that he was phoning to gloat about the match.

"Hey, Dodgy. How's the fourth best golfer on the planet today?" I said cheerfully.

"Shit, thank yer," said Dodgy candidly. "I'm sittin' here logged into my bankin' website. There's been no transfer from Big G. I have ter have the cash by five o'clock and nothin's come through yet. I can't get hold of him either. I've been tryin' all day!"

The money! The gangsters! Bollocks!

"Shit! I forgot!" I said, emphatically. "Have you tried his cellphone?"

"Of course! Silly me! Why didn't I think of that?" said Dodgy, sarcastically. "*'Course I've tried his bloody cellphone!* What did yer think I'd done? Sent a bloody carrier pigeon?"

"Sorry, dumb question. Erm, what about his home phone? Have you got that?"

"No, yer pillock. That's why I'm phonin' you. Can yer give me his number?"

"Erm, not sure. It might be in my phone." Embarrassingly I didn't know how to look for a number in my phone whilst I was talking on it. "Let me look for it and I'll call you back."

"Bloody well hurry up," growled Dodgy. "These bastards aren't exactly renowned fer their patience yer know!"

I hung up and quickly found Big G's home number, but then I had a thought. Maybe he'd had the chat with his wife and it hadn't gone so well. Maybe that's why he was ignoring Dodgy.

Maybe he'd forgotten the money too. Maybe he wanted to be left alone. Too many maybes. I decided to call him myself.

After a couple of rings, his wife answered.

"Hi, Bernadette. It's, erm, Speedy here. Big G's golf partner. He's not around is he?" I said tentatively.

"No, he isn't," she replied, rather tersely. She didn't sound happy at all. "He's out. I'm not sure when he'll be back."

"Oh. Okay, no problem," I said, trying to sound nonchalant. "I'll catch up with him later. It's not important."

Damn! Now I was worried. I tried Big G's cellphone. Straight to voicemail. Then I phoned Dodgy back.

"I don't have his number here, but I'm on my way home now. I'll pick it up there," I lied. I didn't want him to panic.

"Make it snappy, fer Gawd's sake. I'm about an hour away from havin' the livin' shit kicked out of me here!"

"No worries, Dodgy. I'm on it." I had an idea.

I scrolled through my address book once more.

"Come on Speedy! Move it!" I told myself as I scanned the names. Eventually I found it and pressed the green 'call' button.

"Steenberg Golf Club, good-day?" came a rather refined voice.

"Hi. Could you put me through to the bar please?"

"Going through, sir." An annoying pan pipes tune filled my ear, then another polite voice answered.

"Steenberg, good-day? You're through to the lounge."

"Erm, hello. I'm supposed to be meeting one of your members there today and I'm running a bit late. I wonder if you could tell me whether he's still there? His name is Big ..., erm, Greg Gardner."

"Yes, sir, he's here. Would you like to speak to him?"

"No thanks, don't disturb him. I'm on my way over there now."

I dashed out of the office and sped off to Steenberg as though my life depended on it.

Dodgy's possibly did.

27

I pulled into Steenberg in a very different frame of mind to usual. Normally I'd coast in through the gate, admire the fairways and feel all tingly about going to have a lovely round of golf or at least a good practice session. This time my heart was racing and the tingly feeling was one of anxiety not anticipation.

I slowed down for the gate, signed in and pulled away as slowly as I could manage. Once I was around the first corner, however, I sped – yes, *sped* – into the car park and raced into the clubhouse towards the bar.

Big G was perched on a stool with a large whiskey glass and a bowl of brown, gooey stuff in front of him. As I approached I realised that this was probably not his first drink of the day. His eyes were glazed and he was staring blankly into his bowl, shovelling the glutinous sludge into his mouth. I felt a mixture of despair and relief. It wasn't exactly the sight that I had hoped for, but at least I'd found him.

He looked round in slow motion. "Hey, Schpeedy!" he slurred. "Howzit, man! Juscht came here to, erm, ya know, have something to eat and contemplate my navel. I'm just finishing my dessert now." He was clearly plastered.

"Shit," I said quietly. "What the hell is that stuff you're eating?" I didn't have to ask what he was drinking – I could smell it on his breath.

"Schticky toffee pussy. It'sh delischus man."

"*Sticky toffee pussy?* Good grief! You're more pissed than I thought!"

"You got that right. But you were all wrong before, man. I told Bernie, juscht like you schuggeschted. She wasch freakin' furiousch. She's gonna move out. It'sch a bloody schtuff up."

"And that's not all. You forgot about Dodgy. He's waiting for the money."

Big G suddenly seemed to sober up. Well, almost.

"Ssshhhit! I forgot!"

"Yeah, I know you did. That's why I'm here. There isn't much time. We've got to try and save him."

It sounds like a scene from a movie, I know, but at that moment it felt like one too. At the speed my little Honda Jazz could travel, it was only about fifteen minutes to Dodgy's house, but I was still worried that we'd be too late. My plan was to get there before the thugs, or at least intercept before they beat him up. Then we'd somehow get Big G to sober up, he could transfer the money and everyone would be happy.

"Come on Speedy! You've got to drive like you've never driven before!" I urged myself as I swerved along the streets. I pretended I was a film star like Bruce Willis or Vin Diesel desperately trying to reach the scene in time to save the day. I just hoped that this movie would have a happy ending.

When we reached Dodgy's house the signs weren't good. For a start, the gate to his driveway was half open. I skidded to a halt and tried to wake Big G who had passed out on my back seat. But he was spark out. Realising that it was futile, I left him there and went in alone.

Another bad sign greeted me. A padlock was lying in pieces on the ground next to the open gate. As I sprinted up the path the signs got even worse. The front door was open and the wooden frame was splintered. And as I gingerly stepped inside, the signs all screamed '*Too late, sucker!*'

Dodgy was lying face down and motionless on the floor.

I'd never seen a dead body before. At least not a real live one, if you know what I mean. I wasn't sure what to do. I approached cautiously. I'd done a first-aid course years before, but couldn't remember the first thing about it. Besides, I don't think they covered 'what to do if your mate has had the crap beaten out of him by gangsters'.

"Oh no," I whispered. "Why this? Why now?"

I knelt down next to him. There was blood coming from his nose and mouth. I couldn't tell if he was breathing. His arms were both trapped underneath him and I couldn't get at them to feel for a pulse. I decided to try and roll him over, which was easier said than done. He might have been short, but he was no lightweight.

In retrospect, this was probably the worst thing to do. What if he'd had a broken neck? But I didn't think of that. I just wedged my hands under his stomach and heaved as hard as I could. As I did so, I realised he was alive. Either that or I had just witnessed the loudest, smelliest fart ever produced by a dead person.

But dead blokes don't fart, do they? I'd never been so pleased to hear someone crack one off in my life.

Seconds later, he began to groan. I retreated until the stench subsided and then spent the next few minutes trying gently to revive him until eventually he came round to full consciousness. In fact, he was soon a lot more awake than Big G.

"Bleedin' hell," he groaned, rather eloquently. "Me bloody head's killin' me. And me arm. The bastards!"

"What on earth happened here?"

"What's it look like? They beat the bloody shite outta me, that's what happened!"

"I can see that, but what …? Never mind." I'd run out of words. "I'm just so sorry we didn't get here in time."

"It's hardly your fault, is it?" grunted Dodgy as he tried to sit up. "What the hell happened ter our resident knight in shinin' armour? Where the bloody hell is he anyway? Oww, me arm's buggered."

"Erm, well, it's a long story …"

I proceeded to explain to Dodgy what had happened to Big G: the business deal, the woman, the seduction, the phone call, the back nine meltdown, the not-very-impressed wife and, of course, the half-litre of Jack Daniels.

"Why the hell did he tell his missus?" asked Dodgy. "Is he bloody daft?"

"Let's just say that it was based on some sage advice that *someone* gave him," I replied guiltily. "Anyway, that's not important right now. We need to get you to hospital."

I managed to get him to the car with difficulty and got him safely to casualty. Big G didn't stir and certainly didn't look like he was planning to go anywhere, so I left him in the car again whilst I took Dodgy inside and handed him over to the nurses. Despite his obvious pain, he tried to flirt with several of them.

"Oooh, put yer hand here, love. This is where it hurts most," he said, gesturing towards his nether regions.

"Leave these ladies alone," I told him. "They can make your life a lot more painful in here if they choose to. I'm going to go and deal with our sleeping friend, but give me a call when you've seen the doctor."

I couldn't very well take Big G to his own home under the circumstances so the only option was my place. Shelley wasn't exactly thrilled. I explained the whole story to her as concisely and apologetically as I could and, although she was still singularly unimpressed, I managed to convince her that the recriminations could wait.

We still had an issue to deal with: an issue by the name of Big G. How were we going to get him out of the car?

He wasn't *that* big, if you didn't count his trouser-trout, but at around six feet and a hundred and seventy-five pounds, he was still way too big to be dragged out of the car. It had been hard enough getting him to stagger in there in the first place.

There was nothing for it. Desperate times called for desperate measures.

We had to send in Buster.

Being a common or garden Staffie, Buster didn't really have a significant range of feelings at his disposal. I reckon he had about three emotional states: 'I'm happy', signified by wagging his tail nineteen to the dozen and licking everything in sight, 'I'm confused', demonstrated by cocking his head to one side, and 'What the bloody hell was that noise?' followed immediately by barking his bollocks off.

As a result Buster didn't know or care whether Big G was unconscious, asleep or dead. The overpowering smell of second-hand Jack Daniels did nothing to deter him either. One quick leap into the car and the next thing he was slobbering across Big G's face for all he was worth. Approximately half a second later, Big G awoke from his slumber and tried in vain to defend himself against the unyielding assault. He had no chance.

"Arrrgghhh! Get him off. Stop! Help!"

With a tinge of reluctance, I called Buster off – or, to be more precise, I dragged him off – and then helped Big G out of the car. The intense licking session seemed to have sobered him up remarkably. I took him inside and Shelley poured him a stiff brandy.

"Have this and a couple of aspirins," she said to Big G. "*It will get him off to sleep,*" she whispered to me.

"Then I think you should go and hit the hay. You had better stay here tonight. Hadn't he, Speedy?"

I nodded. The question was entirely rhetorical. I knew she wasn't happy about all this, but like me she realised that we didn't have much choice.

So we had a drink and reflected on Dodgy's beating. In a way it was a welcome distraction – it took Big G's mind off his own problems. Now he suddenly seemed to be more bothered about having let Dodgy down.

"I can't believe it. What have I done? It's all my fault," he said as he gazed into his drink with glassy eyes.

"No, Big G, it's not really," I argued. "Dodgy had it coming. You were gonna save him this time, but it's a lesson that's been waiting to happen for a while now. I guess he had to learn the hard way."

"I guess so, but I still feel lousy."

Fortunately the cocktail of aspirin and brandy had the desired effect and we were spared an evening of Big G's wallowing in despair. Shelley ushered him off to the spare room before he passed out again. A few minutes later she came back into the kitchen.

"I bet he's spark out already. That should be him for the night. I don't think we'll hear a peep until the morning."

"Shouldn't we put a glass of water in there for him?" I asked. "Otherwise he'll wake up with a mouth like the bottom of a budgie's cage."

"Yeah, you're right. Let's just wait a while to make sure he's asleep."

We had another quick drink, then Shelley poured a glass of water and went back into the room. When she came back she looked stunned. She was as white as a sheet.

"What's the matter?" I said worriedly.

"He hadn't pulled the covers over himself. I think I just found out why he's called Big G," she said meekly, sinking back into her chair.

In that one instant, my love life got really complicated. I figured that I would have a tough time satisfying Shelley ever again after what she'd just seen.

"Blimey," I said. "That's all I need. You'd better put your eyeballs back in their sockets. Let's try and forget that this happened please."

I didn't bother explaining any of that to Big G the next morning. It didn't seem right. I'd explain another time. Maybe. Right now he had to get home and sort out his domestic problems. Shelley fed him a big cooked breakfast, whilst I resisted the temptation to ask him how his pork sausage was, and then I drove him back to Steenberg on the way to work.

"Thanks for looking after me last night, buddy," he said as he got into his car. "Let me go home and patch things up. I'm sure it'll be fine. We'll put all of this behind us and be on a plane to Augusta before you know it."

He grinned, then slammed the car door. As he drove off he stuck his head out of the window and called, "We can't *not* go, can we?"

That's what he thought.

○

When I arrived home from work that evening Shelley was busy feeding the kids.

"So did you drop your friend and his pet python off successfully?" she asked with a grin.

"Don't even go there," I said. "He's obviously a freak of nature. Besides, people with small ones try harder. You should know that."

"Who's got a pet python?" said Danny. "Can I have one? Please?"

"You'll get one soon enough," I told him. "When you're older. It just might not be as big as Big G's. Isn't that right, darling?" I said with a mischievous look on my face.

But Shelley was staring out of the window vacantly, stroking our ten-inch tall pepper mill delicately with her finger ends. Damn that Big G and his gargantuan manhood!

"Hello? Earth to Shelley! Are you reading me?"

She looked round slowly. "It was *huge!*" she finally whispered, without so much as a blink.

Great. One of my golf buddies was in hospital, the other was on the verge of divorce and now my wife comes face to face with a penis that's probably twice as big as what she's used to. Maybe more.

Today couldn't get any worse.

To take my mind off things I decided to get hold of Dodgy and see how he was doing. I soon wished I hadn't. His arm was indeed broken and so was his collar bone. He wouldn't be able to play golf for months.

The Subscribers' Challenge prize was not transferable.

All four team members had to be able to play.

One out, all out.

The only thing I could think of was that we should ask Dodgy to travel with us, somehow hiding his injury, and then just get him to walk the course when we got to Augusta. That would be better than forfeiting the prize, but would we get away with it?

In the end, we didn't have to try.

When Big G had arrived home Bernadette was gone. She'd left him a note saying she was at her mum's and he could come and collect the kids. Now it looked like he was out too. How could he make the trip with two kids to look after?

With false optimism, I told him not to worry and that Lofty and I would 'make a plan'. This is another annoying South African expression, which basically means 'I haven't got a bloody clue what we'll do', but for some reason it seemed appropriate.

"I'm glad you phoned," said Lofty quietly when I called him. "I was just going to phone you. I've got something to tell you."

"Ha! *You've* got something to tell *me*?" I said dismissively. "Just wait 'til you hear what *I've* got to tell *you*! What a crap twenty-four hours I've had! You're not gonna believe what a disaster it's been. I don't know where to start. Maybe you'd better tell me your stuff first 'cos once I get going it's gonna take forever! Come on, let me have it. It had better be good, mind you."

His voice was barely a whisper as he replied. "Abigail's got breast cancer."

In a way I suppose she'd been lucky, if you could call it that. Abigail had been playing with one of their kids who had accidentally bumped her just under the armpit. It felt tender. She hadn't thought much of it, but decided to go and see the doctor anyway. He had a look, took some blood and also a biopsy – just in case. On Monday evening – just as I was arriving at home with a drunken Big G – she'd got the bad news.

The silver lining was that they'd caught it early. If she started the treatment now then she'd have a very good chance of getting better. It would mean going for chemotherapy, which would make her very ill, straight away. They couldn't afford to waste any time: it was a very aggressive strain. If it went untreated it would spread like wildfire and she'd have six months to live, maybe twelve at the most.

My problems thus paled into insignificance, but the fact was that Dodgy, Big G and now Lofty were all definitely out of the trip. I had to accept it: the trip was off and we'd have to forfeit the prize. With a heavy heart, I called the competition organisers with the bad news and asked one more question: "What happens to the prize now?"

"It will go to the runners up. In the event of a tie there will be a count-back ..."

I stopped listening. I knew there wasn't going to be a count-back. And I knew very well who'd come second. It hurt like hell, but there was nothing I could do about it.

The following morning, I spotted the local newspaper on the counter. Surely there would be some good news out there in the world to cheer me up? I read the headline: 'Local businessman wins golfing trip of a lifetime'.

That sucked.

I scanned the report and stopped when I got to the part where the reporter had asked Bingley to say a few words.

"My partners did their best to try and lose it for us," laughed Derek Bingley, captain of the victorious team, "but in all honesty it was rather too easy in the end. I think my calmness under pressure made a big difference and we actually won at a canter. I was quite disappointed that no-one pushed us closer. The only team that got anywhere near us was disqualified. Disgraceful really."

I felt sick to my stomach.

28

The next few months spelled change. Not only for the Lofties, but also for me.

The first thing I put my mind to after we'd formally bequeathed our prize to Bingley was getting the hell out of African Tobacco. It had been quite a lucrative contract for our consulting firm – they made good margins from my work there – but it didn't really make any difference to me. I got paid the same salary no matter which client I worked at. I couldn't bear to share a building with Bingley anymore, even if it was only once or twice a month.

I would have been prepared to resign if necessary, but luckily it didn't come to that. I managed to get another assignment at an equally bureaucratic corporate. If anything it had even more red tape than African Tobacco, but at least Bingley didn't work there.

The slimy, smarmy, pompous, overbearing, haughty, grandiloquent *prick*. The *wanker* who'd taken *our* prize and gone to Augusta. The *bastard*!

Do I sound bitter? Maybe just a little.

Going back to the Lofties, Abigail had always been the main bread-winner in their family and given that she was self employed, her loss of income hurt them. Even their private health care didn't cover all the bills and it certainly didn't cover her lost earnings. Lofty managed to keep his coffee shop ticking over, however, and in fact it did quite well. He supported them single-handedly and seemed to be made of much sterner stuff than ever before. He was a rock.

After about six months Abigail was over the worst and her treatment was reduced. She had regular tests and, nine months after they'd first found the tumour, they were in a position to make a prognosis.

She had been lucky after all. She got the all clear. She'd beaten the cancer.

Over this same period, golf had become a spectator sport for the Ferkaryer Four. Understandably, Lofty had neither the time, the money nor the inclination to play golf with Abigail's illness looming large. As for Dodgy and Big G, I basically lost touch with them. I texted them both a few times to see how they were doing with their respective challenges and Dodgy seemed to be getting back to full strength, but he stopped coming to Lofty's shop and we stopped seeing him.

Big G stayed equally quiet. He replied to a couple of my texts and the good news was that Bernadette moved back in on a trial basis. I didn't find out much more and eventually I stopped trying to keep in touch.

So that meant there was one member of the Ferkaryer Four left standing: yours truly.

Sadly, without the rest of them, I practically quit playing too. I had the odd game at the club, but I couldn't seem to get motivated to play. After the excitement of the Subscribers' Challenge and the Ferkaryer Four, ordinary golf seemed so mundane. It was like I'd been on a drug and had suddenly gone cold turkey.

In time I accepted it for what it was. I realised that the Ferkaryer Four had been a wonderful experience, one I could be very proud of. We had, after all, achieved what we'd set out to do – we'd beaten Bingley. We'd won, he'd lost. So what if he went to Augusta and we didn't? We'd taken the moral high ground. I was happy to end things on that note.

And if you believe that …

29

Ten months later...

"Greg darling, can I make you a cup of tea before we unpack?"

"That would be great, sweetheart," said Big G. "I'll be inside in a minute. I've just got to get these last few things out of the car."

It had been a great holiday – without the kids, who had been packed off to Bernadette's mum's for the week – and it had given them time and space to get to know each other again. To start over, if you like. It had almost been a second honeymoon.

Big G reached inside the boot and gathered up the last few odds and ends. Something dropped on the ground. He reached down to pick it up. Then he stopped. He looked at the embroidery on the front: 'Ferkaryer Four'. He turned it over and read his nickname out loud. He managed a smile.

Over the next few days he couldn't get it out of his head. Eventually it was too much. He reached for his cellphone, hoping he still had the number in there. He scrolled down. Yes! There it was. He pressed the call button and, seconds later, a gruff voice answered.

"Yeah?"

"Good-day, Mr Rogers. I've got a proposition for you. A very *dodgy* proposition at that."

"Huh? Who is this?"

"You probably don't actually know my real name, but let's just say that I don't get my nickname for nothing. Don't you remember what you saw in the changing room that great day in the winelands?"

"What? Big G? Is that you?"

"Got it in one!" said Big G. "Now listen Dodgy, let's talk about this proposition …"

30

On that particular morning I was woken up in a rather different fashion to usual. Yes, there was a big slobbery tongue involved, but this time it wasn't Buster's. It was a tradition we had on birthdays, as was taking the day off work. It started as a bit of a joke when she asked me what gifts I wanted one year.

"I don't know." I told her. "The usual kind of stuff – some new socks, some new handkerchiefs, a blow job …" and I was pleased that she took me seriously for once. It had become an annual ritual. My only complaint was that it didn't seem to happen at any other time during the year, but that's another story.

Once the ceremony was out of the way, I clambered weak-kneed out of the bed and went to get dressed. "I've got no presents to open, but I prefer it this way," I said.

"Hah! That's where you're wrong," said Shelley as she brushed her teeth. I think it might have been the second time she'd brushed them, actually. "Firstly, the kids have bought you a present each. Some socks and some handkerchiefs, of course. And secondly, I have a surprise for you."

"Wow. Another one! What is it?"

"Well," she said sarcastically, "that's why they call it a surprise: you're not supposed to know what it is. You're coming with me to drop the kids at school and then we need to get you blindfolded."

"But I'm not into that kind of –"

"Oh, stop it. That's way too predictable. Come on, get dressed. We need to get going pronto or we'll be late."

True enough, once we'd dropped the kids at school, she took out her scarf and tied it around my eyes. "And no peeping," she said as we drove off.

I sat there obediently, attempting to follow the turns in my mind's eye in order to work out where we might be going. After the third turn I felt sick so I stopped trying, sat back and relaxed.

About ten minutes later she slowed down, meandered along for a few more yards and then pulled to a halt. I heard the click of the handbrake.

"We're here."

"So we're here, but where is 'here' anyway? Can I open my eyes yet?"

"No! Not until I make sure the others have arrived. And I've got to get the stuff out of the back."

"What others? What stuff?"

"Never mind. You'll see. Just wait here. And no peeping."

I just sat there, listening to lots of clunking and clanking as she got the 'stuff' out of the boot. Did you know that time goes much slower when you're blindfolded? Eventually my door opened and I climbed out gingerly.

"Okay, birthday boy. Here's your surprise. You can take off the blindfold."

I removed the scarf and opened my eyes. I had to do a double-take.

Standing in front of me in Westlake's car park were Big G, Dodgy and Lofty, complete with Ferkaryer Four caps, all grinning from ear to ear.

"What the … What the …? What the *Fer-kar-yer* all doing here!"

"It's a long story," replied Big G.

"I'm all ears."

"We tee off in fifteen minutes. How about we tell you all about it whilst we get ourselves ready?" suggested Lofty.

"Well, my work here is done," said Shelley in a mock serious voice. "I'll see you later," she added, then plonked my Ferkaryer Four hat onto my head and gave me a big kiss.

We wandered off down to the first tee, me still in shock, and I found out what this was in fact all about.

A couple of months earlier, Big G had finally got back together with his wife for good. It had taken Bernadette a long time to come to terms with Big G's indiscretion, but in the end she forgave him. Once she finally accepted that it wasn't going to impact on their daily lives, they had decided to have a romantic holiday together to celebrate. Finding his old Ferkaryer Four golf cap in the boot when they got home had got Big G thinking and he and Dodgy had put together a plan.

Big G had suspected that Bingley would be entering the Subscribers' Challenge again and confirmed as much with a few phone calls. By all accounts Bingley was as keen as ever to win and as usual had been boasting about how easy it would be. It seemed that, despite his claims in the paper at the time, the corporate golfing fraternity had seen straight through him and had made it quite clear that a win as a result of a forfeit didn't count. He wanted to win it properly this time. That was the first piece of the jigsaw.

The second and final piece – okay, so it was an easy jigsaw – was to get the Ferkaryer Four back together and have one more bash at this thing they called revenge. They called Lofty and he was up for it, naturally. Lofty then checked it out with Shelley who suggested that they keep it as a surprise for my birthday. The timing was perfect – the Subscribers' Challenge was just over a month away. Today was our first practice match.

"There's just one more thing, Speedy," said Dodgy.

"There's more? What now?"

"It's me and yer against these bloody Saffers! And this time it's bloody war!" He dropped his guts noisily and strode off onto the tee box.

"Good grief. What have I let myself in for?"

We played our match – which ended in a comprehensive win for the UK team – and then made a plan for the next few weeks leading up to the competition. Our lack of game time showed, if you don't count Dodgy, that is. He'd had a broken arm, collar bone and goodness knows what else, and hadn't picked up a club at all in the last year, but – lo and behold – there were those trademark, metronomic, right-down-the-middle shots of his, just like before.

Given a few weeks' solid practice the rest of us would also be good as new and we decided to practice together a few nights a week, just like we had done the previous year. We had one last chance to open that can of Whup-Ass.

O

The days passed and we slowly got our respective swings in order. Lofty still had his jigger, but we knew not to tease him about it. Last time we did that he had taken money off us. I managed to groove my swing until it felt really good. As good as ever. As a bonus my handicap had gone out to eleven. If I could re-capture my true form then I'd pick up plenty of points.

Eventually the countdown was over and competition day arrived. We'd all managed to get our games in order and I was feeling really good about our chances. I was slightly nervous as I got to the course. It was to be held at Steenberg again, which at least made it familiar. But I was anxious about seeing Bingley. I hadn't seen him for nearly a year and I wasn't looking forward to it, mainly because I would probably try and strangle him. Fortunately, we weren't paired with his director's team this time. In fact, they were playing much earlier than us and were already on the course by the time we got there so we didn't even see him.

Our preparation was therefore very focussed: hitting a few shots on the range, and then over to the green for some chipping and putting. And of course some jigging. Lofty's 'niblick' still caused quite a lot of mirth. But by now he'd REALLY mastered it, so whilst we couldn't resist taking the piss out of him, we all knew that it could prove to be our secret weapon. Or should I say 'one of our secret weapons'? We all seemed to have brought our 'A' games. As long as we maintained our form in the match itself, we would have a great chance.

We needn't have worried.

We won.

Easily.

So easily it was slightly embarrassing. The year before we had qualified for the final with ninety-five points; this year we won with ninety-eight. The second placed team, who also qualified for the following weekend's final, only had ninety-three.

But guess who it was.

I was disappointed that Bingley had got through to the final. I would have liked to have seen him packing his bags after the qualifying game. It seemed a bit of a shame that he would be allowed to enjoy the privilege of playing in the final of such a prestigious event again.

What I didn't appreciate at the time, however, was that had Bingley not qualified, it would have taken the gloss off the *other* little prank which Dodgy had planned: the *coup de grâce*, the icing on the cake, the cherry on top, the payoff, the final nail in the coffin, the masterstroke.

You get the idea.

31

The final of the Subscribers' Challenge was only a week later, but it seemed to take forever to come round. As you'll have gathered by now, every week drags on when you're a management consultant, but this one was ridiculous. Eventually the day arrived and we all jumped into Big G's SUV once more.

Fortunately for us, last year's final at Erinvale had gone off so well that they had decided to use the same venue again. That meant a one-hour drive to the Cape winelands versus a plane flight to Johannesburg or Durban or some other far-flung city. It also meant that we could get back home to our families that same night. That made a big difference to all of us except Dodgy, who had some delusional notion that he was going to charm an unsuspecting beautiful waitress and spend the entire night rewriting the Kama Sutra.

We got there in plenty of time for some last minute practice and strategising. I also wanted to look at the draw to see if we'd got Bingley again. We'd decided to keep the same pairings – me with Dodgy and Lofty with Big G – and, like last year, I was sure we'd get paired with Bingley. I just felt it in my waters.

As the others went over to practice, I went into the tent to look at the draw. I traced the list with my finger and found our names. I was wrong. My waters had been lying to me.

We were paired with 'Pienaar and Johnson', whoever they were. Big G and Lofty were paired with 'Hinton and Dorrington'. Sounded like another consultancy firm. One thing was for sure, I'd never heard of them. It certainly wasn't the African Tobacco directors.

Still curious, I scanned the list again to see what time Bingley was playing. I didn't find him. I checked the list again and couldn't find any of the African Tobacco names. What I did find instead was the names of the team who had come third in the previous week's qualifier It didn't make sense. Where were they?

I hurried back to the practice area to tell the guys. "You're not gonna believe this! The African Tobacco Directors team seems to have withdrawn!"

Lofty's jaw dropped open in surprise. "*What???*"

Big G and Dodgy, however, just looked at each other and smiled.

"Everything will be revealed in good time," Big G promised. "For now, concentrate on the golf and let's win this damn competition – again!"

Now I knew what my kids felt like when I withheld secrets from them. It was enormously frustrating. I promised never to do it again. Nevertheless, I did as I was told like a good boy and played the best bloody golf of my life.

If it had been a boxing match the referee would have stopped it.

When Dodgy rolled in the final putt – for his *fourth* birdie – we knew we'd done it. Fifty points out and fifty points back – in a stiff south-east wind – making a round one hundred. That would have been a great score at any time, but in that gale it was unbeatable.

This time there was no nail-biting finish. We romped home, winning by six points. It wasn't quite as dramatic as the previous year, but it was just as satisfying.

The only difference was that *this* year we would in fact be going to Augusta. There were no gangsters, no seductive women and no dread diseases on the horizon.

We were actually going.

32

"Spill the beans. This has been killing me the whole way round. Quite honestly, I'm not sure how I managed to keep it together to play such *brilliant* golf!" We'd finally made it to the bar and collected our prize. Now I wanted to know why the bloody hell Bingley hadn't pitched. "Let's hear it. I'm through waiting."

"Yeah, me too," said Lofty. "You guys have got some explaining to do."

"Do you want to or shall I?" Big G asked Dodgy.

"Age before beauty."

"Yes, but it was your idea. I don't want to take the credit away from –"

"*Will you just bloody get on with it???* Tell us the story!!"

"Okay, okay! Are you sitting comfortably?"

"No! And neither will you be if you don't bloody hurry up!"

"Right. You know that story about me splitting up with Bingley's daughter?" Big G asked enticingly. Lofty and I nodded impatiently. "Well, I wasn't entirely honest with you. There was a bit more to it."

"Yer can say *that* again!" interrupted Dodgy, but he got the hint when Lofty and I glared at him and quickly clammed up.

"One day – it wasn't long before I went off to university – I went round to pick her up. We were going out to the movies or somewhere. We'd got ten minutes down the road when I realised that I'd left my wallet in her house so I drove back there to get it. As I slipped back inside I couldn't help noticing some paperwork on the table where I'd left my wallet. The header caught my eye – United Tobacco – and I was so curious that I had a quick peek. As I scanned the documents, it became pretty clear that African Tobacco were about to launch a takeover bid for United. There were some draft offer documents, stuff like that. The information wasn't public at that stage. It only came out a couple of weeks later. But then as I dug a bit deeper, I saw something that really caught my attention – a bunch of broker's notes and share certificates. Bingley had been trading United's shares like crazy. It was pretty clear that something fishy was going on."

"You mean like insider trading?" I said.

"That's exactly what I mean. The only problem was that I got caught with my hand in the till: Bingley walked right in on me. He went ballistic. Told me never to darken his door again and that I wasn't allowed to carry on dating his daughter. I took her out that evening and tried to figure out what to do. I obviously couldn't tell her what I'd seen, but I didn't want to just walk away either.

"Shortly after I'd dropped her back home, he called me and re-iterated his words. He threatened me with all sorts. Said he would ruin me if I didn't get the hell out of his life. I was only a kid and I was so shocked by what I'd seen – I let him bully me. I called her a couple of days later and broke up with her. She never understood it. But that whole saga is why Bingley still gives me the creeps even today."

"Wow," I whispered. "That's hectic."

"Hectic it may be," said Lofty, "but what has it got to do with today?"

It was a fair point. I was glad someone else was able to keep up.

"The illegal trading stuff!" Dodgy took over the story enthusiastically. "As yer know, a leopard never changes his spots and neither does a bloody shyster! When Big G called me, he asked if I could do a bit of investigatin'. Yer know, see if I could find anythin' incriminatin'.

"At first I was just goin' ter hack into his email account and send a few fake emails out ter his colleagues. That wudda been simple. But I figured that he might be able ter explain that away too easy like, so I scratched around a bit more. Tried ter get me mitts on some of his, erm, *personal* documents. When I broke into his house, oh boy, did I hit the jackpot!"

"Broke into his house? Are you serious?"

"Oh yeah. It's easy when yer know how. They don't call me Dodgy fer nothin'."

"You can say that again. What did you find?" I asked excitedly.

"Plenty. Luckily he'd been pretty diligent with his record keeping and everythin' was still there, filed away perfectly. There was a lot of other stuff too. The United Tobacco thing was just the tip of the iceberg. He's done more dodgy deals than I have! Anyway, a couple of days ago I got into his office at African Tobacco."

"You did *what*? How?"

Dodgy just tapped the side of his nose with his finger. "Like I said – it's easy when yer know how. I posed as a computer technician. Got all the passes and everythin'. It was a cinch. I got inside his office and logged onto his computer. It's amazing how unimaginative people are with their passwords, ain't it? I sent out a few emails on his behalf – and not the usual boring business documents either. A couple of Bingley's personal files that I'd scanned in, if yer know what I mean. Poor bastard didn't stand a chance. They frogmarched him outta there yesterday mornin'. His bloody feet didn't even touch the floor."

Lofty and I just looked at each other with disbelieving smiles on our faces.

"So what's happened to him now?"

"Dunno. Don't bloody care either. His career's screwed. So is his life, most probably. I just wonder how he likes the taste of his own medicine. Maybe he's started a coffee shop somewhere!" Dodgy lit himself a cigarette and laughed heartily.

"Well, blow me!" I said, unable to think of anything more to say.

"Very temptin', but no thanks. I've got me eye on this little belter over here. Hello, darlin'," he said to the young waitress walking past. He puckered up his lips. "How would yer like ter be able ter say yer've kissed a superstar?"

Astonishingly, she didn't tip his beer over him. Instead she blushed and giggled, "Only if you promise to buy me a drink first. I finish in twenty minutes."

We'd won the Subscribers' Challenge. That was incredible. Bingley would never bully anyone ever again. That was unbelievable. But neither of those events had anything on this: a female looked like she was interested in Dodgy. And she was human too!

What a day.

○

Dodgy phoned in at about ten o'clock the next morning.

"So how did it go last night?" I asked eagerly.

"What can I say?" he chirped. "I wanted ter go home alone, but she kept insistin'. In the end I couldn't keep sayin' no."

"You didn't! You couldn't have! Did you really –"

"*Geddin the hole!*" he declared triumphantly.

○

It's always a bit tough to get fully motivated on a Monday, especially when you've won a trip to Augusta a couple of days before and you'd much rather be watching your collection of US Masters DVDs, but this particular Monday brought with it something other than the usual mundane consultancy assignments. It started with the shrill ring of my cellphone.

"David Holmes, good morning?" I said as professionally as I could with my mouth half full of bacon and avo on rye.

"David, good morning. It's Jim Bradley speaking."

I quickly put down my sandwich. Jim Bradley was the Chairman and Managing Director of African Tobacco.

"Jimbo! What the hell fire do you want?"

Luckily, this was just a fleeting thought and for once I managed not to say it out loud.

"Mr Bradley! Good to hear from you. How can I be of assistance?" I said instead, desperately trying to sound as though I might be important enough to help him and hoping that it wouldn't be something too complicated for me to understand. If he started going on about their market capitalisation or their RONA or whatever, I would have to hang up and pretend it was a technical fault with the handset.

"Well, we've got a bit of a predicament here and I can't seem to get hold of Rivlin or Lloyd."

They were on a week long jolly up the coast.

"Ah yes, sir. They're in a conference all week. Business planning. Can I help at all?"

"I wonder if you can. One of our Director's has, erm, resigned rather suddenly."

I wanted to say "Resigned? You fired his ass!" but thought better of it.

"Erm, I see," I croaked instead.

"His sudden departure hasn't really left us much time to get a replacement in. We have some urgent business planning of our own to do. In short, we need to find an interim Marketing Director. Quickly. I'd like you to help us out if you can."

When things are going right, they just keep on getting better.

"Leave it with me, Mr Bradley. I have the perfect candidate."

O

I negotiated hard with African Tobacco. I wanted to get a good deal for Lofty. He deserved it. I managed to get him great terms, working via our consultancy. A twelve-month renewable contract, five afternoons a week with flexible hours for roughly twice the salary he'd earned there before, plus bonuses. Rivlin & Lloyd would take a small commission but that barely mattered. He'd be able to keep the coffee shop going and earn more money than he'd ever dreamed of. What's more, he'd be safe in the knowledge that Bingley, his career in tatters, would be too embarrassed to show his face anywhere near the company ever again. That's what I call payback.

The final thing that I negotiated for Lofty was the date of his first holiday: our trip to Augusta.

○

I'd seen the course on TV, but that didn't prepare me in any way for what it would be like when I was actually standing there. It was simply breathtaking.

We walked slowly along beautiful Magnolia Lane. It was only about the length of a good drive – maybe two hundred and fifty yards – but it seemed to take us forever to get to the end. At the clubhouse we had all seen so many times on our screens, we were treated like VIPs as we were taken on a tour of the facilities and presented with a treasure trove of Augusta memorabilia.

What seem liked moments later, we were standing on the first tee, ready to embark on the golfing experience of a lifetime.

It didn't seem to matter that the course was almost impossible for us mere mortals. Nick Price apparently once said that he would be happy to play against a mid- or low-handicapper at Augusta, but with a special proviso attached. He would play the course as normal from the back tees. The other guy would have to start each hole from a pre-appointed spot on the green. Yes, the green. Price reckoned that he'd still win and when I got to the first green, I could see why.

At least the course wasn't tricked up the way it would be for the Masters. They don't actually give the greens a stimpmeter reading during Masters week, but if they did it would probably come out at 'bloody quick'.

The stimpmeter is the device they use for measuring the speed of greens. The higher the reading, the faster – and therefore more difficult – the greens. On the US tour, greens normally run at about eleven or twelve on the stimp. Steenberg was probably about ten. But even in May, when they'd been allowed to grow a bit longer, the greens at Augusta must have been running at about eighty. Alright, I exaggerate. Seventy-nine.

Speaking of seventy-nine, that was my target. As a nine handicapper, breaking eighty was always my aim. Sometimes I achieved it, sometimes I didn't, but to do it at Augusta! What an achievement that would be!

I shot a hundred and five.

Big G didn't do a great deal better really. He shot ninety-seven. Mind you, at least he broke a hundred. Even the normally unerring Dodgy shot a hundred and twelve. We stopped counting Lofty's score when he went over a million.

But it didn't stop us from enjoying it thoroughly. It didn't matter that we all either three-, four- or five-putted every green and that Lofty even managed a six-putt. The Ferkaryer Four were finally playing Augusta – and, what's more, we'd screwed Bingley in the process. Royally.

Of course, the occasion would not have been complete without the traditional UK–SA competition. Despite the astronomically high scores, we all played equally badly which kept it competitive. Incredibly enough, when we finally got to the eighteenth green and had got our balls somewhere near the hole, the match was all square.

Even more amazing, however, was that Lofty had a putt to actually win it.

The putt was about four feet. Downhill. With several inches of break. He had about as much chance of making it as I had of dating Jennifer Lopez. Much as I would love to think otherwise, that meant somewhere down the wrong end of the slim and none scale.

As he surveyed the putt a thought occurred to me. "Hey, Lofty? Seeing as you're contracting to African Tobacco through Rivlin & Lloyd, technically you work for us now, don't you?"

"Yeah, I guess so. What about it?"

"I just want you to remember that the choices you make right now may affect your career. You know: your career – it 'won't be affected'," I told him, imitating Bingley's arrogant tone on that long-ago day. "Do you understand what you need to do with this next putt?"

"I'm afraid you're making a mistake," replied my favourite brother-in-law with a grin.

"Really, what's that?"

"You're confusing me with someone who gives a shit!"

With that he rammed his putt into the back of the cup, accompanied by a raucous shout of "*Geddin the hole!*" from – of all people – Big G.

This time I was very happy to be on the losing side.

Acknowledgements

I would like to say a big thank you to the following people:

To Popsie, Freddie, Sneaky, Hannes and Brucie for providing inspiration for this book.

To 'Ju-Ju' Stanbrook and 'Moriarty' Bromhall, my first ever reviewers and fiercest critics. Thank you so much for your efforts.

To my wonderful Editor, Natasha Curry, for her tireless efforts and dedication to the cause. Your part in the film has been reserved!

To Tony 'Galina' Adams (well actually Laura), Pete 'Radar' Curtis and Samantha Marais for the constructive and helpful feedback.

To Bund – thanks for the feedback and the shout.

To Macca, thanks for the title (it's a qoty). Hope you like your cameo.

To Andy Croucher, thanks for the ruling, and good luck with the book.

To Beatrix, I am eternally grateful for all your help.

To the two most handsome and charismatic golf course managers in Cape Town (in no particular order), Ian from Steenberg and Dave from Westlake, for their support.

Last, but by no means least, to Glynne. Thank you so much and I hope you enjoyed the plonk.

About The Author

Frazer Grundy was born and brought up in Huddersfield, West Yorkshire, and now lives in the more appealing climate of Cape Town with his wife Michelle, their children Scott and Ben, and their Staffordshire bull terriers, Buster and Lucy.

Frazer is passionate about golf, and is a member of Westlake Golf Club. He plays off a nine handicap, and is renowned for his rather 'thorough' style of play.

Geddin the Hole! was inspired by his fourball, who play every fortnight for a three-inch high, broken plastic trophy, affectionately known as the Ferkaryer Cup.